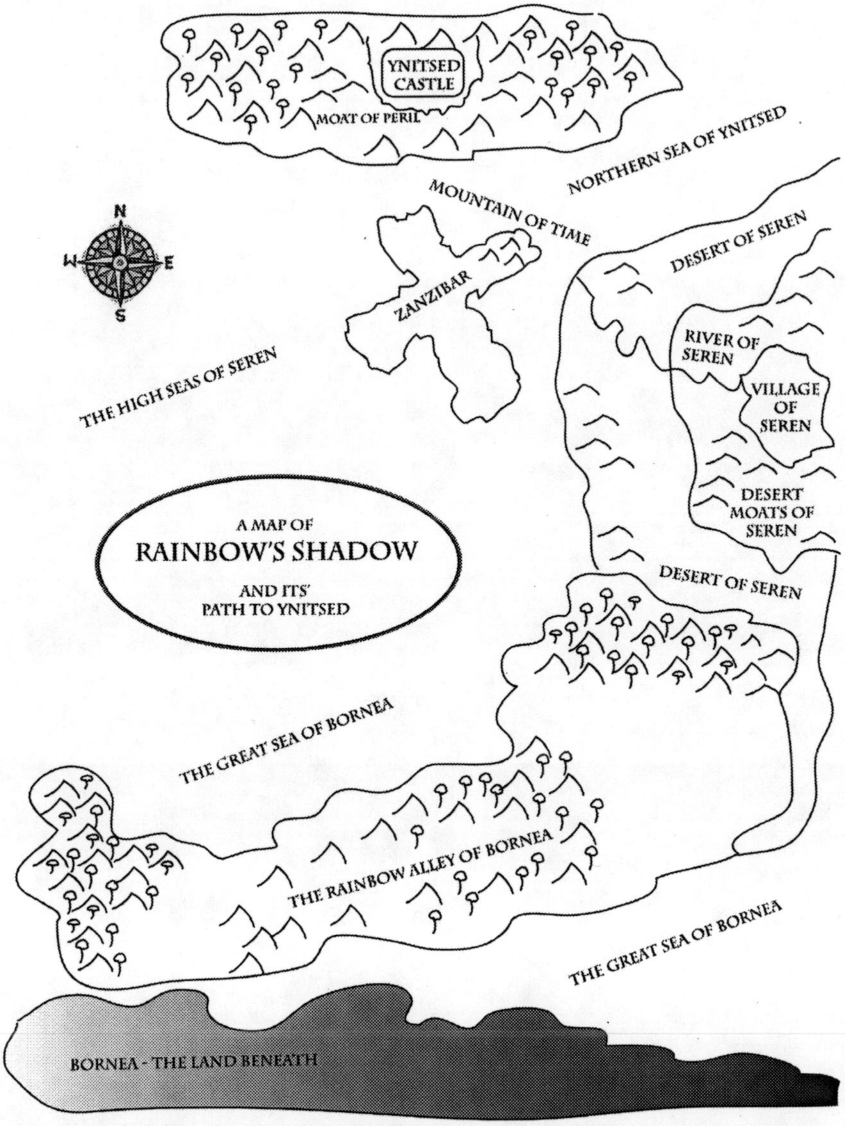
YNITSED CASTLE
MOAT OF PERIL
NORTHERN SEA OF YNITSED
MOUNTAIN OF TIME
N
W
E
S
ZANZIBAR
DESERT OF SEREN
RIVER OF SEREN
VILLAGE OF SEREN
THE HIGH SEAS OF SEREN
A MAP OF
RAINBOW'S SHADOW
AND ITS'
PATH TO YNITSED
DESERT MOATS OF SEREN
DESERT OF SEREN
THE GREAT SEA OF BORNEA
THE RAINBOW ALLEY OF BORNEA
THE GREAT SEA OF BORNEA
BORNEA - THE LAND BENEATH

Rainbow's SHADOW and the tablets of fate

John Cicero

Bloomington, IN Milton Keynes, UK

AuthorHouse™
1663 Liberty Drive, Suite 200
Bloomington, IN 47403
www.authorhouse.com
Phone: 1-800-839-8640

AuthorHouse™ UK Ltd.
500 Avebury Boulevard
Central Milton Keynes, MK9 2BE
www.authorhouse.co.uk
Phone: 08001974150

This book is a work of fiction. People, places, events, and situations are the product of the author's imagination. Any resemblance to actual persons, living or dead, or historical events, is purely coincidental.

© 2006 John Cicero. All rights reserved.

No part of this book may be reproduced, stored in a retrieval system, or transmitted by any means without the written permission of the author.

First published by AuthorHouse 3/2/2006

ISBN: 1-4259-1467-5 (sc)

Printed in the United States of America
Bloomington, Indiana

This book is printed on acid-free paper.

John Cicero

www.rainbowsshadow.com

Table of Contents

Chapter 1
The Shadow Within
1

Chapter 2
Grandpa's Story
7

Chapter 3
The Plan
25

Chapter 4
New Years Eve
34

Chapter 5
Welcome To Rainbow's Shadow
46

Chapter 6
Marabus' Chosen Few
55

Chapter 7
Malkuth's Rule
59

Chapter 8
The Alley
64

Chapter 9
The Unknowing Apprentice
78

Chapter 10
Bornea – The Land Beneath
82

Chapter 11
The Merger
88

Chapter 12
Sibling Rivalry
95

Chapter 13
The Journey Begins
97

Chapter 14
The Unveiling
112

Chapter 15
Marabus Is Discovered
126

Chapter 16
The Road To Seren
128

Chapter 17
Brittani And Bryan Arrive
130

Chapter 18
Crossing The Moats Of Seren
133

Chapter 19
Malkuth's Plan Unvieled
143

Chapter 20
The Village Of Seren
146

Chapter 21
Will Glimpses His Destiny
157

Chapter 22
Malkuth's Rage
168

Chapter 23
The Dungeons Of Bornea
171

Chapter 24
Prelude To Battle
175

Chapter 25
The Battle Of Seren
179

Chapter 26
The Four Scrolls
190

Chapter 27
Escape
195

Chapter 28
The Mountain Of Time
199

Chapter 29
Road To Zanzibar
206

Chapter 30
The First
209

Chapter 31
Devastated Paradise
218

Chapter 32
The First Scroll Directions
222

Chapter 33
The Inhabitants Of Zanzibar
226

Chapter 34
Crossing The Chasm
233

Chapter 35
Reading The Scrolls
247

Chapter 36
The Minotaurs Are Freed
255

Chapter 37
The Prophecy
260

Chapter 38
The Battle Begins
262

Chapter 39
The Miscaculated Battle
266

Chapter 40
The Unveiling
275

Chapter 41
The Rescue Begins
280

Chapter 42
Will And Jimmy Regroup
284

Chapter 43
The Sewers Of Ynitsed
288

Chapter 44
Believe In Your Purpose
291

Chapter 45
The Diversion
294

Chapter 46
The Dungeon Of Ynitsed
300

Chapter 47
Transfer Of Power
305

Chapter 48
The Seventh Tablet
307

Chapter 49
Access Denied
311

Chapter 50
The Four Leafed Wonder
315

Acknowledgements

Debra, Brittani, Joey and Anthony: Debra thanks for always being my rock and giving me the strength and support to continue to pursue my dreams. Brittani, Joey and Anthony, thanks for continually being my inspiration and giving me the drive to keep on telling my stories.

My special thanks to my parents. Dad, you're my number one editor. Mom, Rainbow's SHADOW came together because of the unforgettable stories of the magical land of Zanzibar you would tell us when we were kids. Thanks for kicking off my imagination early on.

*✶*Chapter 1*✶*
The Shadow Within

Slivers of moonlight shine through dense fog as the clopping of horse hooves echoes over a dilapidated cobble stone road. The stench of war is in the air. Darkness riddles the land. As the horses trudge over the deteriorated path, sludge of damp earth mixed with the blood of warriors splatters with every passing moment.

Wounded warriors drape themselves on top of the armored animals. No one speaks as a horse from the front of the pack turns and faces the men. "We rest here," commands the voice of the shadowy figure astride the lead horse.

The weary men slowly stop and dismount their horses. Complete exhaustion filters through the ranks of nearly one hundred warriors as they fall to the ground and huddle around one another. Silence reigns as flasks of liquid pass through the group.

The light from the moon begins to disappear as the fog increases. The lead warrior, a large soldier with broken armor covering half of his body and most of his face, directs his horse towards the men. He surveys

Chapter 1

his legion. Wounded and exhausted, the men simply gaze at their giant, but weakened, leader.

These men have been through something unspeakable. Many nurse broken and severed limbs. More have been left behind, dead. All the lead warrior can do is trot past his men and soak in the utter defeat of souls in front of him.

When he reaches the center of the group, he stops his horse and gazes down at an equally large warrior lying in exhaustion and shock against a tree stump. His right arm has been severed. The wounded warrior looks up to the lead warrior and says, "We are no match for him without Eseph."

The lead warrior remains silent, a look of utter despair on his face. He wipes a drip of blood and sweat from his brow.

Groans of pain and anguish increase as the men continue to settle in for the night. The fog swirls and swells within the encampment. The lead warrior is just about to dismount his horse when he hears a disturbance from the front of the pack. Looking up, he sees hoards of warriors retreating in fear. One of them screams, "He has found us! Malkuth has found us!"

Chaos ensues as the men quickly get up and grab their weapons. The lead warrior shouts, "Stand your ground. Stand your ground!"

The men turn and begin to form a circle.

"Stand your ground, I say!"

As the circle of warriors forms, the fog swells and the misty white cloud begins to engulf the perimeter.

"Where are they? Where are they? I can't see a thing," shouts a fearful warrior in the middle of the pack.

The Shadow Within

Sensing their fear, the lead warrior dismounts his horse and withdraws his sword. He marches with self confidence to the center of the circle and commands, "STAND YOUR GROUND!"

The men can hear the clopping of horse hooves in the distance but cannot see a thing. They remain in silence.

One of the warriors turns to the lead warrior and is about to speak. The lead warrior turns to him and hisses, "Stand your ground!"

As the men stand their ground and ready themselves, the fog in front of them dissipates around a shadowy figure in the distance.

"Stand your ground," the lead warrior repeats.

The men ready their weapons. The figure emerges from the fog but remains unclear. All that can be seen is a shadowy figure with a dark cloak covering most of his body. He stops his horse.

A warrior whispers, "It's Malkuth!"

The men stare in their uncomfortable silence. Malkuth speaks.

"FINISH THIS!"

At that moment, from within the dense fog, an arrow shoots through the cloud and penetrates the forehead of the warrior next to the lead warrior. He drops like a rock.

The lead warrior screams, "ATTACK…ATTACK!"

Hoards of Scolits, greenish-skinned, muscular part-human mutants, emerge from the fog and attack the lead warrior and his wounded troops.

A blow from a Scolits scorpion-like tail begins a shape shifting, morphing process in its victims. When the mutants attack, not only is their uncommon strength a concern, but the very real concern of instant infection from the venom of a Scolits tail is legendary.

Chapter 1

As the men fight the onslaught of the Scolits, it soon appears they are no match for the overpowering strength and numbers of these mutant creatures. One after another, the warriors fall to the power of the Scolits as Malkuth, the shadowy figure in the distance, watches proudly over his conquest.

Suddenly, from behind Malkuth and his saliva-spewing, venom-spraying Scolits, laser beams dart through the trees and the fog. The lasers hit and burn holes through the Scolits. All eyes turn to see where this surprise onslaught is coming from.

Malkuth angrily turns his horse towards the disturbance. One of the warriors shouts, "It's Eseph. He's made it. It's Eseph.!"

From the fog, another shadowy figure emerges, this one astride a white stallion. As the fog swirls around the image…..

A football comes barreling through the air and knocks a book from sweaty, clenched hands. The book falls title-side up. *The Sorcerer's Shadow* lies at the foot of Bryan Collins, a fantasy novel buff. Bryan's caramel brown hair complements his athletic build. A typical sixteen- year-old, Bryan is angry eighty percent of the day for reasons he can't even understand.

His escape from his overwhelming emotions is the world of *The Sorcerer's Shadow*. To Bryan, the series represents an escape to a fantasy world whenever reality threatens to overpower him.

Frustrated by being hit by the football, Bryan looks up and shouts, "What the…"

His little brother, Will, a thirteen-year-old clone of him, and Will's best friend, Jimmy, are running towards him. Will has always looked up to his older brother, but clearly has traits of his own. With their caramel brown hair and athletic builds, it's obvious the boys are brothers.

The Shadow Within

Will is the type of kid who believes he can do anything, no matter how outlandish it may seem. If something is possible, then he can accomplish it. Bryan, on the other hand, is more realistic. No matter how hard Will pushes, he will continually remind his brother of his limitations and the reality of the world they live in.

Irritated, Bryan jumps up. "What in the heck are you two doing? Can't you see I'm reading here?"

Will and Jimmy stop in front of him, out of breath. Jimmy is Will's and Bryan's next door neighbor and Will's best friend. Will and Jimmy don't go anywhere without one another. Jimmy is a pudgy, fun-loving kid who has a funny way of looking at things. And he's not afraid to say what he's thinking. Jimmy would rather worry about his next meal than any world issues.

Will picks up the book from the ground and says, "Sorry Bri, wanna play catch?"

Bryan barks, "Catch? Can't you see I'm reading?"

"Not anymore," Will says with a grin. "Come on, Bryan, we wanna work on some plays. You've been reading that thing all day."

Bryan picks up *The Sorcerer's Shadow* and glares at his brother. "Leave me alone."

He walks away.

Jimmy looks over to a downcast Will and says, "That stinks. Wanna get something to eat instead?"

Will looks at Jimmy in disbelief. "What? No. Hey Bryan, come on." He chases after his big brother. "Come on Bryan. Just play for a little bit."

Chapter 1

Bryan spits over his shoulder, "Look, I don't want to play. You two can do your plays without me. Why don't you go and play in your room with whatever it is you're creating up there. By the way, Mom's gonna kill you once she finds out you painted that crap in the closet."

Will replies, "You better not say a word. You promised. Any way's just wait till Grandpa sees it. He'll love it."

"He may, but if mom finds it, you're toast. By the way, you're getting too caught up in Grandpa's fairy tales again."

Will, defiantly shouts, "They're not fairy tales!."

"Whatever," Bryan says sarcastically. "But if mom finds out, you're toast."

"She doesn't have to know and you better not tell her!"

"Then, don't give me a reason to. Now, leave me alone and let me read my book." Bryan turns away from Will and starts to walk towards the house. Will stands dejected.

Sensing his disappointment, Jimmy walks up to Will and says, "Hey man, my mom just made some cinnamon rolls for the holidays, wanna go steal some?"

Will watches his brother walk into the house and slam the door.

"Some cookies, too." Jimmy forces himself into Will's view. He stares at his best friend with a puppy dog look on his face. Will can't help but crack up. "You are such pig, you know that? Ok, sounds good. Race you."

Will takes off towards Jimmy's house as Jimmy slowly gallops behind him.

✦✶Chapter 2.✶✦
Grandpa's Story

The snow kept changing directions as the houses across the street began to disappear. The holidays were here and everyone in the Collins household was sneaking peeks at the front windows, delighting in the first real snowfall of the season.

Will should have been in bed an hour ago, but Grandpa Joe – Will and Bryan's mother's father, had promised to continue his story about Rainbow Alley tonight. Every holiday, Grandpa Joe would come to the Collins home and share stories of a wonderful land he claimed to have visited when he was a child. Rainbow Alley was a legend in the Collins family. Every Collins child had to listen to Grandpa's ramblings about this amazing place.

It was Will's turn now. He had finally turned thirteen, the magical age that Grandpa claimed was one of the four important elements necessary to gain access to the golden portal of Rainbow Alley.

The other three elements were hidden in his stories he told them. They had to listen carefully to his passages before he would ever let on

Chapter 2

to what they were. He always seemed to change the elements with each telling.

To some of the kids in the family, it appeared that Grandpa might be losing it. Most of them just figured he was just making the whole thing up anyways.

But not Will. After listening to portions of the story on Thanksgiving, Will told Bryan and the cousins that it was a puzzle and Grandpa was giving clues to the pieces. They would all laugh at him and tell him he's getting caught up in Grandpa's fantasies again. Will just shrugged at their rudeness and counted the days until his next Rainbow Alley session with Grandpa – Christmas Eve.

Tonight was the night. It was Christmas Eve, and Grandpa Joe was finally ascending the stairs to continue his story. Grandpa was the type of grandfather that fits like a warm glove. With his worn-out sweatshirt that he bought back when the Indians made it to the World Series, to his five o'clock shadow, which seems to last 24/7, Grandpa exudes a warmth that appears to come naturally.

With Grandma gone now, he simply lives for his children and grandchildren. As he makes his way up the stairs, he skips steps to quicken his pace. His olive skin is set off by snow-white hair. Although Grandpa is in his mid-sixties, he carries himself like a teenager with a physique of an athletic 30-year-old.

With hands roughened from many years working as a carpenter, and forearms Popeye would be proud of, Grandpa has always been an idyllic figure in the eyes of his grandchildren. Will, especially, thinks that he is the luckiest kid to have this man for a grandfather.

Grandpa's Story

"Hurry, Grandpa! I have the room all set up for us," Will urges. Grandpa sees Will is wearing a sweatshirt which reads 'Catch a Rainbow'.

He chuckles, "Perfect my boy…just perfect." When the old man peers into Will's room he sees that it has been transformed into a sea of tented sheets draped in every direction. The sheets create a maze, and Grandpa has to crouch down to enter.

A rotating disco ball left over from the 1970s and strategically placed, soft laser lighting has created a mini cosmic New Age experience in the room for his storied reading.

"This is great, Will, when did you do this?"

"I've been working since Thanksgiving on this. Bryan keeps on knocking it down, so I had to put it together about a hundred million times already."

"He has, has he? Well, I think you have done a wonderful job. This is the perfect atmosphere to create the Golden Portal. Your brother should be proud of what you're doing here instead of knocking it down."

"Not Bryan. He cares more about that stupid *Sorcerer's Shadow* book than anything about Rainbow Alley."

"Well, that can change. Just give it some time."

"I don't think so…not Bryan."

"That's ok, so where do you want to begin?"

"Over here, Grandpa. I made the four step clover entrance just like you told me." Grandpa, crawls on his hands and knees through the maze of bed sheets, and sees an opening to Will's closet. Inside the closet, Will has created a mini shelter that has green clover-like wall art on each side. A sign above it reads: Forerunner.

Chapter 2

The lights shooting through the cascading bed sheets create an eerie effect that even has Grandpa a little jumpy. He notices several murals on the wall that depict scenes from stories he has told the children through the years. The murals depict magical landscapes, murky caves and complicated water slides built into mountains.

Impressed Grandpa chuckles and asks, "You did this by yourself, kiddo?"

"Well, Jimmy helped a little."

"Jimmy?"

"You know, Jimmy, my best bud who lives next door."

"Oh …sure, Jimmy. Has your mother seen it?"

"Not yet."

Knowing that this would not go over well Grandpa says. "Ok, well if the, you-know-what hits the fan, I'll help you clean it up. This is great though."

Grandpa moves to where he can gain a little extra head room in the closet and announce, "Ok, this will do."

Will continues to fuss with the displays and Grandpa sees a small step stool in the corner of the closet. He grabs it, sits atop the stool, and looks at Will.

"Are you ready, bud?"

"Almost, I need to show you something first."

Will rummages through the numerous shoeboxes in his closet. Grandpa hears something in the back of the bedroom. He gazes backward and immediately a sly smile appears on his face.

"Found it!" Will pulls something from a small shoebox.

"What do you have there?"

Grandpa's Story

With a smile so proud, his ears are about to burst, Will keeps his back to his Grandfather and says, "I found the second element, Grandpa."

Taken back a bit, Grandpa slowly looks up towards Will.

"You found what?"

Will turns towards Grandpa and says, "The second element, Grandpa! Last time you told me the Rainbow Alley story, you talked about the clovers being one of the four main elements you need to gain access to the golden portal. After thinking about it, I remembered you mentioned the clovers four times in a row. I thought it was part of the story. Bryan said you were getting old and repeated yourself a lot."

Glancing toward the back of the room, Grandpa says, "He did, did he?"

"Yeah, but I told him it was a puzzle, you know like a clue. And I know I'm right, Grandpa. The four times was not just repeating, it was your clue to find a four leaf clover, wasn't it?"

Grandpa smiles.

"Check this out!"

With the laser lights from the room crashing against the disco ball's rotating light projections, the closet has a mystical presence to it. Will reaches in his shoe box and pulls out a perfectly formed four leaf clover. Grandpa reaches and gently opens Will's hand.

"Well done, my boy, well done. You remembered, when things appear unclear, clues are everywhere; all anyone has to do is open their eyes and see what the clues are telling them."

Will places the clover in his grandfather's palm. He is so proud of himself; he can't help but wipe a small tear from the corner of his eye.

Chapter 2

"Am I ready now, Grandpa?"

"You sure are, Will. What do you say we begin?"

"I'm ready, Grandpa."

"Should we include your brother in on this session?"

"Bryan? No way! I told you he cares more about *The Sorcerer's Shadow* than anything from Rainbow Alley."

"Well, maybe we should ask him, though."

"Come on Grandpa, he'll just make fun."

Peering into the room, Grandpa says, "Is that true, Bryan?"

Will looks into his room from his closet and screams, "Bryan, are you back there?"

The tented sheets begin to ruffle as a muffled roar is heard from the room.

Not wanting to show any fear, Will screams with rage again. "Bryan, you're such a jerk…is that you?"

Grandpa looks over at Will's concerned expression and whispers, "It's him."

Will looks at his grandfather and stands tall.

"He's such a jerk."

At that moment Will's older brother, jumps into the closet screaming, "Aaaaaaagh!"

Will jumps back and shouts, "You are such a jerk, you know that?"

"You were so scared," Bryan says with a smirk.

Will settles back down and spits out, "I was not. What are you doing here, anyways? You care more about that stupid thing than

Grandpa's Story

Grandpa's stories." Will points to the book in Bryan's hand. Its title reads *The Sorcerer's Shadow*.

Bryan, on his hands and knees, settles down next to his grandfather.

"That's not entirely true, Grandpa. This story is just so cool though. And I've heard all about Rainbow Alley already."

Grandpa looks at the book in Bryan's hand.

"You have, have you? Well, maybe we can hear about yours."

Will jumps up in anger.

"No! That's not fair Grandpa!"

Grandpa looks up at Will and winks.

"Let's just see what this one is all about, what makes it so cool and all."

Will's balloon is a bit deflated.

"Aw, man."

Bryan looks over at the dejected Will, and then quickly back to Grandpa.

"Grandpa this book is so cool, the whole series is…here check this out."

He hands the book to Grandpa. Grandpa looks at the dark image on the front cover. It depicts a dark castle with a shadow of a sorcerer.

"Hmmm…interesting."

Grandpa turns the book over and begins to read the back of the book.

"Living in the shadow of an ancient curse had always put Marabus, the Goddess of Magic at odds. The reason she invested a portion of her divine might in mortals is not known. Some feel that Marabus foresaw

Chapter 2

the Time of Troubles and chose to give some of her power to mortals to ensure that her successor would have a number of nearly immortal allies in the struggle against the schemes of Abra and Malkuth who precipitated the Time of Troubles by stealing the Seven Tablets of Fate.

These seven tablets contain the portfolio and obligations of all gods and all Fathers. These seven tablets hold the lost information from the "One" that provides a blueprint to the past, present and future. These seven tablets are essentials for the Balance of the Cosmic Order.

Will interrupts, "Come on, Grandpa, its Christmas Eve...you promised."

Grandpa looks over to Bryan and then back to Will.

"Bryan, what do say? This seems very interesting, but can you sit through one more chapter of Rainbow Alley. Hey, you never know, this just might be the night your eyes are opened."

"To what?"

"Well your brother found another element you know."

Will jumps up and shouts, "I did, didn't I? I knew it! I knew the four leaf clover was one of the four elements."

"What's he talking about...four leaf clover?"

"Look," Grandpa says as he shows Bryan the four-leaf clover.

Bryan looks at the clover and then to his brother.

"That's not real."

"It sure is. I found it at Jimmy's the day after Thanksgiving. There was no snow, so we could search all day. I finally found it."

Bryan looks up at his grandfather.

"Is this real Grandpa?"

Grandpa's Story

"It is. It's the real thing."

"Well so what? There are probably a million of these. What's it suppose to do anyways?"

Grandpa looks at the now interested Bryan.

"It's not what it does alone. It's when it's combined with the other three elements that it creates the golden portal."

Bryan starts to get a little uncomfortable as the lights run across his face.

"Come on, Grandpa. None of this stuff is true."

"Would you like to hear how true it is?"

Bryan looks over to Will who is on his knees listening to his grandfather.

"What do you mean?"

Grandpa puts *The Sorcerer's Shadow* down next to one of the spinning disco light balls and picks up his Rainbow Alley notes.

"Well, you have to remember, Rainbow Alley is not your ordinary land. In fact, I'm not even sure it is truly a land. I'll never forget the day I gained access to the portal. It was a day like today surrounded by a holiday theme. There was newness in the air and my parents were setting up for everyone to come over to our house that night. I was playing in my room, much like we are today, and I, too, had found a four leaf clover."

Will, all proud of himself again, and his brother, Bryan .actually appear to be listening.

"Mine was by accident though. The clover actually found me. You see we were playing football in my front yard and I must have been rolling around the grass and the clover somehow hooked onto my pants.

Chapter 2

I was thirteen years old then and I always loved magic. Harry Houdini was the big name during my era. Everyone wanted to be like Houdini. So naturally, when I found the clover on my trousers I figured it was sent to me for a reason. I had to conduct a séance like Houdini had done. He claimed he could talk to the dead. In fact before he died, he convinced believers he could be contacted after his death. Many believed him. Even to this day people try to contact him on his birthday. I thought I could speak with my Uncle Peter, who had passed on. So I took the stem and grabbed one of those tiny snow globes. You know the ones with the little worlds inside. When you shake them, the tiny snow crystals float around. Well, mine was one of the earlier models and it had this beautiful mountain scene in it with a miniature town inside. Anyhow, I placed the clover atop the snow globe and just stared at it for a few minutes.

"The moon was full that night and the sky was cloudless. I noticed that the moon generated beams through my bedroom window. I quickly picked up the snow globe with the clover and placed it in the middle of my room. It was now in the direct path of the moon's beam. I watched it for a while and was just about to begin my séance when the snow crystals started to change colors! I could not believe what I was seeing! It appeared to me that my clover had been sucked into the snow globe and created something magical.

"I didn't know if I should scream for my parents or run for my life. Instead, I chose to move closer to the globe. The closer I got, the more I could see. The crystal had transformed its inner contents into a magical land. I could see beautiful waterfalls flowing, and smell lush vegetation. I turned the globe to see more. I could see tropical settings with palm

Grandpa's Story

trees and what appeared to be farms that actually seemed to grow candy. At one point, it looked like people inside the globe were eating ice cream off of the trees and dipping their fingers into a river of melted chocolate covered rivers. I thought I was looking at the Garden of Eden.

"I moved closer and closer to get a better look. All of a sudden, the crystal began to shake and generate a rainbow of colors from its inner core. There were so many colors. I remember that distinctly. I saw red, blue, purple, green, orange and yellow. The colors quickly took over my entire room. I felt that I had been sucked into the belly of a rainbow. These fireworks lasted for what seemed to be minutes, but probably was only seconds.

"When it was complete, I couldn't believe my eyes. In the center of my room, where the snow globe had once sat, was a giant golden portal. It looked to me like a giant slide of gold without an ending. I crept closer to gaze inside. Although I couldn't see the bottom, I had a feeling everything was ok. I really felt that I was in very safe hands. So, I told myself, this had come to me for a reason. I had to continue on."

Bryan and Will can't take their eyes off their grandfather as Will intones, "You dove in, didn't you?"

Grandpa looks at Will and smiles.

"I dove in. You wouldn't believe the ride I had. This golden portal shot me through a vortex of colors so beautiful I wanted to <u>taste</u> each and every one of them. I was having a ball riding this slide, but as fast as it appeared, it ended. I felt myself falling through the air and heading directly toward a green field. This was it. I was sure I was dead. As the ground came closer, I screamed louder. As I was just to hit the ground, I closed my eyes. I thought I was done!"

Chapter 2

"What are you saying, Grandpa? Did you hit the ground?" said Bryan.

"I did. But it was so strange. The ground absorbed me as if it was catching me with a soft pillow. I didn't feel a thing. It actually was very comforting."

"No way!" said Bryan.

Grandpa looked at Bryan, smiled and said, "Way!"

Bryan starts to get up, but stops.

"How could the ground <u>catch</u> you?"

"From that point further, everything that I thought should be never was. This magical land transformed my senses into a minefield of jelly. I couldn't believe what I was seeing. The happiness that shot through my body was unbelievable. This is when I met Bethel and his people. I spent the afternoon wandering the land and meeting the inhabitants of this unbelievable setting. The courtesy Bethel and his people gave me was truly unforgettable."

Bryan interrupts, "Grandpa, this is exactly what I mean. We hear about this all the time. It's same story. The rainbow, the chocolate, Bethel…none of it seems real. Can't we hear something new?"

Grandpa looks to Bryan and says, "Things don't have to seem real to be real, Bryan."

"So it's all made up, the whole story?"

"To some…maybe. To others…not a chance! For me, it was the most real event of my life. One I will never forget. And one I think it's time to share with you."

At that moment, Grandpa reaches into a tiny velvet bag he had carried up to the room with him.

Grandpa's Story

Confused, Bryan asks, "What's that?"

"It's the third element."

Grandpa pulls out a snow globe.

Will is immediately impressed.

"Aw, look at that. Grandpa, is this *the* original snow globe?"

"Yes…yes it is. But before we can do anything, the year has to be new for the final element to become full."

"I don't understand. I thought this was the last element. Is this real or not?" Bryan says.

Will jumps in.

"Of course it's real. Let's show him, Grandpa. Let's go to Rainbow Alley tonight. I have the clover and you have the snow globe."

Grandpa looks over to the Will.

"Oh, I don't know Will. I'm getting too old to make the trip. Besides, we're still missing one very important part of the fourth and final element."

Bryan looks at the snow globe.

"We have everything you said we needed. Let's see what this does."

He runs over and grabs the snow globe from Grandpa.

"It won't work, boys, we're still missing the full mo…."

"Bryan, listen to Grandpa; let's get all the right elements, before we try," Will shouts.

"Give me that clover, Will," Bryan says.

He grabs the clover from Will and places the globe in front of the window so the moonlight beams through. As Bryan rushes to place the ball down, his erratic behavior causes the clover to fall through a

Chapter 2

crack at the base of the globe. The globe tips over and slightly cracks the base, causing it to become unbalanced.

"Aw, Bryan, look what you did. Now how are we going to do it?"

"We need something to brace it. Give me something."

Will leans over and grabs Grandpa's Rainbow Alley notebook. At the same time, Bryan quickly grabs his own book, *The Sorcerer's Shadow*. He places his book first without Grandpa or Will noticing, then grabs Grandpa's notebook and places it underneath the globe to brace it. Grandpa, distracted by the moonbeam, does not notice that Bryan's book has been placed under his Rainbow Alley notebook.

Grandpa looks at the globe and peers over to the three quarters moon shining down into the room. He notices a tiny beam of light generating through the window.

Bryan belts out; "Now we can see if this thing is all made up or not."

"You really think so?" Grandpa asks with a grin.

"Grandpa, I don't mean to be disrespectful or anything, but this whole thing is just getting old," the older boy says.

Grandpa watches as the beam from the moon inches closer to the ball.

"Maybe so." He keeps staring at the moonbeam.

Will notices the beam next. He points to the light.

"Look!"

Bryan glances over and sees the crawling beam. "Oh come on. It's not gonna work".

Grandpa suddenly reaches for the brothers. "Boys! Grab my hands quickly."

Grandpa's Story

The globe's snow crystals begin to shake.

Bryan appears nervous. He bites his lip and murmurs, "Grandpa, what's going on?" he says fearfully in a fearful state.

"I'm not sure myself. We do not have all the elements. This shouldn't be happening."

"What do mean? What shouldn't be happening?" says Bryan.

"We're still missing the full moon. This isn't right."

At that moment, the beam hits the ball and sends a surge of white light around the room. It darts around the perimeter of the room like a pinball and jolts through Grandpa chest and careens off of Will's shoulder. The beam instantly settles back around the globe, creating a halo-like effect.

Concerned for their grandfather's safety, the brothers scream in unison, "Grandpa, are you ok?"

Grandpa looks down at his chest, amazed at what just happened. He appears to be ok, and tries to reassure the boys. "I'm ok, boys. I'm ok. Will, are you all right?"

Ignoring his grandfather's concern, Will shouts, "Grandpa is this it? Is this Rainbow Alley?"

Startled at what he is witnessing, the old man answers, "I'm not sure what this is, Will. It shouldn't work like this."

Bryan shouts, "Look!"

He points to a halo-light surrounding the globe. Images are beginning to form within the center of the light.

Will looks at his grandfather and says "This has got to be it, Grandpa. It's Rainbow Alley, I know it is!"

Chapter 2

Grandpa bends over the light and begins to smile slightly. He quickly sits back and stares directly at the boys with a stern look on his face.

"Boys, this doesn't make any sense to me right now. We have to be very careful about this."

As the light from the halo distracts the three of them, the snow globe suddenly begins to absorb the contents of Bryan's *Sorcerer's Shadow* book and Grandpa's Rainbow Alley notes. It is as if the entire content of the books are morphing through each other up through the center of the globe. The words within each of the books appear to be getting sucked out from their pages and into the inner core of the globe in unison.

Bryan, a look of absolute horror on his face gasps, "Grandpa, I'm not sure I like this. What's going on?"

Will looks over to him and says; "Don't be afraid, Bryan. This is Rainbow Alley. Everything is perfect here."

At that moment the globe finishes absorbing Grandpas notes and Bryan's entire novel. None of the three notice.

Bryan pushes back.

"What are you talking about? You don't have a clue what's going on."

At that moment, the moon beam disappears and as fast as the room lit up, it loses its intensity. The next moment, everything is back to normal.

Will looks around the room.

"What happened? What happened to the light?"

Grandpa surveys the scene. He looks at his chest, which now has a dark red burn in its center.

Grandpa's Story

He then turns to peer at the moonlit sky. Suddenly, he turns and heads towards the globe. He slows with caution as he gets closer.

His delight quickly alters to one of concern. As he peers into the globe, his eyes become transfixed. As much as he tries to pull himself away, he cannot. Then, as if he were hit with bolt of lightning, he is jolted back with a fear he cannot explain. He looks back to the moon and then to the globe.

"Boys, we need to stop. We need to stop now!"

Grandpa grabs the globe and shoves it into his velvet bag.

"Grandpa, what are you doing? We're so close!" Will yells.

Beads of sweat begin to form on his forehead as Grandpa says slowly, "Will we have to stop. I shouldn't involve you boys in this type of stuff anyhow. The tablets have been compromised."

Will looks at him and says, "What? What tablets?"

At that moment, Grandpa notices that his Rainbow Alley notes have a perfect hole burned though the center of the pad.

"Oh my lord, what did I do? Boys, we're done. Get this place cleaned up before your parents get upset. I'm going downstairs."

He grabs his notebook and the globe, and gets up from the stool. Sweat stains his shirt.

Will tries to stop him.

"Grandpa, please."

"No, Will. It's time to stop."

Grandpa strides out of the room without a backward glance.

Will looks to Bryan and says, "Aw man. We were so close. Did you see that? That was awesome!"

Chapter 2

Bryan, still fearful, only vaguely pays attention to Will. He is amazed at what he just witnessed. He stutters, "Wha...what did you say?"

"Did you see that, Bryan? We were so close? We gotta do that again!"

Bryan gets closer to the area where the globe was resting. He slowly pulls back the cloth he placed over *The Sorcerers Shadow,* the book has vanished.

Will is still excited about the experience.

"That was so cool! We're doing this again on New Year's."

Hearing that, Bryan quickly turns around and with as stern as a voice he can muster, mutters, "You will not go near that thing again. Do you hear me? Just forget about this. Do you hear me?"

His brother's demeanor takes Will back.

"What's your problem?"

"Did you hear what I said? You have to promise me you're going to let this go."

"Promise you nothing. You're such a baby. You never want to have fun."

"Will, this is not fun. We don't know what this thing is."

A blood-curdling scream interrupts his next thought.

It's their mother.

"Dad! Something's wrong with Dad!"

The boys rush out of the room and to the top of the staircase. As they look at the base of the stairs, they see Grandpa lying on the floor. Their father is administering CPR. Their mother is on her knees, crying.

"Call 911, someone call 911!" she screams. Grandpa isn't moving.

Chapter 3
The Plan

Christmas Day came and went without a trace of merriment this year. With Grandpa in the hospital in a bizarre comatose state, the Collins family had the unenviable task of trekking to the hospital, instead of choosing the next toy to assemble.

Will and Bryan were still in shock about what had transpired a week ago in their bedroom. The week between Christmas and New Year's had come and passed, and the boys were basically told not get in the way at this point. Their mother, Grandpa's daughter, is taking it the hardest. It seems that she has not slept since the tragic night.

Bryan has avoided Will for the most part since the episode. This is his way of dealing with things like this. Will, on the other hand, can't let it go. Ever since Grandpa went down, his mind began to spin and he hasn't stopped asking himself questions.

With the morning snow no longer trickling down, Will is still sleeping as his head spins with questions. 'Why did this happen to Grandpa, why now? Did Rainbow Alley have something to do with

Chapter 3

it? Did I cause Grandpa's stroke? What can I do to make it easier for my mother?'

As he tosses and turns, images of his grandfather, the penetrating beam of light and his four leaf clover race through his mind. His restlessness keeps up for a few moments as he begins to sweat. Suddenly, his restlessness turns to a soothing calm. A bright white light shines down upon him and he opens his eyes.

Not knowing if he is dreaming or not, Will tries to raise his head but can't seem to move. He tries to scream out, but words do not seem to flow from his mouth. Helpless, he stares straight ahead and watches the white light. Slowly he begins to see an image. The image is soft and looks like a cloud forming into a human form. As the image forms it begins to look more and more like a woman in a white silky cloak.

The image is angelic in nature and Will tries to reach outward towards it, but cannot raise his arms. As if he were also in a comatose state, he is helpless as the image gets closer to him. With his mouth tightly closed, he watches as the image utters softly, "Come through the alley, he will be healed."

Now frightened, Will tries to pull away. It is as if a two hundred pound weight is resting on top of him. He cannot move. He tries to scream out again but his muffled yell is drowned out by his fear.

Once again the image says, ""Come through the alley, Forerunner, and he will be healed."

Fighting through the fear, Will feels stronger; he is now able to free his arm and reach upward towards the cloud-like vision of what he believes is an angel. As he rocks back and forth he begins to fight with his own weight to free himself. His muffled scream is deep within his belly as he drums up enough strength to free it from its dream-like capture.

He screams out and at the same time is able to free himself. The image vanishes and Will is left sitting upright in his bed in a state of shock, gazing at the ceiling. He stares for a few moments and looks around his room. Nothing is around. It must have been a dream, he convinces himself. Why else was it so difficult to move?

Yes, he was dreaming, he tells himself as he gets up and heads towards his bathroom to start his day.

LATER ON THAT MORNING

Wills' mind keeps on spinning with questions. First, that was one crazy dream, he tells himself. So real, but surely it was a dream. He also begins to think about his grandfather and what he can do to help. Maybe it wasn't a dream. Maybe he did cause his grandfathers stroke. Maybe he should just follow what the image said. There had to be a solution to this all. A grim end result of his grandfather losing his battle was unacceptable to Will.

No, he had to do something. Whether it was a dream or not, something in him-- or something out of him-- was telling him to follow his heart and do what he knew his grandfather would want him to do. With unmatched determination, Will decides to go for it. It was now or never in his mind and based on his parents' demeanor the last few days, time was obviously of the essence. He knew his grandfather was fading and the idea of sitting back and not contributing was simply not an option.

Chapter 3

With Bryan giving him the cold shoulder and his parents out of touch, Will had no one else to turn to other than his partner in crime, next door neighbor and best friend, Jimmy Foster.

As Will walked over to Jimmy's, he did not have to wear his boots. Ever since Christmas Eve, the weather had taken a turn and all of the snow that had been built up on Christmas had all but vanished due to the rains and warmer weather.

From inside the house, Bryan watches his brother walk over to Jimmy's. He has to get up to look closer to see what he is carrying. Will is carrying an oversized duffle bag with him as he trots across the yards to the front step of the Fosters. Curious, Bryan tries to keep an eye on his entire walk. Once Mrs. Foster opens the front door and lets Will in, Bryan loses his sightlines and has to run to another part of the house to spy on his brother.

"Hey Will" Jimmy screams from the top of his stairs.

"Hey Jimmy." Will looks up and sees his best bud.

"Come on up."

Will runs upstairs like a lightning bolt, all the while carrying his oversized duffle bag.

"Hey Will, you wanna play my new Madden 2006? I made it to the playoffs already."

"You didn't really make it to playoffs. You must have cheat codes."

"Yeah, so? I still made it. You wanna see?"

"Not today, I have something bigger." Will walks over to a bench in Jimmy's room.

"Bigger, what can be bigger than Madden 06?"

The Plan

"Look at this." Will falls to his knees and pulls the duffle bag off of the bench.

"Come here and close your door."

Curious, Jimmy quickly closes his door and rushes over to Will.

"Look what I have." Will begins to slowly pull out Grandpa's velvet carrying bag.

"What is it?" Jimmy says.

"This is my grandpa's. I have all his stuff, even his notebook."

Jimmy jumps to his feet.

"To Rainbow Alley?"

"Yep."

"I thought that it wasn't real. I mean, that's what Bryan always says."

"Oh it's real. Bryan doesn't know anything other than his Sorcerer's junk."

Jimmy begins to laugh, as it is a common joke.

"Yeah, yeah what is it, Rainbow Alley's a joke, but *Sorcerer's Shadow's* real."

"In his mind."

"Well it is kind of cool, sometimes, when he tells us how to bring down a sorcerer."

He starts to get excited as he begins to tell Will about Bryan's Sorcerer's story again.

"You know what I love is when the Eseph character is down and the sorcerer gets the surprise attack from the…."

Chapter 3

"Jimmy...stop! We don't have time for Bryan's stupid book stuff. I need your help. Because we're going there to save my grandpa. You and me."

Jimmy is confused.

"What are you talking about, save your grandpa? Isn't he in a como?" Jimmy stops.

Will says. "It's a coma, foodbag. But I think I know how we can help him and maybe bring him back. You see I had this dream last night and...well never mind that...look at this." Will pulls the snow globe from the bag.

"Wow. Where did you get that?"

"It's my grandpa's. It's one of the missing elements. And I have the others."

Jimmy looks inside the globe. "Huh," he says with a confused expression.

"What's wrong?" Will asks.

"Is it supposed to be that dark inside?"

Will grabs the globe and says, "That's just the lighting in your room."

Believing him, Jimmy responds, "Oh...ok. So what do we do with this?"

Will looks him in the eyes. "Not what....when. Look at what else I was able to get." Will pulls his grandfather's Rainbow Alley notebook out from the duffle bag. It has the hole burned through its center.

"What happened to that?" Jimmy says.

"I don't know. It was ok before everything happened the other night. But when the darting lights stopped, this is all that was left."

The Plan

"Wow!" Jimmy says

"Check this out. I've been reading it and look what this says."

Will opens up the notebook and begins to read.

"It's a little tough to read because of the hole and everything, but check this out. It says something about these two guys named Abra, and Malkuth who stole something called the Tablets of Fate. It cuts off here but goes on to say that this power would sleep…see it's cut off again. I think it says the power would sleep in mortals…see it's broken up here, too, but it says it would give the Chosen the ability to heal quickly, and would give them life spans far greater than those of ordinary mortals. Life as a…see it's broken here again. I'm guessing it says would be easy for these mortals when….and it cuts off."

"What do you mean it cuts off?"

"It cuts off, look."

He shows him the notebook with the hole and the text that has been deleted.

"I don't get it," Jimmy says.

"Look."

From his pocket Will pulls another piece from the notebook. This one also has a hole through it, but this document features a map.

Jimmy looks at the map and says, "Where'd you get that?"

"It was falling out of the notebook. But check this out, it shows us everything. All we have to do is follow this."

Jimmy is still confused.

"Follow this, to what?"

"Don't you see? We need to open up the golden portal on New Year's Eve and go to Rainbow Alley so we can find these Tablets of Fate.

Chapter 3

It's all right here." He points to areas in the map. "If we find the tablets, then we can be one of the Chosen and heal my grandfather."

"Why on New Year's?"

"Because my grandpa said we need a full moon to open the portal. I checked the calendar and on New Year's Eve, guess what?"

"Full moon?" Jimmy says.

Will looks at him with a smile. "Full moon!"

"Are you sure about all this, Will?" Jimmy looks over all of the stuff in the duffle bag and then folds up the map to place it back in his front pocket.

"Sure I am. Grandpa has been telling me about this for years. Rainbow Alley is a very special place, with very special people. They'll help. This is my Fate and I'm going to get these tablets to continue my grandpa's Fate. You guys are still coming over on New Year's Eve right?"

"Yeah, I think so."

"That's when we're going."

"Going. Going where?"

Will looks to the snow globe. Jimmy's eyes get wider.

"You're serious aren't you?"

"Yep. I know if we get to Rainbow Alley, they can fix my grandpa. We *gotta* go."

"Even if we can make it to Rainbow Alley, how are you so sure they can fix him?"

"I just know. Plus my dream told me too."

"Your what?"

The Plan

"Nothing. Let's just say I know they can fix him, and we're going."

"What about Bryan?" Jimmy says with a bit of fear.

"Don't say a word to Bryan. He'll just try to stop us."

"That's fine with me. Ok, this sounds pretty cool. I'm in. We gotta make sure we bring enough snack though. You wanna play Madden now?"

"Yeah…you got the cheat codes?"

"Yep!"

As Will and Jimmy put the snow globe away, inside his room next door, Bryan peels the binoculars from his eyes. He has been watching the two of them the entire time.

⋆Chapter 4⋆
New Years Eve

The snow has begun to fall again as the white-carpeted landscapes of the neighborhood glisten in the afternoon. The Fosters were coming over to the Collins' house tonight to support, rather than celebrate. This would be a tougher New Years for the Collins, and the support of their friends was direly needed at this point.

It was 5:00p.m. and the sun was still out. The nighttime sky wouldn't arrive until around 5:45p.m. The weatherman had been reporting that the snow would stop and clear skies would develop through the night. The full moon would be seen.

The Collins home was very subdued today. Will and Bryan's mother, had been moping around all day. She really wasn't in the mood for company, but knew her dear friends could possibly help on a night like this. Their father had told Bryan and Will to stay out of mom's way for the next few weeks, especially tonight. Since it was another holiday, Grandpa usually would arrive early to help set up for the company. But tonight was different and everyone really felt it.

New Years Eve

Will had been keeping clear of not only his mother tonight, but Bryan too. He knew he had to get everything set up for his journey, but he also wanted to make sure his brother wouldn't ruin it. He needed to gather up all of the elements for the trip. He had Grandpa's snow globe, he knew the full moon was coming, but he still needed his four-leaf clover. Since Christmas Eve, he had been searching for the remnants of the clover. But with the reaction from the intense lights they had, all that was left was a charred stem.

It was getting later and Will knew he had to find a new one when the doorbell rang. The Fosters had arrived. Like a lightning bolt, Will ran down the steps, grabbing his boots and jacket.

"Hi, everyone!" he screams.

He runs directly up to Jimmy.

"Come on, we have some work to do."

"What kind of work?" Jimmy says.

"Come on!"

He grabs Jimmy by the hood and drags him outside. The Fosters laugh it off as Will and Jimmy run to the side of their houses.

Jimmy's father yells, "You guys have 'till it gets dark, then get in here!"

Will replies, "We won't be long."

As they run to the side of the houses, Bryan sprints to his bedroom window to see what they are up to.

"What's this all about, Will?"

"Jimmy, I can't find the four leaf clover. We have to find another one."

Chapter 4

"Another one? The last one took us two weeks to find. We're not going to find another before tonight."

Starting to get a bit panicked, Will shouts, "Just start looking!"

The boys begin to clear as much snow as they can to uncover the grass below. They begin to search the frozen grounds for the elusive four-leaf clover.

INSIDE WILL'S CLOSET and underneath a pile of clothes is his duffle bag. Bryan had searched the room, but for whatever reason elected not to move the pile of clothes. The snow globe rests within the bag and sits on top of the notebook.

With absolutely no light penetrating the bag or the clothes above, the globe begins to illuminate itself. It is, as if the snow crystals within are coming together forming a soft, gentle illumination. This illumination grows ever so slowly for a few moments, then changes abruptly to dispel a dark and milky film that fogs up the globe. Faint sounds of people screaming spill from its inner core as the darkness fills the inside of the bag.

THE SUN IS all but down and the nighttime sky is beginning to rise. Will and Jimmy have basically shoveled the entire strip of grass between their two houses. Will is starting to feel the pressure when he hears Mr. Foster yell for the third time.

"Boys, it's time to come in now!"

Jimmy hears his father's calls and looks to Will.

"Will, we better go in now."

On his hands and knees searching the frozen ground, Will looks up with tears beginning to form.

"We can't. This is our only night. We have to find one now."

New Years Eve

Jimmy looks at him with a discouraging expression.

"I think it's too late, Will. I think we're too late."

Will begins to brush away the snow faster.

"We are not too late. I know we can find it."

They hear Mr. Foster's yells once again.

"Boys, I mean it now…let's go!"

"Will, we *gotta* go."

"You go. I'm staying until I find one."

"JIMMY! GET IN HERE!" Mr. Foster roars.

"Just hurry will ya? I'll try to hold them off."

Will looks up at his buddy.

"Thanks, Jimmy."

Jimmy runs inside.

Will continues his feverish brushing of the snow.

"It's gotta be here. There has to be more than one in a patch."

Will searches for the next few moments on his hands and knees. He is beginning to feel the chill of the night now. He is also beginning to feel the hopelessness of his quest. Finding the clover is as far-fetched to him right now, as it is to go and find a miracle for his grandfather. After five minutes more of intense brushing and searching, Will begins to cry. He is defeated by the darkness of the night and he knows it. While resting on his knees he raises his head to the sky and screams.

"Why can't I find it? Why can't I find it?"

As he stares into the dusky sky, he sees tiny snowflakes trickle down upon him. The gentle flow of the snowflakes takes him away for a moment as he begins to daydream. He thinks of his grandfather again and the night he collapsed, when suddenly he hears the angelic

Chapter 4

voice again. It says, "Come through the alley, Forerunner, and he will be healed."

Will quickly looks around and sees nothing.

He screams, "Who are you? Where are you?"

Again the voice intones, "Come through the alley, he will be healed."

Out of frustration, Will screams "How can I come through the alley, I need the clover. Where are you? Who are you?"

He waits a few more moments and receives no response. The snow begins to trickle downward more frequently.

Drained, Will screams one last time. "Who are you?"

Out of desperation he falls back, helplessly staring at the rising full moon. Tears flowing, he says, "Why can't I talk to you, Grandpa? Why can't you help me find it? Why, why?"

He lies on his back for a few moments watching the moon rise. Then suddenly hears, "Looking for something?"

Will has to clear the tears from his eyes before he can see who is in front of him. His demeanor immediately changes as he begins to rise. He sees a four-leaf clover staring right back at him and resting in the hands of his brother, Bryan.

Completely stunned, Will says, "Wha…where did you get that?"

Bryan looks at him and say,. "It's not mine."

"What do you mean?"

"This is your clover from the other night. I took it that night after all of the craziness."

"You *what*?"

New Years Eve

"You heard me, I took it. And I placed that burned up stem in your room. I didn't want you to do anything crazy tonight. But as I can tell, I might be a little late."

"Bryan, you have to give me that. We don't have that much time."

Bryan looks at him almost father-like and says. "No way, Will, this stuff is too dangerous. You saw what happened the other night. Anyways, Mom and Dad have to go back to the hospital again. I think the Fosters are going with them. It doesn't look too good, Will. I don't think Grandpa's gonna make it. We gotta go in now. Brittani should be here in a few minutes. She's dropping some pizzas off that her family made."

On his hands and knees, Will looks up to his brother and says. "Bryan, you gotta help. It's our only way to get Grandpa back".

"Grandpa? What are you talking about? Nothing's going to help Grandpa now, Will. He's almost gone."

"No, he's not."

Sensing that his brother is a bit out of it, Bryan looks to him with comfort and says, "Will there's nothing we can do to bring him back. I wish there was. But it just doesn't work that way."

Will looks at him with confidence.

"Oh, yes it does. It says it all in his notebook."

"What are you talking about?"

With determination increasing through his bones, Will stands up.

"The Tablets of Fate!"

Bryan can't believe what he has just heard.

"THE WHAT?"

Chapter 4

"The Tablets of Fate! It's all in Grandpa's notebook. It talks about how we can get to heal someone quickly. We just need to find them and…."

Bryan's head is beginning to spin. He immediately feels a sense of urgency.

"Where is this notebook? I need to see it now."

Will looks at him and smiles with a sly look.

"You give me my clover, and I'll let you see the notebook."

Bryan looks down at him and says, "How 'bout, you give me the notebook, and I let you walk inside instead of dragging you?"

"You could drag me if you want to, but no clover, then no notebook."

Bryan's adrenalin is beginning to kick in. He realizes he could argue with Will all night. He knows his brother all too well and really is not in the mood to take on his stubbornness. With a deep sigh he hands the clover over to Will.

"Show me this notebook."

With an enormous smile, Will grabs the clover and begins to runs inside.

"Come on!"

Bryan watches his brother run inside and looks up at the rising full moon. It looks as if it is shining directly onto the house. The moonbeams almost look to be pointing directly into their bedroom.

"What is going on here?"

He turns and heads inside.

WILL YELLS FOR Jimmy as he darts inside and rushes quickly upstairs. Bryan is trailing right behind him. On his way upstairs, he

New Years Eve

yells to his parents, "Mom and Dad, we'll be upstairs for a while playing PlayStation."

The parents are in the family room rushing about. Their father yells back, "Bryan, wait!"

Frustrated, Bryan stops on the steps and listens to his father.

"Bryan, we have to get the hospital now."

Trying to get upstairs Bryan turns and inches closer to the top.

"Ok, Dad. Call us, ok?"

"We will. Be good. Keep an eye on Will and Jimmy, try and keep them out of any mischief. Remember, Brittani is dropping off some food, please be nice to here. "

"Ok, Dad."

The parents hustle outside. In their haste, they forget to lock the doors.

WILL JOLTS HIS door open and rushes inside his bedroom. Jimmy and Bryan quickly follow behind. Will runs directly to his closet. Bryan demands, "Alright, where's this notebook?"

Will grabs the duffle bag and carries it over to a desk in front of the window. He begins to unzip the bag and immediately a foul odor oozes from the bag. Jimmy almost faints from the smell.

"Whoa! How old are those socks in there?"

Will, holding his breath, says "There's no socks in here. Just this stuff."

He takes everything out of the bag. First he pulls some of Grandpa's pens out of the bag.

"He used these pens every time he wrote in the notebook," says Will.

Chapter 4

Bryan is beginning to get impatient.

"Let's go, runt!"

Will stops.

"Don't call me runt."

Bryan pays no mind to him.

"Just get me the notebook."

"Don't call me runt."

"I won't...the notebook please."

Jimmy just watches as the two brothers stare each other down. This is a common occurrence. If he had a quarter for every time these two stared each other down, he would be quite wealthy by now.

Reluctantly, Will reaches in the bag and pulls out the notebook. Bryan quickly grabs it from him and moves towards the bunk beds. He begins to read the pages.

Will looks inside the bag and can't believe his eyes.

"Check this out!"

"Wh...wh...what?" a nervous Jimmy stutters.

"Look at the globe!"

He pulls the snow globe out from the bag. It is completely dark inside. He can barely see the inside of the city within.

"What happen to that thing? Jimmy asks.

"I don't know. It's pretty cool, though. This is what my grandpa used to go to Rainbow Alley."

"That place sounds so cool. Do they really have ice cream on the trees there?"

Will looks at him and says, "Do you wanna find out?"

Jimmy begins to smile.

New Years Eve

Will stands up and moves everything from the desk. He has the four-leaf clover in one hand and the snow globe in the other. He looks up towards the moon and its beams of light appear to become stronger. Just behind Will and Jimmy, Bryan feverishly pages through the notebook and is unaware of his brother maneuvers. He appears more and more frantic after each page. As he reads, Will is positioning the globe in front of the window.

Bryan can't believe what he's reading. The pages in Grandpa's notebook now mirror his favorite book of all time the *Sorcerer's Shadow*. Knowing every aspect of *the Sorcerer's Shadow* and understanding the macabre world of wizards, sorcerers, Minotaurs and Scolits, Bryan senses that this can not be a good sign. He looks up and sees that Will is placing the clover over the snow globe. He notices that the moon outside their bedroom window is completely full and the rays are shining directly through the pane.

"STOP!"

Will turns towards his brother and, as if time begins to morph into slow motion, the four-leaf clover is sucked from Will's finger by an intense vacuum force from within the snow globe. Will turns back to the globe and watches as the glass begins to melts into itself and becomes almost jelly-like. As a mysterious wind begins to kick up inside the room, Jimmy screams, "What's going on?"

OUTSIDE THE COLLINS home Brittani Divine, their eighteen-year-old neighbor, is getting out of her car. As she walks up to the front door with a tray of food in her hand, she notices an odd beam of light projecting from the sky onto the boys' window. Immediately concerned,

Chapter 4

she looks as though she has seen this phenomena before. She knocks on the front door.

"What are they up to now? Boys it's me…Brittani."

WILL CAN'T SEEM to move or even utter a word back. The globe has begun a metamorphosis and Will appears to be part of it. He can only muster the strength to look to his brother and mouth the word "BRYAN!"

Bryan throws the book down and tries to run towards Will, but the force of the wind within the room pushes him away from his brother. He fights the pressure but he can't seem to get closer.

"Get out of there. This is NOT what you think it is!" Bryan screams.

Jimmy, on the other hand is trying to run from the scene, but has been pulled into the vacuum of pressure that has overcome Will. His hands clutching the bedposts, he is almost airborne as a portal begins to form underneath Will.

"Help me! I don't want to do this anymore!" screams Jimmy.

Will is beginning to be drawn into the formation of the portal. His re-actions have been slowed down considerably and he is practically helpless. The wind increases again inside the room. It is as if a tornado has spun its forces into the core of their bedroom.

"Will, hold on!"

Bryan is trapped behind the forces of the wind and Jimmy is losing his grip on the bedpost.

"I can't hold on anymore," Jimmy screams.

Bryan looks over to him and tries to reach out his hand. He yells to Jimmy, "Grab my hand!"

New Years Eve

Jimmy tries to grab Bryan's hand, but the force is too intense as the eye of the portal reaches its peak. Horrific wails shoot upward from within the dark hole.

Will looks back to his brother one last time. He can barely hear his screams for help. He looks into the portal and suddenly, he is sucked into the dark hole. Bryan screams, "Noooo!"

He looks over to Jimmy and sees that he, too, is on his way into the portal. Bryan cannot believe what he is seeing. He continues his fight to drive into the wind but he can't seem to win. The pressure is too strong. Just when he's feeling that he is gaining some momentum, Bryan notices that the portal is shrinking.

"Noooo…No way!"

The wind is decreasing and so is the portal. Bryan feels he can still make it. He begins to drive forward and makes it to within three feet of the shrinking hole. He tries to dive into the center and as fast as it appeared, the portal vanishes. Bryan hits the ground. There is no sign of the portal, Jimmy or his brother, Will.

He falls to his knees and scrapes the ground, screaming for his brother.

"Will…Will…!"

Chapter 5.
Welcome To Rainbow's Shadow

Red, yellow, green, purple, all the colors of the rainbow shoot by in jet-filled streams of light. Will and Jimmy are flying though the colorful portal much as they would slide down a water slide at their favorite water park. Intermixed within the colors are moments of darkness that shield the boys from the bright lights of the portal.

Even as the bright colors appear between dark spurts, the boys try to grab onto to one another. There is no sound within the core of the portal. The boys attempt to scream to another, but only erratic gestures of anxiety come from them as they roll around the banks of the brightly colored gateway.

Colors begin to intensify as they continue down the portal. Seamlessly, the bright pleasing colors of red, yellow, green and purple morph into four distinct bands of colors of red, white, green and black as the boys travel through the portal. The boys also begin to hear sounds of horses galloping. The brightness and the sounds overwhelm

Welcome To Rainbow's Shadow

them and they both close their eyes to act as shields. Then, as quickly as they began, the lights and sounds suddenly disappear. The boys look to one another in amazement, as they appear to be floating in a cosmic-like state. There is nothing above or below them and the darkness of the moment provides a somber, almost soothing feeling.

Will grins toward Jimmy. Jimmy, still full of anxiety, tries to speak but no words come out. He looks at his buddy's grin and then looks around. The boys have stopped falling and are hovering in what appears to be outer space. Will taps Jimmy on his foot. He mouths to him," Watch me!"

Confused, Jimmy watches Will.

Like an astronaut in outer space, Will executes a backward flip. He rotates one complete revolution and remains floating in the same spot. He looks back to Jimmy and the two begin to laugh. Jimmy mouths to Will, "Watch this!"

He also does a flip. Jimmy's flip is forward and, because of his larger size, his revolution is more of a side twirl. In any event, Will slowly claps for his friend as the two begin to play in the zero-gravity state.

Flips and twirls take their mind off of the situation. The boys are beginning to enjoy themselves in their newfound surroundings. They still cannot speak to one another, but they each mouth to each other when they try to communicate. Jimmy taps Will after Will does a double flip and says, "Watch me now...WILL!"

Stunned, Will hears his name. "I can hear you!"

Confused, Jimmy says, "So can I...."

At that moment, the boys begin to fall again. This time there are no colors, only land below. Looking down, Jimmy screams.

Chapter 5

"Oh no...we're going to die! Aghhhhhh!"

Will looks to the land below and remembers Grandpa's story.

"It's going to be ok. Just hang on."

Jimmy doesn't buy into this at all.

"Nooooooo."

The boys are falling like rocks straight towards the base of a canyon. As the ground gets closer, Jimmy loses control.

"Aghhhhh. Why did I listen to you? This is it, it's over! This is going to hurt so bad!"

Will's wisdom.

"Just hang on!"

"Aghhhh!"

The boy's decent is quick and just as they are about to impact, the lack of gravity they experienced a moment ago, is back. They hover over the surface of the land and slowly descend to the base of the canyon. Once safely on the ground, Jimmy looks up and says," That was awesome. Can you believe that?"

Will looks at Jimmy and then looks upward. There is no sign of the rainbow portal. He looks back at Jimmy and begins to laugh.

Jimmy raises his arm and points behind Will.

"Look."

Will turns around and can't believe what he sees.

"Oh my..."

The boys stare out into the canyon and gaze upon a lush meadow filled with vegetation which the wildlife is feasting on. Palm trees riddle the area. In the foreground an oasis twinkles with crystal blue waters flowing from a gentle waterfall. From the looks of it, the boys

Welcome To Rainbow's Shadow

have found paradise. Surrounding them in every direction is another beautiful sight. From soft white sand to the warm winds that kick up the rolling tide, the boys cannot believe what they're seeing.

Jimmy jumps up and tries to walk; he immediately falls down like a drunken sailor. Will laughs and says, "What's wrong with you?"

"I don't know. Every time I get up, my legs just give out."

"Are you hurt?"

"No, I'm fine. I just can't seem to walk normal."

"Here, I'll help you."

Will gets up and he, too, falls. The two cannot walk! Their legs give out every time they get up. Jimmy falls over again, then Will. This goes on for several minutes until they finally acclimate themselves to the land.

Jimmy looks over to Will, who has finally gained his balance. "What's going on here?"

Will, hands out as if he's standing on a balance beam says, "I don't know. I feel really light. Almost, as if, I can float."

"Me too. This is wild."

Jimmy looks at the waterfall. "Do you think we're there Will? Is this Rainbow Alley?"

Will looks at the waterfall, and with a huge smile on his face says, "No question about it. This is it; this is exactly like Grandpa described it."

Feeling stronger about his sense of balance, Jimmy begins to walk towards the stream.

"Where are the ice cream trees and the river of chocolate?"

Chapter 5

Will pulls the map from his front pocket. "I don't know. But that's not why we're here. We have to find the 'Tablets of Fate'. We have to get to here."

Will points to a section on the map labeled 'Ynitsed'. Jimmy studies the map.

"Where are we now on that thing?"

Will looks at the map and then at his surroundings. He does this a few times. Nothing seems to match.

"Will…you *do* know how to read that thing?"

"Of course I do. I'm just trying to find the match."

Will surveys the entire map. The only place on the map that resembles anything like where they are is the waterfall. He runs his finger over the area a few times and then looks up at the falls, but shakes his heads in confusion.

Sensing his frustration, Jimmy says, "What up Will?"

"A…I'm not sure. The only place that looks like this is…this area here. But look at this, it's not a waterfall on the map. It's more of a river of something…I can't read the description on it. It's cut off because of this hole. Looks like we just need to find this path through Zanzibar and then on to Ynitsed."

Jimmy looks at him and asks sarcastically, "What did you say?"

Not paying attention to his sarcasm Will hands him the map. "Right here, it's all on the map…read it!"

Jimmy looks at the map and says, "I had a feeling that was going to be a problem with a hole in our map. I mean, didn't you ever think that would be a problem? Not that I'm scared or anything, this is a pretty nice place and all, but didn't you ever.…"

Welcome To Rainbow's Shadow

"Shhhhh."

Will stops Jimmy's rambling and whispers, "Do you hear something?"

Jimmy listens. He looks around the canyon. He sees nothing out of the ordinary.

"What...what did you hear?"

Will begins to walk toward the waterfall and he stops in his tracks.

"I thought I heard something up there." He points to the top of the falls. Jimmy looks up toward the flowing water and still sees nothing.

"Maybe it's just the water."

Will stares at the ridge.

"Naw...I heard something. There's something up there. Let's go check it out."

Jimmy is still gazing up towards the falls.

"You want to go up there?"

"Sure...let's go see."

Reluctant, Jimmy starts to look around the canyon.

"You sure you heard something up there?"

"Yes, now come on."

Will begins to walk towards the falls. As he gets closer, he notices that the water appears to be flowing upward rather than plunging downward into the clear pool below. Perplexed by this phenomenon, Will moves closer to the flow.

Jimmy is moving much more slowly than Will, and he, too, decides to go towards the water. Jimmy moves closer to the pool than the flowing falls.

Chapter 5

The environment surrounding the boys is one of beauty and bewilderment. It appears to be a tropical setting, but the land has an awkward dark feel to it. With caverns and canyons as far as the eyes can see, the terrain blends an unexplained evil with serene and picturesque beauty.

Will finally makes it up to the waterfall. He looks back at Jimmy, who is wandering near the pool below. Gently, he takes his hand and reaches it out towards the upwardly flowing stream. The water splashes up against his hand as he marvels at the bizarre aspect of the reverse flow.

"I see it, but I can't believe it," he says to himself. He looks towards Jimmy, who is now sitting on a rock in the middle of the pool below reaching to cup some water into his hand. Will senses that he is not alone. Once again, he hears something from above. He looks back to Jimmy.

"Hey," he says in a loud whisper.

Jimmy, enjoying a taste of the clear, fresh water, doesn't seem to hear his buddy. Will tries again in his loud whisper, "Hey!"

Jimmy hears this time and looks up towards Will, who has now climbed up about halfway.

"What?" Jimmy says with a leisurely, leave- me alone type stare.

"Are you coming or what?"

"Up there?"

Whispering loudly again, Will says, "I don't think we're alone."

Jimmy replies," Good, I'm getting hungry. Maybe we can find some of that candy you told me about."

Frustrated, Will bellows, "Get up here!"

Welcome To Rainbow's Shadow

Jimmy throws the water from his hand. "Ok...ok, I'm coming."

Will watches Jimmy get off of the boulder he was resting upon. As he peers down toward the pool, he has that awkward feeling again. He surveys his surroundings. He looks upward to the top of the falls and notices that the sky is beginning to cloud over with a dark, more ominous look. He looks down the canyon and then back to Jimmy.

The sounds of solitude are quickly vanishing. He hears cracklings from above as well as below. "Jimmy hurry up!"

Jimmy slowly approaches the upward falls and suddenly Will screams, "Jimmy, look out!

Out of nowhere a Scolit jumps out at Jimmy.

Will screams, "Jimmy!"

Stunned by the attack, Jimmy is thrown to the bank of the pool. He looks up at the beast hovering over him.

"What do you want? What do you want?"

The Scolit doesn't respond. A rattlesnake-like sound comes from its tail. Jimmy is frozen with fear.

Will screams, "Leave him alone!" He begins to hurl rocks toward the Scolit, but the rocks merely float in the light air.

The Scolit tail gets closer to Jimmy. Will, grabs a broken branch and heads down toward Jimmy.

"I'm coming, bud!"

Watching the Scolit hover over him, Jimmy is helpless and in near shock as the Scolits tail begins its upward motion towards his temple. Jimmy closes his eyes and waits for the blow.

Will is about a hundred feet away when Jimmy screams as the Scolits tail strikes the left side of his head. A small gash on his temple

Chapter 5

oozes a tiny stream of blood. The Scolits tail projects a greenish milky substance that blends into the blood. Both Jimmy and the Scolit have the blood and the greenish liquid on them.

At that instant, the Scolit is lampooned by a spear underneath its right arm. The spear-- actually Will's branch-- punctures the right side cavity of the mutant. The creature falls to the ground.

Will, full of adrenalin, can't believe he has just put down this monster. He stares as the mutant lying motionless on the ground. Remembering his buddy, he rushes over to Jimmy.

"Jimmy, Jimmy are you ok?"

Jimmy, still in shock, reaches to his forehead, looks at his fingers and sees droplets of his blood.

"Yeah…yeah. I'm ok. What was that?"

Will looks over at the Scolit. "I don't know."

Jimmy says," We gotta get out of here."

"Yeah. Yeah. Let's go. Are you sure you're ok?"

Jimmy feels his head again and says, "Yeah, let's go."

Will helps Jimmy up and the two quickly move away from the Scolit and begin to head back up the canyon. As the boys move up the canyon and far enough away from the Scolit, the Scolits form begins to morph. Aspects of Jimmy's facial features begin to form on the Scolits face. Resting next to the Scolit is Will's map of Ynitsed. It had fallen from his pocket when he speared the beast.

Chapter 6
Marabus' Chosen Few

The castle crowned the Mountain of Time for centuries. It wasn't until the 19th century that it was discovered by mortals. It took two more centuries for the gateway to be opened.

Stumbling upon the gateway had proven to be quite advantageous to Marabus, the Goddess of Magic. It was during the Times of Troubles that Marabus had been challenged for the very first time by her brothers, the evil sorcerers, Abra and Malkuth. It was Malkuth who saw the value of the Tablets of Fate. He knew that possession of such powerful tablets of knowledge would allow him to rule all worlds.

Abra had less of a desire to rule, but the idea of possessing the tablets and ultimately destroying them tempted him. The act would grant them eternal strength. It was this desire that brought the siblings together.

Marabus, the outcast of the cult, had always gone her own way. Her cunning and desire not to follow in the evil footsteps of her siblings had always pitted her against her brothers. Malkuth had always known that Marabus would not follow their lead against their father, and could

Chapter 6

potentially dilute his ability to rule. But he did not act on his suspicions until Malco, their father and God of Destiny, vanished on the eve of the Time of Troubles.

It was on the eve of the Times of Troubles that Malkuth invaded the castle, which stands at the crest of Ynitsed Mountain. The invasion brought Marabus to her knees. He managed to steal the Tablets of Fate on this dark night, as well as to channel most of his sister's magical powers into his own being. All that was left for Marabus to battle was her will and her ability to harvest mortals and give them fractions of her being in an effort to form a resistance against her evil brothers.

Marabus has been living in the shadow of her brother's ancient curse for quite some time now. The passion and motivation she possessed to release a portion of her divine powers and pass along to unsuspecting mortals is not known. Some feel that Marabus foresaw the Time of Troubles and her own passing and chose to give some of her power to mortals to ensure that her successor would have a number of nearly immortal allies in the struggle against the schemes of the gods. Others say, this was a direct effort to maintain the tablets and witness to all the powerful truths within.

It was also on the eve of the Times of Trouble that Marabus informed her father) that some of her power must be put into the hands of mortals who would then become known as the Marabus' Chosen, or the Sorcerer's Shadows. This power would sleep within the bodies of those mortals, in this case, singling out one, the Forerunner, to lead the chosen few, allowing Marabus to call on them only with her permission. It would give the Chosen, the Forerunner, the innate ability

Marabus' Chosen Few

to confidently challenge the evil forces fighting for the destruction of all that is good.

INSIDE THE DUNGEON OF TIME...

With the Times of Troubles looming over the land, Marabus plotted her destiny in a dark and cold dungeon on top of Ynitsed Mountain. Her evil brothers, Malkuth and Abra, continued to rule and pillage the land she once cherished.

The dungeon, a dark and cold lower level within the castle, reeks of musty, stale air. The pungent odor of rotting flowers and damp clothing filters through the dark hallways as a stream of light barely becomes visible in a tiny corner alcove. Flashes of intermittent brightness flicker up and down the hallway.

As the flicker of light increases in intensity, a shadowy figure becomes apparent within the alcove. It isn't until the streams of light become a static flame that Marabus appears in the corner of the room. Her shadowy figure is difficult to make out until she gets closer to the glow.

Even though the darkness of the room hovers all around her, the lack of light cannot dampen the beauty she possesses. Marabus has a glow within her that is purely angelic. Her soft golden hair glistens in the darkness as it captures the light crystals within each strand of her locks.

Her brother, Malkuth, sentenced Marabus to a life of solitude, but she has managed to create a world within her incarceration. Amongst the pebbles and twigs beneath her feet, she has managed to simulate a

Chapter 6

landscape that resembles the journey Will and Jimmy are embarking upon.

The landscape model she has crafted is modest in the sense it has been created with the raw materials within her shelter, but it is accurate enough for her to simulate the canyon and the rivers outside of her fortress. Her landscape resembles the road to Ynitsed and the map that Will had left behind.

Her calmness is soothing as she continues to work diligently on her creation. The base of the canyon model even has water flowing, which mirrors the many waterfalls throughout the land. As she runs her fingers through the waters, they begin to rise. She backs away and waves her hand over the model. Above the mountainous range she had created waves of cloud formations. Within the clouds appears a perfect circle or gateway accessing the land below.

As she waves her hands over the clouds, the circle begins to close. It is as if this is a closing of the gateway into her world. The clouds form one solid mass above the land and Marabus backs away to sit calmly in the center of her tiny cell She stares at the base of the canyon at the approximate location that Will and Jimmy have entered.

Chapter 7
Malkuth's Rule

The Moat of Peril surrounds the palace on Ynitsed Mountain. When Malkuth took control of his father's land, he knew he would have enemies. He created the moat to defend himself'. To the onlooker, the moat appears to be a lush stream with vibrant vegetation and crystal clear water. However, the acidity of the liquid quickly eats away anything and everything from vegetation to flesh.

Most know of the wicked waters of Ynitsed Mountain, but even after Malkuth's reign, enemies of evil who manage to get passed his militia still try to cross the stream. Once immersed, they find themselves in a world of pain.

With the anniversary of Malkuth's rule fast approaching, Marabus only has until midnight, or when the shadow becomes full on the sundial of time, to stop her brother from his pillaging and complete devastation. If Malkuth manages to stay in control when the shadow reaches it fullness on the sundial, his ascension would be complete,

Chapter 7

the Tablets of Fate would be destroyed, and all that is good would be sentenced to damnation.

Malkuth has until the shadow becomes full.

INSIDE THE PALACE...

With a neatly groomed goatee and a bulky cloak wrapped over his shoulders, Malkuth stands in front of large, concave wall of stone. The wall has a rough exterior to it and is very plain. Malkuth, who is taller than most, has a stature of a royal. His demeanor is one of arrogance, and if one could read his true character upon his face, it would be that of pure evil, deceit, and cunning manipulation.

He stands motionless for a few moments staring at his wall. He appears to be in some sort of trance. After a few minutes, he moves forward towards the wall. His eyes are closed, and it would seem that he will run straight into the barrier. Mumbling incoherently, he continues to pace directly towards the wall.

Just as he is about to hit the exterior, the wall morphs into a gelatinous substance not unlike barrier of Jell-O. Malkuth takes himself inside the stone and into an entirely different dimension. Surrounding him is a reddish jelly-like substance that slows his movements down considerably. He is now completely inside the wall.

Once inside, he begins to look around a completely high tech environment, which resembles an ancient but modern torture chamber. Outside the wall and on the Mountain of Ynitsed, people live as if they are in the 10th century. They have no modern amenities what so ever. However, inside the Wall of Dimension, Malkuth is transformed to a future state were technology is in abundance and the latest amenities are at his disposal. The technology possessed by Malkuth has been summoned from his newfound powers and his ability to retain the Tablets of Fate.

Inside the Wall of Dimension is a vast and dark place. The reddish atmosphere at times clouds the vision, but the technology that supports the system overrides any discomfort that is evident. Malkuth, obviously accustomed to the environment, makes his way through the jelly-like chambers with ease.

As he glides down the dimension's chambers, he passes over a glass bridge supported by two glass rods. The bridge appears to hover over an empty and endless pit. If it were not for the strategically placed rods, the bridge would plunge into the abyss.

As Malkuth passes over the bridge, faint sounds of moans and shrieks of pain filter through the muffled lair. Once he is over the bridge his gaze turns to an area next to the pit and underneath the bridge.

Lines of men hang with their arms outstretched over a trench of sludge and greenish liquid. They are shackled with iron chains and leeches cover portions of their bodies. Some victims are half submerged in the murky sludge.

The line goes on for as far as the eye can see. The men number well into the hundreds. Malkuth strolls by each of them with a sly smirk across his face. His demeanor is that of a victor admiring his conquest.

Normally Malkuth doesn't acknowledge the men as they scream for his mercy. Today, he stops suddenly and peers down upon one man,

Chapter 7

obviously a warrior, who is hanging under the bridge. The warrior looks up at Malkuth while leeches crawl upon his helpless body.

Malkuth looks down upon him and says, "Nothing can stop me now, not even you Eseph. The tablets are now mine."

Dropping his head from exhaustion, Eseph does not respond. Malkuth continues his stroll through the lair and heads towards a dark alcove with a light shining through. The alcove appears smaller as he gets closer.

Once in front of the faintly lit niche in the wall, Malkuth stops. Surrounding him is his newfound sea of technology and what appeared to be an altar within a larger tabernacle. From present day computers to futuristic gadgets, Malkuth is in the middle of a tech world created by his sorcery and his expanded knowledge of the Tablets of Fate. He passes the altar and tabernacle and heads to his personal sanctuary within. He reaches forward and presses a key on one of the computers, and the walls open and streams of light jet across the room.

Malkuth marvels as the light streams around him. He tinkers with the gadgets as a child playing with his toys. He walks over to a chair in the middle of the room and sits down, head propped up, staring at the streaming lights above him. He laughs like an infant staring at a mobile above his crib.

The lights above begin to portray images of bloody battles. They recap the story of his ascension into power and depict how he has overcome his sister, Marabus, with technology and the powers given to him from the Tablets of Fate.

Marabus' seraphs did not have a chance against Malkuth's evil and futuristic fighting machines. Much like scenes from Armageddon,

Malkuth's Rule

Malkuth's Scolits use their lasers to riddle the sky and bring down Marabus' army.

Malkuth watches the scenes above him, which periodically show Marabus huddled in her dungeon. Finally, he looks over to a console in his room of techno gadgets and resting above it, encased in an electronic field which houses an ancient looking ark, are his Tablets. He stares at them for a moment with a grin, then looks back up to continue with his joyful viewing.

Chapter 8.
The Alley

The road to Ynitsed is simulated to perfection within Marabus' miniature creation. She continues to add pebbles ever so softly to her landscape. Her calmness is apparent as she gazes over her tiny countryside. She sprinkles water over the mountainside. The water blankets the landscape as it flows from the makeshift clouds in her dungeon. She stares at the base of the mountain as the droplets feed into the ridge of the mountains.

Closer to the Ridge of the Mountains

Will and Jimmy find themselves half way up the mountain, climbing towards its peak. Will is well in front of Jimmy as the boys continue their trek. Will looks back towards Jimmy as a light drizzle of rain begins to fall.

"Are you coming?"

Jimmy looks up, obviously winded and says, "Aw…great, rain. What's next? Yeah…I'm coming. Just keep on walkin'."

The Alley

Will decides to sit on a nearby boulder to wait for his buddy. He searches his back pockets. Jimmy sees this and says, "I said, I'm coming."

"I know, I just want to see where we go from here." He continues to search his pocket and begins to get a concerned look on his face.

"Hey, do you have the map?"

Jimmy, still winded, stops and looks up. "What…what map?"

"The map you fool. The map to Ynitsed!"

Now only a couple feet from him, Jimmy finds another boulder to sit on and looks at Will with confusion. "What are you talking about?"

Frustrated, Will says, "Will you just check to see if you have a map in your pocket?"

Jimmy quickly checks his pants. "I don't have anything."

"Aw. We gotta go back."

Jimmy looks at him with disbelief. "Back where? Down there?" He points down the mountain.

"Yes, we left the map down there."

"Oh, no way! "I'm not going back down there. That thing's still down there."

Will looks down the mountain, "That thing is dead, I think."

"You think. Will, I'm not going back down there. Besides you know that map anyways."

Will looks down the mountain they have just climbed. "I don't know Jimmy."

"What dya mean, you don't know! I'm not going back down there."

Chapter 8

"Jimmy, I really don't know that map all that well. We could get lost."

Jimmy looks at Will in disbelief.

"Will, less than an hour ago we transported into some bizarre land through a hole in your bedroom. I'd say we're already lost. Anywhere you can take us from here is a plus."

"I don't know."

Jimmy gets a weird look on his face.

"What's wrong, Jimmy?"

"Do you hear something?"

Will stops to listen. He looks around.

Jimmy says, "Hey Will, did you notice water up here a few seconds ago?"

Will looks at Jimmy, perplexed. "Up here? No. Why?"

Jimmy points to a crack in the canyon above them. "Look."

Will slowly turns his head upward and sees the gentle flow of water above him dripping into the mountain's ridge.

"It's just a little stream, Jimmy. Nothing to worry about."

Jimmy starts back down the mountain. "I don't know Will, can't you hear that?"

Will listens as the droplets begin to increase into a more solid flow. "I don't hear anything."

Jimmy resumes his descent. "Let's get out of here."

"What's wrong with you? I don't hear any…wait!" At that second, Will hears rumbling. He slowly turns back towards the canyon as the gentle water flow has turned into a crushing current headed right towards them.

The Alley

Jimmy turns to look back up at Will. His eyes bug out. "Will look out!"

The water rush is too quick and powerful for Will to even have a chance. It picks him up as if a hand of fate was directing it. The surge is so fast and heavy it shoots down the mountain and begins to chase Jimmy who is running to avoid the rush. Jimmy looks over his shoulder to the rushing waters. If he can make it to a curved ridge about one hundred feet ahead, he may be able to jump over the ridge and help Will.

He looks back again and notices the waters increased density as it tosses Will around and down the mountain. He has to hurry if he is going to have a chance. He's only fifty feet from the curved ridge. Sprinting like he has never done before, Jimmy reaches twenty-five feet from the ridge as the water continues to close in on him. He knows he only has seconds. Only twenty feet away, he notices the ground beneath him is beginning to carry more and more water. Splashing through puddles, Jimmy is only ten feet as he hears the roar of the water approaching him.

He only has three feet left with the rushing tide on his heel. He jumps with all his might towards the ridge and grabs onto a tree branch as the rush of the current begins to thrust up against him. He manages to look above the tides and sees Will shoot by him and around the curved ridge. Will is screaming Jimmy's name as he goes by.

At that moment, the waters overpower the tree Jimmy is holding onto and the branch snaps. Jimmy enters the flow and shoots around the ridge and into a cavern he has just seen Will disappear into. The

Chapter 8

two are being carried down a slide-like canyon within the mountain as if nature had designed a water park just for them.

The water turns into a speedway as the boys fight to keep their heads above the flow. After traveling through the channel within the canyon, they are hurled over a tiny cliff that has turned into a mini-waterfall. Thrusted over the falls, the boys land in a pool at the base of another canyon. They have traveled over a mile down the mountain and through the channel, ending up east of their original location.

Submerged in the waters below, Will flaps his arms to push himself to the surface. Once above, he frantically looks around for his buddy in every direction. The water is too deep for him to get a good look, so he feverishly paddles towards the shallow waters to look for Jimmy.

As he paddles, he tries to shout Jimmy's name, but the rushing waters drown out any sound. He keeps paddling. Once able to stand, he quickly surveys the waters again for Jimmy. There is no sign of his buddy.

Out of breath, he tries to scream out his name. "Jim…Jimmy!"

No answer. Will walks toward land when he sees something out of the corner of his eye. He quickly turns and sees a body floating face down in the waters. "Jimmy!" He screams as he darts over to the lifeless body. "Jimmy! He reaches the body and quickly turns him over to try and save him. Almost instantly he drops it and screams. The body is that of the Scolit the boys left back in the canyon.

Will, who has jumped back at least ten feet, was scared out of his wits. But he slowly approaches the dead Scolit to look at its odd facial features. The Scolit actually looks quite a bit like Jimmy. Will stares when he hears his name being called weakly.

The Alley

"Will" Will turns and sees Jimmy on top of a boulder about 50 yards from him.

"Jimmy is that you?"

"Yeah...are you ok?"

Looking at the Scolit's face, Will says in a bewildered tone,"Yeah... yeah are *you* ok?"

"Yes, you gotta get over here. Come and check this out."

Will looks back at Jimmy and sees him waving to him with great intensity.

"Ok," Will says with hesitation. He steps closer to the Scolit for a final look, when Jimmy shouts, "Come on. You're not going to believe this!"

"Ok! Ok!" Will stares at the Scolit one last time and then quickly backs away and begins to swim towards Jimmy and the large boulder. As he makes his way towards the boulder, Jimmy urges, "Hurry up. This is unbelievable."

Will quickly makes it to the boulder and begins to climb his way up.

"Help me, Jim..."

Jimmy is at the top and turns around to lend him his hand. "Will, you're not going to believe this." He reaches down and with unusual strength, pulls Will up to the top of the boulder with one hand. Will is hoisted to the top of the boulder and nearly falls back down because of the quickness of the jolt. Gaining his composure, Will looks up at Jimmy in bewilderment. He sees Jimmy staring with amazement.

"What are you looking at?"

Chapter 8

He pulls himself up and looks in the same direction as Jimmy. Will's mouth drops open in utter disbelief. He can't believe his eyes.

"Oh my God. It's true. It really is true."

Will and Jimmy stand on top of this great boulder and stare outward towards the end of a Rainbow which has seamlessly embedded itself into the landscape as well as reaching upward toward the sky. As far as their eyes can see, gigantic swaths of color are embedded into the landscape. It looks as if the colors of the rainbow are melded into the land. However these colors are distinct in their orientation. There are red, white, green and black purplish tones to the rainbow stream. Perplexed for a moment by the odd colors, the boys look past the rainbow and into the land adjacent to it.

Outside of the rainbow bridge is a land of splendor. Everything Grandpa Joe has told Will about this great land seems to be in front of them now. The land actually appears to be edible. Trees appear to be made of candied branches; bushes resemble strands of sweet vegetation. The streams look like they've been plucked from a factory. White milky streams flow directly into dark chocolate lakes. There is also an abundance of green moss filtering though out the landscape. The flow ultimately produces natural landscapes of what appears to be edible grounds. The boys cannot contain themselves.

Jimmy whispers, "Am I dreaming?"

Will looks at Jimmy, who appears to have developed a bit of facial hair. He does a double take then shrugs it off to look back at the landscape.

"We're not dreaming. We're in Rainbow Alley! It's everything Grandpa said it was."

The Alley

Jimmy grins at Will. "You hungry?"

"Starved."

"Then what are we waiting for?"

The boys take off for the edible land. They literally attack the landscape at a fever pitch and begin to eat their way through the landscape. Loose in a land of candied dreams makes the boys feel that they have died and gone to heaven.

Jimmy runs directly to the candied bushes and begins to pull the licorice–like strands of branches off and shoves them in his mouth. Will darts towards the pinecone shaped trees and bites--out squirts a raspberry jelled filling. The boys run around sampling the landscape. Every tree, bush, boulder and liquid is naturally made of a candied sweet substance.

Jimmy, knee deep in the white-chocolate lake, plucks blueberry filled chocolate acorns from a large sprawling tree that leans across the lake. He looks at Will jumping up and down on top of a marshmallow patch and says, "This is unbelievable, Will. I can stay here forever!"

Still jumping, Will shouts, "This is great Jimmy!"

As the boys run around tasting things, a stirring outside of the rainbow bridge is evident. The bushes begin to ruffle, and the water begins to morph from milky white chocolate to a florescent reddish glow. Will notices the subtle changes in the landscape.

"Jimmy..."

Jimmy stops jumping and looks over at Will. "What?"

"Look."

He points to the water, and Jimmy rushes over. They both stand on top of a boulder and watch the waters transform. A reddish tint begins

Chapter 8

to flow slowly across the banks of the river and they both get an eerie feeling. Looking up they see that the sky also shows hints of red haze.

Will looks at Jimmy. "This isn't something you see everyday."

The bushes begin to ruffle again. First to the right, then to the left, then behind them. Jimmy, turning in each direction, screams, "Who's out there?"

"I don't like this Jimbo. What dya say we get back on our trail?"

Looking at the shifts of the landscape and the increasing ruffling across the bushes, Jimmy says. "Ah, yeah...I think that would be a good idea."

The boys begin to head towards the river's edge. Tiptoeing on the bank, they begin to walk across the moss covered rockscape. After a few moments of walking, they hear grunting. Jimmy hears it first. "Are you hearing what I'm hearing?"

Will keeps on trekking. "Just keep walking."

"I don't see anything, but it sounds like it's right on us."

Will looks around. "Just keep walking."

The boys keep their pace through the moss-covered rocks. The grunts get louder.

"Will, I don't like this!"

"Me either. Don't stop, though."

As the boys walk, the rock formations begin to move ever so subtly. Neither of the boys notices at first. Then Jimmy slips off one of the rocks and hears a louder grunt. Will grabs his buddy and helps him up. They stop for a moment and look around at the sky becoming a soft red tint.

The Alley

Underneath their feet and within the moss, eyelids begin to open. While the boys continue to trek across the boulders, they don't realize that they are actually walking over moss-covered rock creatures that are slowly waking from their sleep. Each step evokes another grunt and moan while more eyelids pop open. As the moans and grunts get louder, Will stops to assess the situation. He looks towards the sky, the rainbow and then back to the pond.

He decides to continue when he hears a crackling sound behind him. He turns and sees nothing. Then he notices a rock formation move. Squinting for a better look, he sees what looks like an arm of rock and moss move about twenty feet from him.

"Ah....Jim...Jimmy."

Jimmy is walking a head of him.

"Yeah?"

"We gotta go."

"What dya think I'm doing?"

"I mean *now*. We gotta *go*!"

"What is you're prob...," Jimmy turns sees the rock formations coming to life.

"Oh my..."

He looks down at his feet and sees an eyelid open directly underneath his foot.

"Aghhh....Let's go!"

The boys take off as the rock creatures begin to stir in earnest. They tear their way towards the outer banks of the river and hear someone yelling from the distance.

"Over hear quickly!"

Chapter 8

Looking around, the boys see nothing. "What...where?"

"Over hear!" The scream is much louder.

Jimmy turns to his left and sees what looks like the cross between a rabbit and a human waving towards the boys. The creature is a Chimera, a hybrid that contains human and rabbit DNA.

"Will look!"

He points towards the chimera. It screams again, "Quickly, here or they'll get you!"

The rock creatures are beginning to stand.

Jimmy looks from the rabbit-like creature to the rock creatures. "What dya think Will?"

A rock creature almost trips Will as he runs.

"Hurry!" says the Chimera.

"Let's go!" says Will.

The boys take off toward the Chimera as the rock formations begin to hurl boulders towards them. Sprinting and jumping across the rocks and water the boys finally make it to the river's edge where the chimera is standing.

"Hurry, this way and you'll be safe."

The boys follow the Chimera as it scampers into a wooded area just to the side of the rainbow. Running as if the rock creatures are right on their tail, the boys sprint with all their might to keep up with their rescuer. About 100 yards into the forest the rabbit-like human jumps down a hole the size of a manhole. The boys stop and look at their surroundings. Out of breath, Jimmy looks at Will.

"What dya think?"

The Alley

Will looks back and sees branches breaking on the trail they just ran through.

"They're coming. We have no choice. Let's go."

Will jumps down the hole and Jimmy quickly follows. As soon as the boys make it down the hole, the chimera pops its head out to look at the trails. Quickly, she covers the opening of the hole with a camouflage of mud and leaves. She lowers herself back into the hole and huddles below with the boys. They all listen to the rumbling above ground.

She addresses the boys, "Shhhh, they'll be above us in a matter of seconds."

Terrified, the boys don't utter a sound as they listen to the sounds above and begin to really look at their newfound rescuer. Theysee traits of a human and rabbit mixed together. The chimera appears to be young and is female with long dark hair flowing over her rabbit ears.

Jimmy tries to talk, "Are they…"

"Shhh, they're above us," she says. She glares at Will and then does a double take on Jimmy. The boys quickly become quiet. They hear and feel the ground rumble above them. This last for a few minutes, and then slowly fades away.

They all sit motionless for what seems like an eternity. Restless, Jimmy moves and says, "They're gone."

Frustrated, the chimera quickly turns and says, "I said shhh!"

At that very moment a powerful arm of rock and moss comes shooting through the land above narrowly missing her furry ears.

She screams and orders, "Move, move move!"

She takes off down the hole and through a tiny passageway. The boys follow her as the rock people from above begin to thrust their

Chapter 8

arms through the land attempting to grab them. Narrowly escaping the first plunge, Will trails behind Jimmy and their new guide. Just as he is about to make it to the passageway, his ankle is grabbed by one of the rock creatures.

"Aghhh, Jimmy, help me. Jimmy!"

Even though Will has gone about twelve feet already, the rock creature's arm begins to pull him effortlessly back towards the surface.

"Jimmy! Help, help!" Will screams with a vengeance.

Will claws at whatever he can get his hands on as he is being hoisted back up the hole. Jimmy hustles back to Will, grabs onto his hand and pulls Will back down the hole. Will can't believe that Jimmy is actually pulling him back down.

He also feels unusual strength on his hand as Jimmy squeezes it while pulling him away from the creatures. The tug-of-war last for a few moments when suddenly the chimera shoots a powdery white substance up from the base of the hole. The substance covers the boys and the rock creature. The rock creature screeches as if being burned by acid lets go of Will's leg. The boys roll down the hole and land at the base of the bunker.

The darkness at the base of the bunker makes it difficult for the boys to see. They look in every direction. Finally they see a fluorescent illumination in front of them. The chimera holds a crystal rod that produces a violet illumination. The boys see only the face of the chimera. "What was that stuff?" Will asks, brushing the white powder off his face.

The Alley

"Glylack, it is used to ward off the creatures. It is only temporary. We should hurry. They can come back. Follow me and you'll be safe."

Will looks at the chimera and asks, ""What's your name?"

"They call me Danaë."

"Where are we?"

"There will be time for that. We must go. Quickly follow."

Danaë takes off down a corridor passage. The boys look back towards the surface and then down the corridor. Jimmy says. "Do you feel good about this?"

Hearing some ruffling at the surface, Will looks upward. "I feel better about this, than that…Let's go!"

The boys reluctantly begin to follow Danaë down the passageway that winds underneath the mysterious land above.

Chapter 9
The Unknowing Apprentice

Brittani Divine had been living next to the Collins family for the last few years. In fact, she used to baby sit Will when he was younger. Now that Will is older and Bryan is at an age he can monitor his brother, her services have not been necessary for quite some time. However, considering the circumstances with Grandpa Joe and her closeness with the family, Brittani decided to come by and see how everyone is doing. At the very minimum, she might help keep the family company in this time of need.

Brittani attends the same school as Bryan. Secretly, Bryan has had a crush on Brittani ever since she used to baby-sit Will. Even though he would run to his room and fake playing PlayStation every time she would come over, he loved knowing that his secret sweetheart was in the house while he hid in his bedroom.

Brittani also developed a bond with Grandpa Joe during her years of babysitting. Their relationship was so strong, she would sit and listen

The Unknowing Apprentice

to his stories. With Grandpa Joe in the hospital, it was only natural Brittani would be by sooner or later to lend her support.

Tonight was different, though. There would be no running to his room. His little brother and next-door neighbor were somehow sucked into a vortex in the middle of their bedroom. It was incomprehensible to Bryan.

As he lay on the bedroom floor, head pounding and spirit weak, Brittani pops her head into the room. She cannot believe the mess.

"Hi Bryan, what's going on?"

Bryan doesn't acknowledge her. He merely continues pounding the floor to the rhythm of his headache, slowly and weakly.

"Bryan? Hello?"

"He's gone. He's just gone. My parents are going to kill me."

He turns to Brittani with tears in his eyes. "This is why I tell them I didn't want to watch these guys!"

Stunned, Brittani drops her coat in their doorway.

"Bryan what's wrong? Who's gone? Where?"

Bryan sits up and looks directly at her. "Will! Will, and Jimmy both. They were just both were sucked through the hole. I tried to stop it. But the force was too strong. It was just too strong."

"What? What are you talking about? Bryan, you have to calm down and tell me what's going on. I'm sure you're brother is just playing a trick on you. You know how creative he can get."

"This is no trick. I'm telling you Will and Jimmy were sucked through a hole in the floor. They're gone."

Confused Brittani says, "Did you check the basement?"

Chapter 9

"Brittani, you don't understand. My grandfather, his stories, they're true."

Brittani looks at him in amazement. "Rainbow Alley?"

"Yes, whatever he was calling it. It's true. Will found all the elements needed to open the door. He did it. He thinks he can save Grandpa. I don't know it's all crazy."

Brittani listens closely, almost as if she expected this day would come sooner or later. Since she had spent many nights over the Collins' house, she had become well versed with the story of Rainbow Alley. It was all Will could ever talk about.

Just a few years ago Will snuck into his grandfather's bag and took his journals and kept them for a few weeks. He let Brittani read all of it. The detail and the beauty of the story captivated her. It stuck with her and proved to be quite a life-changing experience reading Grandpa's writings. In the following weeks Will and Brittani would dissect Grandpa's writing much like a group would do at Bible study.

Then, Brittani approached Grandpa to learn more about this unique and wonderful story. From that point on, Brittani became a tag-along listener every chance she could get. She was well versed in the writings of Grandpa Joe about Rainbow Alley.

As Bryan lies on the ground moping, Brittani springs into action. "Do you have the clover?"

Bryan looks at her in confusion. "What did you say?"

"The four-leaf clover, do you have it?"

Still confused, Bryan says, "How do you know about that?"

The Unknowing Apprentice

"Never mind. I'll be back in five minutes. Start to set the room up again, exactly how your brother did. We may be able to do this. Hurry! We don't have much time, we must get there as soon as we can!"

Still confused, Bryan looks up at Brittani. "Huh?"

"Just set the room up how Will did before they were sucked into the vortex. I'll be right back."

Brittani grabs her jacket and sprints down the stairs.

Still confused, Bryan watches her leave. "What?"

Chapter 10
Bornea – The Land Beneath

The boys follow Danaë through the corridors lit only by florescent rods strategically placed across the base and ceiling of the passage. They notice many side passages throughout their descent. Each passage appears to lead downward, with the same sort of florescent rods illuminating the alternative routes.

As they pass each alternate passage, Will can't help but think that wherever they were going better lead to a way out. If he had to try and trace the way back up the maze of passages, it would be an impossible task.

During the descent, the boys notice symbols on the walls. Though they are meaningless to them, they note that as they pass them, Danaë places her hand over her heart in the form of worship. Finally Will says, "Danaë, stop, please."

Danaë stops and slowly turns towards Will. She doesn't utter a word.

Bornea - The Land Beneath

Out of breath, Will looks around and turns to were they came from. He looks back to her and asks," How much longer?"

Reassuringly, Danaë looks into his eyes and says, "We're here--look!"

She backs up about four feet and moves to the side. Pointing her arm upward with her palm raising up, she stands at a massive sculpted arch entrance.

The boys look at each other and then slowly begin moving forward. With every step they take they begin to appreciate the size of this magnificent arched entrance. As they move closer, they see that beyond the arch lies an underground paradise.

The boys gaze out on a wondrous metropolis of beauty and activity. Though they have traveled far underground, what they see is a city that appears to be above ground. They see cliff dwelling structures and rows of hut-like homes lined across the terrain. Roads have been clearly paved to lead the inhabitants throughout the land below.

The only way into and out of the city is a bridge. These bridges resemble giant pipes of metal that support the crossing platforms. The platforms provide walking foundations for travelers, but are separated from each other. Each platform is approximately fourteen feet in length and seven feet in width. As soon as one of the platforms ends, the other starts up. A two-meter gap yawns between each platform. When traveling over the bridges, the chimera typically hops over the gap, obviously accustomed to the structure.

The bridges lead to a center tower in the middle of the city with archaic peaks built on top of it. Each peak is higher than the next with

Chapter 10

a total of five peaks protruding upward. An additional two peaks curve outward and provide platforms for featured speakers.

At the base of the city, merchants conduct their daily routine. Hovering motorcycle-type vehicles careen though the streets.

Will and Jimmy gaze in awe.

"Can you believe this, Jimbo?"

Jimmy responds, "This is unbelievable, what are those floating things below?" He turns and sees Will looking at him in an awkward way.

"What?" Jimmy says, obviously irritated.

Will sees that Jimmy's complexion appears to have changed. "Aah… nothing. What floating things?"

Danaë turns to them and says, "Graviports. They help us pilot through Bornea."

Will looks at her. "Bornea? Is that where we are?"

Danaë says proudly. "It is. Welcome back. Please come with me." She begins to walk over one of the bridges. Jimmy looks at Will. "Did she say welcome back?"

Confused, Will says, "Yeah she did."

They watch as Danaë walks across a bridge and hops effortlessly over the two meter gap along the way. Will starts to follow and Jimmy tags along. The boys walk across the bridge and gingerly jump over the gaps along the way.

Bornea resembles a place that dreams are made of--lush vegetation punctuated by gentle waterfalls and colorful blossoms. Will and Jimmy can't get enough of it as they walk and hop across bridges and gaps to the center towers

Bornea – The Land Beneath

Danaë has made it across the final bridge and waits tranquilly for the boys. Jimmy lags behind while he surveys the land. He is still in awe at the vast and complex underground city. From the graviports to the sophisticated dwellings below, he still can't believe what he sees. All the while, his appearance is ever so slightly changing with every second that goes by.

Will finally makes it across the last bridge. He sees Danaë standing at the edge of the bridge underneath a bright spotlight. For a split second he stops, overtaken with her unique beauty. She looks absolutely angelic in front of him. His body begins to get warm and tingly. This is the first time he has actually seen her in a bright light. She is beautiful.

Trying not to show his obvious infatuation, he turns quickly towards Jimmy. "Hurry up man."

Jimmy looks up. "I'm coming."

Will turns back to Danaë. She is only an arm's length away. Startled, Will awkwardly says. "Aah…where to now?"

Danaë steps aside and points to the tower. "I must stay here. You are to enter. You are expected."

Stunned, Will protests. "What? What are you talking about? How can I be expected? Why can't you go up there? What's in there?"

Calmly and soothingly Danaë slowly points to the towers and says, "It will be fine. You are expected."

Jimmy finally makes it across the final bridge. "Expected for what?"

Danaë looks at Jimmy and says. "Not you. You must come with me." Pointing to Will she says, "You must go see Him."

Jimmy protests, "What do you mean not me, and who is Him?

Chapter 10

Will looks at her and says, "We're not splitting up. You tell Him that we're not splitting up. Who is he, anyway?"

Danaë looks at both of them reassuringly. "Abra is the one who knows all. It is he who you seek. He is expecting you."

Jimmy is beginning to get agitated. "Expecting him? How can that be? It's not that we made plans to be here or anything."

Danaë looks at Will with her soft brown eyes and hypnotic gaze. "It is he who you seek."

Jimmy says, "I don't like this, Will. This doesn't seem right."

Will looks at Jimmy, then back to Danae's soft brown eyes. "I think we're gonna be ok, Jimmy. "Turning to Danaë he asks, "Where will you take him?"

Danaë says softly, "He will be with me. He is safe, you have my word."

Jimmy can't believe what he's hearing. "Will, don't leave me."

Will looks at Jimmy. "Jimmy, it'll be ok."

"How can you know that?"

Will looks back at Danaë. "I just do. I don't know. I just do."

"Oh, this is crazy." Jimmy moans.

"I won't be that long. I think this might be what I'm looking for."

Will steps on the path toward the towers. Jimmy tries to follow, but Danaë moves in front of him and says," You are to be with me."

Jimmy tries to get around her. "Will!"

Will turns around and says. "Jimmy, it'll be ok. Just stay with her."

Jimmy watches Will walk on. He looks over at Danaë and mutters, "This is nuts. All right, where are we going?"

Bornea - The Land Beneath

Softly, Danaë says, "Follow me."

Danaë begins to walk in the opposite direction of Will, towards the base of the city.

Will stops and watches Jimmy and Danaë begin their descent. Reassured, he tentatively resumes his walk towards the castle-like towers.

*∗*Chapter 11*∗*
The Merger

Moving like a snail, Bryan's lackluster approach to setting the room up is dismal. Bryan would rather be working on his downloading more videos to his iPod™ than attempting to follow his little brother into a mythic vortex in the center of his room.

He slowly picks up pieces of debris on the floor and tosses them over to his bed, creating a much larger mess in a different location. He slowly reviews each piece before tossing it. He does this for most of the mess that was on the floor.

As he nears the bottom of the pile, he starts to see shreds of his grandfather's Rainbow Alley notebook. It's pretty torn up at this stage, and has a hole burned through its center. He tries to pick up the notebook piece by piece.

Just as he was going to toss the book over to the bed he notices something different. Puzzled, he sits on the edge of his bed and pages through the book. At each page he grows increasingly focused.

The Merger

Trying to decipher his grandfather's writings he is struck by an eerie familiarity within the content. He has read this before. There is only one other book that has affected him so strongly--a book that he has literally memorized from beginning to end. A book that has shaped his thinking and, in many ways, his personality, the last few months. As Bryan pages through his grandfather's notes on Rainbow Alley, he is also reading excerpts from his all-time favorite novel, *The Sorcerers Shadow*.

The most amazing aspect to Bryan's discovery is how *The Sorcerer's Shadow* story is interwoven into Grandpa's notebook. It is as if Grandpa wrote the story himself. The stories appear seamless. As Bryan reads them, he is particularly struck by how the diagrams and maps of Rainbow Alley closely resemble those in *The Sorcerer's Shadow*. They have hauntingly merged into one story.

After reading Grandpa's tattered notebook, Bryan is even more confused about this night. He drops the book back down in its original spot on the floor, and stares out of the window at the full moon lighting up the winter sky. Only a few moments go before Brittani runs back into the room holding her own notebook. "Ok Bryan, I've got it."

Bryan continues to stare at the moon.

"Bryan, come on I've got it!"

Deflated, Bryan turns to Brittani, "What? What do you have?"

"Come here, I'll show you."

Bryan gets up and Brittani moves in to where he was sitting. She throws her notebook on the desk." Look at this."

Bryan looks down at the notebook and reads "Grandpa Joseph and Rainbow Alley. What's this?"

Chapter 11

Brittani sits next to Bryan and grabs his hand. Immediately Bryan's hormones shoot up like a wild monkey running up a tree. Regardless of the situation, he is still a young-blooded teenager. Having any girl grab his hand at this age is cool, let alone someone he had fantasized before! He tries to maintain his cool.

"Bryan, your grandfather was an amazing man."

Bryan interrupts. "*Is* an amazing man."

Humbled, Brittani continues, "You're right. I'm sorry. *Is* an amazing man. Anyhow, every time he would come over and I was here, I would listen to the story he was telling you guys. I really enjoyed our time together and I think he really liked that I was so into his story telling. At first, it was just that. Just story telling. He had a wonderful way with words. But then, as he would continue with the stories, they became more real to me. I had to learn more. He must have sensed this, because one of the days he was telling the story, he asked if I would take notes. I wasn't sure why he did this, but it became more evident as over time. He was forgetting important parts to his own story! He needed someone to take notes and write his story. I did this for a couple years."

Bryan points to the tattered notebook on the ground. "You mean that's not Grandpa's writing?"

Brittani smiles and says, "No, it's mine. I was his official note taker."

Bryan looks back to the desk. "What's this, then?" He points to the notebook Brittani brought into the room.

"A copy. An exact copy, I must say. He asked me to make an exact copy of the original in case...well, in case something happened to it.

The Merger

"Looking over to the charred notebook pieces she says, "Something did happen to it. And I did make a copy."

Bryan glares at her and grumbles, "I don't think it's an exact copy, at least not now."

Confused, Brittani asks, "What are you talking about?"

"Check this out."

Bryan leans over and hands the charred notebook to Brittani. She pages through the first couple pages, slowly skimming from top to bottom. Her pace quickens. She tries not to tear the charred pages. She is obviously confused about what she reads.

"This doesn't make any sense. Marabus and Malkuth? I never wrote those names in the book."

Bryan sits down next her. "That's the weird thing about this. I know these characters all too well. I know them very well. They're all characters from the *The Sorcerer's Shadow*."

"The what?"

"*The Sorcerer's Shadow*. The book is awesome. It's one of my favorites."

"Why did your grandfather write it into his notebook?"

"That's even weirder. I just told him about this book the other day. He must have really liked it to do this."

Confused, Brittani pages through the charred book and says, "Huh…that just doesn't seem like something he would do."

"Then who…Will? No way. Rainbow Alley was sacred to him. He would never do this to it. Naw, it had to be my grandfather."

Brittani, still reading the book, looks at Bryan with a frightened glare, "Bryan who is Abra?"

Chapter 11

Bryan looks at Brittani, excited that he knows the answer. "Oh, Abra, he's a nasty one. He's the brother of this evil ruler, Malkuth. He puts on this nice guy front so he can deceive anyone who comes to him. He's like a caretaker for Malkuth. Those two together are nasty! The stuff they do to people is, well, just nasty!"

Concerned, Brittani puts the charred book down. "Bryan, I'm not sure what's going on here, but I think your brother may be in more trouble than you think. We need to start this now."

Bryan looks at her in disbelief. "Start what now?"

"Look at the last page in the book."

Bewildered, Bryan slowly picks up the book and turns to the last page. He reads aloud, "As the two young strangers from above descended deeper into Bornea, Abra prepared for the return of The Forerunner." Bryan looks up at Brittani. "You don't think…"

Brittani stares at Bryan. "I don't know. It's just all too weird right now. I do know we have to do something before those clouds cover the moon."

Bryan looks out the window and sees a group of clouds heading towards the full moon. "Why?"

It's one of the elements, the Glare of the Moon Rays. If they're gone, so are our chances. Your grandfather was very specific and he made me memorize each of the elements in their proper order. The age of teen or a teenager, the four leaf clover, the snow globe and the full moon on the new year"

Bryan looks at Brittani, sadly. "You mean to tell me he told you all of the elements. He never told any of us. He just had all these crazy clues for us?"

The Merger

Smiling, Brittani says, "I know he told me that, too. He made me promise not to say anything until the time was right. Well, I guess the time couldn't be righter."

Startled, Bryan screams, "Whoooaaa". He quickly drops the charred book and jumps back.

"What's wrong?" Brittani says.

Eyes wide open, Bryan moves back towards the book he had just dropped. "Check this out."

Confused Brittani says, "What?"

Bryan very tentatively picks up the notebook. Trying not to hold the book too firmly, he moves closer to Brittani and says, "It's writing itself."

"What are you talking about?"

Bryan shows her the last page. "Look."

As Brittani looks at the book she sees words appearing on the page. It says:

As the two young strangers from above descended deeper into Bornea, Abra prepared for the return of The Forerunner. Abra knew that the young Forerunner was desperate. This would be easy for him as he....

"As he what? It stopped! As he what?" Bryan shouts.

Brittani looks at the clouds moving towards the moon. "Bryan, we have to hurry."

"This is unbelievable," Bryan says. "Ok Ms. Element lady, what do we have to do?"

From her jeans pocket, Brittani pulls out a four-leaf clover encased in a tiny plastic case. Bryan looks at the clover and then back to Brittani.

Chapter 11

His lungs fill with air and he lets out a stream of air from his nostrils. "Are you sure you know what you're doing?"

She looks at him with soft brown eyes. "I trust in your grandfather, Bryan. His writing will show us the way."

Satisfied, Bryan grabs the four-leaf clover. "That's good enough for me. Let's do this thing!"

Chapter 12
Sibling Rivalry

Malkuth's ascension to power was riddled with deceit and cunning evil. Once the proud son and clearly the chosen one, Malkuth had long been on track to rule the land. If only his patience had persisted, none of the unnecessary carnage would have occurred.

Even in his earlier years, Malkuth had plotted his ascension with or without his fathers blessing. He knew that once the Tablets of Fate were out of his father's possession--and out of the minds of the people-- his siblings would not stand a chance against him.

In his warped sense of reality, his siblings' gentleness was the central weakness to their aspirations of power. Neither of them even hinted for the right to ascend to their father's throne. It was something that wouldn't have crossed their minds. They were satisfied knowing that their father was the One Power, the One Being who would make everything pure. But when Malkuth deceived them all, everything changed.

Chapter 12

Quickly, sides were chosen. Wars between Malkuth's and Marabus' armies commenced. The two sides collided and nothing pure could continue to exist. Although Marabus' armies fought valiantly, Malkuth had once again outwitted his sibling. It would take a miracle for Marabus to overcome her brother, reclaim the Tablets of Fate, and restore honor to her father and wholesomeness back to the land.

Marabus would have to develop an army that would overcome, not through force, but through purity. To fight Malkuth in a conventional manner had proven fruitless. Countless warriors had been dealt an uneven hand and now lie deep within the catacombs of Malkuth's castle. Marabus would need to find the pure of heart to lead her people from this bondage of evil. Her quest had been all but lost, but for the ancient tablet prophesies that would inspire her to call upon her chosen few.

Nestled deep in her cell Marabus plots her next move as she cleverly allows her siblings to play into her hands.

Chapter 13:
The Journey Begins

After crossing the bridge, Will feels very alone as he travels deeper into this oasis in the center of Bornea. Looking back, he can still see Danaë and Jimmy traveling downward towards the city, but they are growing smaller as the distance between them grows.

Trying to keep his courage about him, Will walks toward the tower. The outer layer of the circular formation is smooth and solid. Will wonders how he can gain access. From a distance it appeared to be a hovering cylinder linked to the bridges. Now, that Will is within central structure it, it is even more puzzling.

It doesn't seem to have an entrance as he follows the outer layers of the formation. He runs his hand over the edges of the wall to see if he might feel a chink that would be part of a doorway. The smooth exterior wall feels almost soothing to the touch. Will circles the structure completely, dragging his hands across the wall.

After a few moments, Will begins to lose his sense of direction and hypnotically follows the wall with his hand still dragging. What

Chapter 13

had seemed like a never-ending journey around one circle has actually become a winding maze of perfect circular formations. He actually appears to have entered the circular maze opening without even noticing. When Will finally gains his senses and removes his hand from the wall, he realizes that he is near the center of this odd formation and cannot see the city below him anymore. He is now deep within the coil-like opening.

Trying not to panic, Will is just about to turn back when he hears a faint sound up ahead. He stops to listen, but can barely hear the soft voice. Taking a deep breath, he continues on. The deeper he enters the coiled entrance, the clearer the sounds become. What he's hearing now sounds a lot like a preacher giving a sermon.

Deeper and deeper he travels into the coiled opening. A light begins to shine at the end of the circular maze. The preacher's voice is becoming more and clearer as he makes his way out of the coiled entrance and toward the light.

Tentatively, Will peers out of the maze and into the light. He sees a group of young adults sitting up on a hill listening to a speaker. The speaker leans against a tree as his young audience stares and listens hypnotically to him.

The speaker has hair that rests over his shoulders and covers his ears. His beard and mustache are dark and his stature is gentle. As he rests against the tree, he almost seems to become one with nature as his unassuming way and soft-spoken tones draws his enrapt audience in.

The speaker says, "It is not thou that brings us to this task, but it is the evil forces that surround us. We must come together and fight for what is ours and bring peace back to our land once again."

The Journey Begins

Will creeps closer to the group. The speaker subtly glances his way, but continues his speech.

"Our land has been ravaged and pillaged by the evil ones. The frightening part, my young friends, is not what they have done. It's what they intend to do. We have not yet seen their wrath. What has come to us thus far is nothing compared to what will come."

Will sits down in the back of the group. He notices that the audience is filled with young warriors. The average age of these warriors cannot exceed eighteen. Their demeanor and their intense concentration on their leader intrigue Will.

The speaker continues, "My young warriors, our time is limited, when the newness of the day arrives and the night time is full, the true intentions of the wrath of Malkuth will filter through our land. We have seen what it has done to your elders. You, my young friends, will be next. We must stop them and we must stop them now."

A young warrior in the center speaks up, "How will we stop them, Father? As you have said, look what they have done to our elders. We are less then them, how can we stand with Malkuth armies and his sorcerer's magic?"

Will is stunned at the mention of a sorcerer.

The speaker looks directly at his young warrior and says, "It is written: *When evil strikes to devour the land, the Forerunner shall impart the keys to recovery.* It is the Forerunner who can defeat the evil one. It is the Forerunner that will free us all."

He glances at Will as he finishes his sentence.

Will quickly flashes back to when he was creating the closet vortex for his grandfather on Christmas Eve. He was told by Grandpa Joe to

Chapter 13

create a sign that said "Forerunner" on it. Will sees himself creating the sign and then affixing it to his closet door in anticipation of his grandfather's visit that night. He quickly comes back to his senses and listens.

The speaker begins to walk away from the crowd, when the one young warrior again speaks up, "Abra, how will we know when the Forerunner arrives? How will we know?"

Abra stops and slowly turns to the crowd. Then he stares towards Will.

"It is he who will know, and it is he who will come forth to show us the way."

Abra turns from the crowd and begins to walk inside his tower.

Will watches as the crowd begins to separate. They all appear to be in a noticeable worried state. The young warrior who had spoken up remains as the rest of the kids slowly walk down the coiled exit.

Will sees the warrior alone, and empathizes with his plight. The young warrior has had his confidence completely stripped away. His head down, shoulders drooped over, he remains motionless.

Will slowly walks over to him. "Are...are you ok?"

He slowly gazes up towards Will and says, "We have lost our will. The end is near."

Confused, Will replies, "End? What end? What is going on here? What is this place?"

Dressed in native garb the warrior looks more closely at Will and sees the obvious differences between the two. He smiles and says, "Are you the Forerunner?"

The Journey Begins

Will quickly responds. "I'm no Forerunner or what ever he was talking about. I'm just a kid who's looking to save his grandfather. Now what is this place and who was that guy?"

"You are within Abra's Temple of Knowledge," says the young warrior.

"Abra? Was that Abra?"

"It is."

"I think I'm supposed to be talking with him. Danaë sent me in here and said he was expecting me."

The warrior smiles hugely and shouts, "You *are the Forerunner!"*

Will protests, "I am no Forerunner, or whatever you want to call it. Now can you take me to see this guy? I need to get moving. My grandfather doesn't have much time and I need to find the Tablets of Fate."

Enthusiastically the warrior responds, "You are the Forerunner! Oh! Yes…yes, I would be honored to"

He quickly walks towards the tower, practically giddy with excitement.

"Come! Quickly follow me! Follow me! It's the Forerunner, the Forerunner here! He's here, oh my, he's here to deliver us. The Forerunner's here."

Will doesn't quite know how to take this, but remembering Danaë's directions, he can't help but follow the young warrior. As he walks toward the center of the tower's entrance, he begins to sweat. With every step closer to the entrance streams of heat begin to flow around them. It is as if they have walked inside a furnace as Will paces himself behind the young warrior.

Chapter 13

Will can actually feel the heat penetrate his body. It quickly produces streams of perspiration which slide off his forehead. He looks over at his companion. "Is it always this hot in here?"

With a sad expression, the young man turns to Will and says, "No. Ever since Malkuth began his wrath, the climates have changed. It's his sorcery. It has no equal."

Will stops in his tracks.

"You said that earlier. What are you talking about? Who is Malkuth?"

The young man looks directly into Will eyes, "It is not for me to say who or what he is. All that I know is that we must prepare to stop him."

"What do you mean by prepare? And stop him from what?"

The warrior points to the base of the canyon.

"Look."

Will looks down into the canyon and sees a grouping of young warriors at the base of the city. They have all gathered for what looks like the beginnings of a competition with the graviports.

"What are they doing?"

"Training," a deeper voice than the young man's replies.

Will quickly turns and sees Abra standing before the entrance to his temple.

"Training? Training for what?"

Abra walks softly over to Will and peers down into the city below.

"A war that cannot be won."

Will watches as the young men begin to race and duel with their graviports in remarkable feats of maneuverability. They look like they

The Journey Begins

are riding flying motorcycles as they careen up and down the city walls, flying, dipping and dodging one another.

"I don't understand. If this war can't be won, then why even train?

Abra looks at Will and softly says, "Come with me and you will understand."

He turns and walks towards the temple entrance. Will watches Abra walk inside, then glances again at the warriors below. He looks over to the young warrior who had escorted him in.

"Please, follow him. He will show you everything."

Apprehensively, Will looks back at the city below once more and then walks towards the temple's entrance. He looks back at the young warrior.

"Aren't you coming with me?"

The young warrior has stopped as if an invisible fence barricaded him.

"This is as far as I may go. Please continue on. It is not for me to enter the sacred temple. It is for your eyes only."

Will turns back to the entrance and mumbles, "My eyes only? This is getting weirder by the moment."

Then he enters the temple.

As quickly as the swirling heat had swarmed over his body outside, a refreshing coolness surrounds Will in the interior of the temple. The foyer features a smooth white surface with a glimmering ceiling that is at least twelve feet high. Once Will gets to the end of the foyer, the ceiling opens up and he enters a circular temple. He is awestruck.

Chapter 13

As archaic as it is outside the walls of the temple, the interior is futuristic in every facet. From holographic images of the graviport training in the city below, to large and opulent decorations throughout the structure, the temple is magnificent.

Will gapes as he walks around trying to absorb this futuristic site. He stops to watch some of the holograms of the training below. Within one of the holograms he sees Danaë and Jimmy watching the training. They're smiling as the other warriors careen past them at speeds beyond comprehension.

"Quite impressive aren't they?" Will hears Abra voice once again.

He turns and sees Abra sitting at a long dining table in the center of the temple. He is feasting on grapes and other fruits and candy-like flavored vegetables.

Will says, "They sure are. I can't believe they can make those things climb the walls the way they do."

"That's only a small portion of what the graviports can do," Abra responds.

"Really? What else can they do?"

Abra smiles, "What would you like them to do?"

Will looks at him, confused.

"I'm not sure I understand."

Abra motions for him to join him at the table.

"You will, my son, you will. Come now and join me."

Will walks closer to the dining table. The graviports almost appear to be inside the structure as they careen through the sides of the walls in a holographic mirage. Will is mesmerized.

He tentatively sits at the opposite end of the table from Abra.

The Journey Begins

"Eat. They are quite fresh, I assure you."

Will looks at the feast on the table.

"I, ah, I guess I can have some."

He grabs a handful of grapes and chunks of the candy-flavored vegetables and indulges himself. Abra smiles as he watches Will feast at the table.

With his mouth full, Will mumbles, "So what is this place? And why did they say you were expecting me? Who are you? Are you the one that can take us to Ynitsed?"

Smiling, Abra says, "You have many questions. Many, that I would like to answer and will. However, I must ask you one first. Will you tell me how you found us?"

Confused, Will looks up. His mouth is still full. "Found you? You guys found me. Danaë rescued us from those rock things above."

Abra looks at him sternly. "Not inside Bornea. I mean, how did you find our land, how did you find the Alley?"

Fearful that he might be about to get scolded, Will responds softly, "Oh. That. Well, you see, um, there was this waterfall and...."

Abra sits up in his chair and interrupts Will, "Did you come through the portal?"

Confused again, Will responds, "The portal?"

"It opened again, didn't it?" Abra says.

Will looks at Abra as he puts his food down and says. "Look, in all honesty, I really don't know how I got here. We came through something; I'm not sure what it was. But I do know I have to be here to save my grandfather. I have to get to Ynitsed. And I don't think I have that much time."

Chapter 13

Abra sits back in his chair with a satisfied look on his face. "It is the Forerunner. The prophecy is being fulfilled."

He gets up and begins to wander away from the table while staring at the holographic images.

Will looks up at him, "Can you help us? Can you show us the way to Ynitsed?"

Abra begins to laugh, "The road to Ynitsed? My son, my son if we don't act quickly there will *be* no road to Ynitsed."

"What are you talking about?"

With his back still to Will, Abra raises his arms towards the holographic images surrounding them, and says, "Perhaps a brief history will provide answers for you."

Suddenly the images of the graviports below disappear and the thunderous roar of a waterfall is seen and actually felt inside the temple. Startled, Will's eyes open wide as he watches the walls depict scenes from up above Bornea.

THE DAY THE ALLEY WENT DARK…

The waterfall roars as the sun shines brightly down upon the Alley. Streams of rainbows shoot across the horizon as the gentle chimeras of the Alley go about their daily routine.

The younger chimeras are playing their games near the stream as the elders pick their crops off the lush vegetation. For as far as the eye can see, the landscape is full of edible candy-flavored trees, bushes and grasses. It is a virtual and endless paradise for the young and the young at heart. Happiness abounds on this more than beautiful day.

The Journey Begins

Young couples are camped out underneath chocolate-filled foliage. Danaë and her siblings run through the spraying waters of the falls. The setting could not be more beautiful and content.

Playing tag in the waters, Danaë runs past her siblings and tags them, then darts under a licorice tree that's home base. While she laughs at her brothers running clueless through the waters attempting to tag the other kids, a dark shadow suddenly covers the sun and erases the rainbows from the sky.

Confused, Danaë looks up towards the sky. Instantly the Alley is rocked by a barrage of boulders crashing into the landscape. It is as if a meteor shower has hit the small Alley paradise.

Crushing stones impact the sides of the terrain with such force that the people of the Alley are thrown from their idyllic settings. The barrage of stones from nowhere seems to last for an eternity, as the residents attempt to run for cover.

As the people run, it seems the boulders sense their retreat and fall strategically in front of them to stop their flight. Slowly but surely, the barrage creates a circle that surrounds and encloses the residents of the Alley.

The barrage suddenly stops. They are all in the center of the stream with boulders encircling the group. The silence that follows is deafening as the creatures of the Alley try to gain their senses.

The elders begin to push the younger generation to the center of the stream in an effort to protect them from any other flying boulders. As soon as the last child is pushed to the center, a loud, irritating squeaking sound emanates from the boulders. Holding their delicate ears for protection from the painful sounds, the elders turn towards the boulders

Chapter 13

and see that each of them is opening up. Droves of Scolits emerge from the crevices of each boulder. There are too many to count, and the gladiator-like Scolits run directly for the center of the stream.

Reacting as quickly as they can, the elders form a chain to try and protect one another. With the Scolits only feet away, they brace themselves for battle. At that moment, the Scolits leave their feet and leap towards the elders.

Danaë watches in horror as each of the Scolits jump on top of an elder and mysteriously disappear, taking the elder with it. One after another jumps on top of an elder, and they both disappear. The process only lasts for a few moments. As soon as Danaë and her siblings gain their senses, they see that half of the chimeras have vanished. Most of those are the elders of the tribe.

The youngsters are stunned as the sky grows darker and rain begins to fall. The same rocks that carried the Scolit gladiators now morph into the rock creatures that chased Will and Bryan.

Danaë quickly takes the lead and leads the survivors to the forest and the entrance to Bornea'. While running Danaë looks back. Some remaining elders are trying to fight off the creatures.

This battle only last for seconds as the rock creatures crush the remaining elders. Shocked, Danaë quickly pushes the younger ones down into the entrance of Bornea'.

The hologram images go dark as Will sits in awe at the table. He looks over to Abra.

"Wow. All this happened here?"

"Yes. And I'm afraid it will continue."

"What are those things?" Will says.

The Journey Begins

"Scolits. They are truly an interesting breed. They're a product of Malkuth's sorcery, and their powers are vast. One sting from a Scolit can start a very interesting process in the victim. The creature's shape-changing characteristics, ability to morphing and, as you can see, the ability to vanish, make them formidable opponents."

Thinking a bit, Will says, "Really. So where did they vanish to?"

"We believe Malkuth's castle on the mountain of Ynitsed."

"Ynitsed! Did you say Ynitsed?"

Abra nods, "Yes."

"I have to get there. Can you take me?"

"It won't be that easy, as you have seen," Abra replies.

Determined, Will blurts out, "I don't care. I have to go if I have any chance of saving Grandfather."

Abra looks at Will and says softly, "He must be a special being for you to go to such extremes."

"I would do anything for him. Can you take me?"

Abra begins to pace.

"If I were to show you the path to Ynitsed, what is it will you do for me?"

Sensing the worst, Will asks, "What could you possibly want from me that I can give you? I am lost in this land of yours and I need your help more than you need mine."

Abra turns towards Will, "On the contrary, I believe you have exactly what I need."

Confused, Will says, "I don't understand."

Chapter 13

Abra walks briskly up to Will and grabs his shirt. Ripping downward he reveals a mark of the four-leaf clover on his chest, just under his left shoulder.

Will instinctively jumps backwards, "Hey what are you doing?"

He looks down at his chest and cannot believe what he's seeing.

"What in the…?"

He tries to rub the clover mark off his chest, but it is as if it was a birthmark that has decided to display itself just now. It is one with him.

"How did this get here? I've never had this. What's going on here?"

Abra settles back and says, "The Forerunner. The prophecy has been fulfilled."

Will looks at the marking on his chest, and then back to Abra, who now has an unusual look on his face.

"Hey, I don't know what you're thinking here, or what this thing is, but I'm not who or what you think your looking for. I'm just a kid."

Abra drops to his knees without paying attention to Will's ramblings.

"It is written, so it shall be."

Abra bows his head in front of Will and says, "Deliver us from this evil and we shall be at peace once again o' great Forerunner."

Will is extremely uncomfortable at this point.

"Hey, I don't know what's going on here, but this is crazy. There's no way I am this Forerunner thing you're talking about. I just need to help my grandfather, that's it," he pauses to gather himself. "Now, you said you could get me to Ynitsed. Right?"

The Journey Begins

Abra looks up at Will and says, "We will follow you until death delivers us."

Startled, Will asks, "Ah, we don't have to go *that* far, do we?"

Like a ball player who has received a pre-game pep talk, Abra stands up and begins to ready himself.

"The time has come to fulfill what is written. You must join the others to prepare for your journey."

"Journey?"

"To Ynitsed."

Excited, but even more concerned, Will slowly gets up from his seat. He looks down once again at his newfound birthmark and murmurs, "Ok, what's next?"

Chapter 14
The Unveiling

The graviports careen through the underground city as Danaë walks Jimmy over to a docking station. Jimmy is now wearing a warrior's garment. He looks like a motocross racer prepping for a big race. His facial features are also different. He has more facial hair and his complexion has darkened.

Danaë doesn't pay much attention to his appearance; her attention focuses on the graviport riders zipping through the city. The docking station they are on hovers over a mini-cliff in the center of the city. One wrong step will send them into the ravine below.

Jimmy looks like a natural as he casually walks close to the ridge of the docking station. Danaë looks down the ravine and back towards Jimmy, and can't help but be impressed by his lack of fear. Jimmy looks as if he is getting ready for a ride on a rolling coaster at his favorite amusement park. He watches the other riders dart in and out of the city on the impressive flying machines.

Jimmy pipes up, "So, how fast can these things go?"

The Unveiling

Just as Danaë is about to answer, a voice bellows from the inside the docking station.

"How fast do you want it to go?"

Jimmy looks over to the station and sees a handsome young man, also dressed in warrior-motocross attire, walking out from the station. Danaë looks over and smiles.

"Allow me to introduce one of our top instructors. This is Juno. He will be taking you for a ride through the city so you may learn the unique features of our graviports."

Juno stands proudly in front of Jimmy. With a sarcastic smirk on his face, Jimmy looks at Juno and then to Danaë.

"Oh come on. How hard can these things be? I mean, I've been watching these guys for over an hour now. It's just like my dirt bike, only this one flies."

As he talks, Jimmy walks over to a graviport and throws his leg over the seat. He tinkers with the controls.

Juno walks over with concern, "Ah, wouldn't do that if I were...."

At that instant, Jimmy turns and smiles at Juno and hits the ignition.

"Oh, no you don't!" Juno says. He runs towards the graviport. Jimmy hits the accelerator and hovers about fifteen feet above the docking station and the flustered Juno.

Juno shouts," You don't know what you're doing!"

"I've been watching these guys. This is a piece of cake. I'll bring it back, I promise."

Chapter 14

He hits the throttle and darts forward about twenty feet. He hovers for a moment, and then drops sharply. The graviport swirls out of control.

Juno screams, "Noooo! Hit the yellow throttle to your left."

Frantic, Jimmy looks for the yellow throttle as he drops. He can't find it.

"Where is it?"

"To your left! Your left!"

Still swirling, the graviport drops perilously close to the base of the ravine. The ground rapidly approaching, Jimmy finally sees the yellow throttle. He has to move his left leg to grab it. Just as he is about to grab it, his pant leg gets caught on the throttle. Panic stricken, he grabs his pants with his left hand but still can't shake loose.

At this moment, Will walks into the docking station area and quickly notices Jimmy plight.

"Oh my God!" He looks to Juno. "What's going on?"

"He took it on his own. He doesn't know what he's doing."

Jimmy is now a mere 70 feet from impact.

Frantic, Will shouts, "Do something! You gotta do something!"

Helpless, Juno shrugs his shoulders. "His leg is stuck on the hover throttle. He's doomed."

Will responds quickly, "Where's the hover throttle?"

Juno looks at him in despair, "He's doomed."

Will grabs Juno by the shoulders and shakes him. He screams in his face,

"WHERE IS THE HOVER THROTTLE?"

Juno only repeats,, "He's doomed."

The Unveiling

Jimmy is 50 feet from impact.

Will runs to the edge, grabs his head in anguish and screams, "Jimmy, pull your leg from throttle now!"

At that moment, Jimmy's pant leg is freed from the throttle. He grabs the lever just 30 feet from impact.

Will screams, "Pull up Jimmy, pull up!"

Jimmy pulls up on the throttle and the vehicle immediately stops in mid-air. He is almost thrown because of the sudden stop. Gaining his composure, he looks up to the docking station and sees a relieved Will and Juno.

"No problem guys, I got it all under control."

Will screams down to him, "Get that thing back up here."

Surveying the controls, Jimmy gains his confidence again. He looks back up to Will and says. "I got it now, bud, I'll be right back, I got to try this thing."

He hits the forward throttle once again and floats around the base of the city. He starts off slowly. Gaining confidence, he turns it up.

Will looks down and sees that his friend has the hand of things.

"Unbelievable."

Jimmy hits the engage throttle and takes off like a pro. He turns it up to impressive speeds and careens through the city like the warriors before him. Will can't believe what he is seeing. He turns to Juno, "Can you believe him?"

Juno is on his knees bowing before him. Confused, Will asks," Are you ok?"

Juno doesn't look at Will. He says, "It is true, you are the one, you are the Forerunner."

Chapter 14

Will rolls his eyes and says, "Oh, come on, not you, too?"

Juno, speaking into the ground says, "You stopped the graviport with your tongue. It is written, you will be our deliverer."

Ignoring this, Will looks back down to the city and sees Jimmy darting around like a maniac.

"I didn't stop any...." He stops in mid-sentence as he sees Danaë come to the docking station platform. She is wearing a warrior's outfit and is strikingly beautiful with her hair now shoulder-length and covering her ears. Will is, as before, a bit taken back by her beauty.

"Hello, again." Will says.

Danaë looks over the edge and sees Jimmy careening through the city. She smiles and looks over to Will and says, "He's a quick learner, I see. It must be the morphing."

Confused for a moment, Will looks at Jimmy as he takes the graviport up and over a small building below.

"Morphing? He's a nut, is more like it."

Danaë looks at Juno, who is still on his knees in front of Will.

"Juno get up please."

Juno sneaks a glance at Danaë and whispers, "It is him."

Danaë reaches down and picks Juno up. "I know, I know, but we have work to do. You must go and prepare the graviports and gravipods for departure. We have limited time."

Juno gets up and is still finding it hard to look directly at Will. Seeing this, Danaë shouts, "Go! Now!"

She pushes Juno away from Will. He runs towards the station like a child who has just seen Santa Claus for the first time. Watching this,

The Unveiling

Will looks over to Danaë and says, "You know this is getting weirder every moment."

"Yes, I know. But you must understand what my people have been through."

Will sees some young children walking within the city. No elders accompany them.

"I think, I'm starting to."

Danaë grabs Will's hand and guides him over to a look out a tower within the docking station.

"Come with me."

The two walk over to the tower. Abra, on top of his platform, watches as they approach some rocks next to the tower. Jimmy continues to careen through the city.

"Let's sit here," Danaë says.

Will looks around. "This place is really amazing. You guys really have something special here."

Danaë looks at him with her soft, sad eyes and says, "It was special, very special, up until Malkuth and the Scolits came."

"Who is this Malkuth and why is he doing this?"

Danaë looks over the city. "It's all about power. What he has and what he still wants."

"What else can he want? It seems to me that he has most everything." Will says.

"One would think so, but as long as the shadow of the sorcerer exists, Malkuth can not obtain his full power."

"What did you say?"

Chapter 14

Danaë explains, "The shadow of the sorcerer, the one who would rise from shadows to defeat the evil ways of Malkuth. The one also known as the Forerunner."

Will doesn't know quite how to take this. He mumbles to himself, "The shadow of the sorcerer? *The Sorcerer's Shadow*? It can't be."

He looks to Danaë and says, "How can this Forerunner help? This doesn't make sense."

Danaë puts her hand on Wills leg. He immediately squirms. She explains, "It is the purity of the Forerunner which will cleanse us all--much like an offering at the Altar of Destiny. The Forerunner is the only one to stop his wrath."

Confused, Will says. "An offering?"

Danaë begins to get into an attack position. "We will assemble our armies together."

Will sees that many of the warriors are coming into the loading station.

Danaë speaks more intensely, "Once our armies are sound, nothing can stop us. We will be free."

Will senses the worse and looks up to see Abra staring down at them. He looks to his left, and then to his right, and sees more and more warriors assembling.

As he takes her hand away from his leg, Will says, "Ah, this is all great news. I need to talk with Jimmy for a moment."

Danaë says sternly, "Your friend is infected; he can not partake in the quest."

Shocked, Will says, "Infected? What do you mean?"

The Unveiling

He looks towards Jimmy and sees that a few graviport warriors are following him.

Will tells Danaë, "I need to talk with him."

"There won't be time. We must go."

Backing away, Will mumbles, "Ah, yeah."

Danaë senses his retreat. She shouts to the warriors, "Cholla, Cholla!"

The warriors descend upon Will.

Will screams, "JIMMY!"

Hearing the screams, Jimmy sees Will running through the landing dock and scampering past warriors as if he is a tailback running for the end zone. He hears Danaë scream, "Cholla, cholla, get him now!"

Jimmy says to himself. "I knew it!" He hits the throttle and veers towards Will and the dock. He notices three graviport warriors on his tail. He looks back and says, "Oh, boy"!

He takes off like a dart, navigates through the city's stalagmite maze and shoots like a rocket towards the docking station. Once on top, he surveys the area for Will. He screams, "Will! Will, where are you?"

There's no answer.

Again he screams, "WILL!"

He hears a muffled sound and looks up. On top of the ridge above the docking station, Abra is holding Will. He has one arm around him and another holding a jagged knife above his throat.

Jimmy roars, "Will!"

Abra retorts. "It was not supposed to be like this. We would have given you every opportunity to say goodbye to one another. This way is just, uncivilized."

Chapter 14

Jimmy sees more graviport warriors circling him.

He meets Will's terrified eyes.

Will breaks the gaze to stare at the knife at his throat. It begins to melt into a molten gel in Abra's hand.

Jimmy watches in amazement. Raising his arm he notices that hair has grown on his knuckles and arms. He experiences an adrenalin rush of confidence he has never felt before.

"We're outta here!" he shouts to his buddy.

He hits the throttle on the graviport like a pro, and darts towards Will and Abra. His reflexes are so keen he is able to shoot past the graviport warriors and fire up toward Will in a flash.

Seeing this, Abra tries to hang on to Will, but the heat from the molten gel is burning his skin. He has to let go, and Will frees himself.

Jimmy zooms up to the ridge and screams, "Get on!"

Startled, Will looks at Jimmy and his Scolit –like appearance and says. "What happened to you?"

Jimmy features are now half human and half Scolit.

Jimmy screams again, "Get on!"

Will glances at Abra and then the approaching graviport warriors, and then back to Jimmy, who now looks like a creature from one of his comic books. He says to Jimmy tentatively. "You better not eat me or anything!"

Jimmy looks at him in disbelief. He growls through clenched teeth, "Will you just get on already?"

Will jumps on and screams, "Go! Go!.Go!"

The buddies take off and careen through the city.

The Unveiling

Abra screams to the graviport warriors. "Get them!"

Will screams to Jimmy, "Are you ok with this thing?"

Shouting over the roar of the vehicle, Jimmy says, "I know this sounds weird, but I feel like I've done this before."

"Then get us out of here man, they're on us."

Jimmy looks around the city.

"Where to?"

"Get to the edge of the city; we'll get out the same way we came in."

"All right. Hang on!"

Jimmy navigates through the city as if he has done this a hundred times. He maneuvers through the stalagmite structures with ease and even amazes himself with his newfound reflexes.

The graviport warriors engage in a remarkable chase. They try to knock Jimmy off course, but he is holds his own with these warriors. One after another, they crash into the stalagmite obstacles through the city.

The chase takes them through the entire city. With over fifteen graviport warriors chasing the boys, Jimmy maneuvers through unlikely obstacles the warriors are not used to.

Will is amazed as Jimmy and his newfound body and senses make the graviport warriors look like the children chasing after a seasoned warrior.

He shouts with glee, "This is wild!"

The few warriors left appear to be closing in. Will looks up and sees the entrance the boys originally came in through. "There's where we came in! Push it, man, push it!"

Chapter 14

Jimmy aims for the entrance, but senses a disturbance. He sees that another grouping of warriors hover by the entrance.

He shouts, "No good. Hold on!"

He pushes forward on the handlebars of the graviport and navigates downward towards the city's base. He does this with such quickness that the warriors still chasing him on graviports have to navigate up rather than down. They are now forced to go around a structure to follow them.

Will screams, "What are you doing?"

Jimmy screams back, "The entrance is closed, need a new plan."

Will looks up and sees the warriors at the entrance.

"Get to the base!"

Jimmy steers the graviport to the base of the city where they manage to stop for a moment and gain their composure. They look up and see the warriors circling around. They note that a few more are readying themselves by the entrance with graviports.

Jimmy barks, "This isn't looking too good. Where to, genius?"

Will looks around hopelessly, "I don't know."

Suddenly, Will shudders as he has a vision of a boulder landing on top of the warriors. The vision also shows an opening the boys could dart through.

Jimmy looks at Will and asks, "Are you ok?"

Will looks around and sees the same boulder in his vision next to the docking station.

"There! Go there!"

Jimmy looks to where Will is pointing. He sees fifty to one hundred warriors in between.

The Unveiling

"Are you nuts?"

Confident, Will says, "Trust me, it feels right."

"That's what you said about coming here to begin with," Jimmy gripes as he hits the forward throttle. A cadre of warriors approaches. Jimmy hits the throttle again, and goes in the opposite direction of where Will directed him.

The chase ensues as the warriors get much closer this time around. At one point, one gets so close that Will is almost knocked off the graviport. As they dart through the city, it becomes more evident that they are cornered in every direction.

Will begins to get the visions of the crumbling boulder again. This time he sees Juno triggering the explosion from within the docking station. When the vision fades, he looks back towards the docking station sees Juno running across the platform.

The boys are now circling as the graviport warriors close in on them. The graviports are close enough that they can identify the individual warriors.

Frustrated, Jimmy hits the hover throttle and they hover closer to the base of the city.

"Not looking good, bud."

Will looks back at the docking station. He sees Juno by a control panel.

"Jimmy, go straight for the station."

"No way, man. That's *really* crazy."

"Jimmy, I'm telling you, go straight for the station."

Chapter 14

Jimmy looks at the hovering warriors and sees that Abra is getting into position on top of his tower. Abra has a superior smirk on his face.

Frustrated, Jimmy shouts, "This is nuts!"

He hits the throttle, turns the graviport upright and begins to navigate straight towards the docking station.

Abra can't believe that he is being engaging directly. At that very moment, Juno hits a lever on the control panel and a tiny explosion follows. He immediately runs to the center of the dock.

Realizing what is happening; Abra quickly turns and screams "JUNO, NOOO!"

The explosion sets off a self-destruction mode within the city. The giant boulder Will had envisioned comes loose. Seeing this, Will screams, "Go straight for the boulder!"

Jimmy screams," I hope you know what you're doing."

The loosening boulder creates an avalanche. Pandemonium ensues within the city. Jimmy sees the opening.

"There it is! This is amazing! Hang on."

He hits the throttle and darts directly towards the opening. As they pass by the docking station, Will sees Juno standing helplessly on the deck. He smiles as they pass by.

Will shouts in Jimmy's ear, "No wait!"

"WHAT?"

"Wait! Go and get him."

"You are nuts."

"Jimmy, he helped us. Get him. He won't be safe here anymore."

"So what? We'll be safe somewhere..."

The Unveiling

"Jimmy, go and get him. He can help us get to Ynitsed."

Frustrated, Jimmy snarls, "I can't believe you."

He turns the graviport around and darts toward the docking station. The avalanche intensifies and rumbles like an earthquake. The boys reach the deck of the station and Will screams to Juno, "Get on! You won't be safe here anymore!"

Unsure, Juno looks at Will. "You will be my savior, won't you?"

Will looks at him and shouts, "If you wanna be saved, man, you better get on NOW!"

Juno jumps on the graviport and the boys take off. As they shoot upward, Will sees Danaë staring at the boys. She has a looks of utter frustration on her face. Will looks at her for just a moment. Then he screams to Jimmy. "Get us out of here!"

The boys dart up and out of the entrance that has been created. The rest of the graviport warriors never have a chance to follow because of the boulders raining down upon them.

Once out, and finally above ground Will looks back to Juno and shouts, "Which way?"

Juno points north.

Jimmy sees his hand gesture and the three begin to ride north towards Ynitsed.

✱Chapter 15✱
Marabus Is Discovered

Nestled inside her makeshift sanctuary, Marabus continues to tinker with her model of the land. Her hand is cupped over a crevice within her model as she slowly rains pebbles down and into the crevice. She has a look of satisfaction on her face as she drops the tiny pebbles into the hole.

When the pebbles begin to overflow, Marabus runs her hand over the covered hole. Just as she is about to seal the tiny hole, a loud crash is heard behind her. Startled, she turns to see Malkuth standing in the alcove with three of his henchman.

Disgustedly he sneers at her detailed model and says, "I should have known better than to leave you by yourself."

Frightened, Marabus responds, "It's not what you think, brother."

Malkuth interrupts, "Don't even waste your breath, my sweet." He looks over to his henchman and commands "Crush it."

Immediately, the three henchmen approach the model and tear it to shreds.

Marabus Is Discovered

Marabus screams, "Noooo!"

The three soldiers pay her no mind as they complete the destruction. Broken, Marabus merely watches. Then she looks over to Malkuth and says smugly, "You're too late, it has already begun."

Malkuth looks at the destroyed landscaped at the feet of Marabus.

"No. You're the one who is too late, my dear sister. My process is nearly complete. Soon the prophecies of the tablets will be fulfilled and within my power completely. Your reign is over." He starts to walk away, then stops and turns towards her. He snarls, "Make that, your reign never began. It will be stricken from all that is written."

Without looking at the henchmen, he barks, "Take her to where I can see her at all times. I don't want to take my eyes off of her until the shadow is full."

The henchmen grab Marabus and drag her away as she turns towards Malkuth. She smiles and says, "What will be written is what has already been delivered. The tablets will overcome and you, my dear brother, will fall deep within."

Angrily, Malkuth shouts, "Take her away."

The men drag her away and Malkuth slowly turns towards the remains of the landscape Marabus had built. He looks closely at the details. He appears impressed, but at the same time, a bit concerned. With a look of confusion and concern, he studies what's left of the tiny landscape. Not sure what he is actually looking for, he gets up in frustration and darts out of the alcove to follow behind his men.

⋆Chapter 16⋆
The Road To Seren

As the graviport glides above the landscape, Jimmy and Will gaze in awe. Everywhere they look they see once-beautiful landscape in various states of destruction. The mixture of paradise and destruction disconcerts the two. This is not what they saw when they came through the portal.

The changes in the land and the atmosphere are drastic and confusing. What they thought was the paradise of Rainbow Alley has now become a war-torn country. What's even more upsetting to Will is that the landscape resembles the cover of Bryan's favorite book *The Sorcerer's Shadow*. As he watches the land below darken and become eerily familiar, he can't help but think of Danaë's last words to him:

As long as the shadow of the sorcerer exists, Malkuth can not obtain his full power.

Will gains his senses again as the graviport begins to putter.

"What's going on?"

Juno looks to the back of the vehicle.

The Road To Seren

"We should land. We are coming close to the electron fields," Juno shouts above the noise.

Will looks at Juno and says, "The what?"

"The electron fields. Look." Juno points directly ahead.

The boys look forward and see what looks like heat lightning.

Will tells Jimmy. "We better land." He then turns and yells to Juno, "Is it safe down there?"

Juno eyes a tiny village below.

"This is the village of Seren. The Serenians are quite peaceful beings. Yes. We'll be fine here."

Will studies the quiet village. Tiny huts form rows upon row of structures. They connect in a giant circle that looks more like a barricade than a town. Nonetheless, with the graviport puttering their options are limited.

Will shouts, "Bring us in, Jimbo." As he turns to catch Jim's eye, Will is startled by his appearance. Jimmy has morphed more into a Scolit. His human features are nearly unrecognizable.

Will shouts, "Whoa! It is you, isn't it, Jimmy?"

Jimmy hits the throttle, points the graviport downward and says, "Keep it up ,Will, and I'm taking us straight into the ground."

"Just kidding man," Will replies. "But just wait until you see yourself. We gotta find something to fix you up."

"Fix me up? No way, I never felt better or stronger. Let's go."

He hits the throttle and the boys quickly descend towards the village of Seren. The heat lightening continues to electrify the sky.

Chapter 17
Brittani And Bryan Arrive

Palm trees sway softly in the wind. Water trickles gently off of a cliff into a brilliant blue pool below. Birds sing and tiny animals frolic on the edge of the river's basin. Whispering winds playing about the mouth of a small cave join the sounds of paradise.

A blood-curdling howl breaks the peace inside the cave. Wordless screams frighten the animals as Bryan and Brittani shoot through the portal and splash down into the river below.

They hit the river hard and plunge deep into the water. Gaining his senses, Bryan grabs hold of Brittani, who's thrashing about. Once above the surface, he turns Brittani away from him and uses a lifeguard technique to float to the river's edge.

It takes less than a minute, but seems like an eternity. Once at the edge, Bryan makes sure Brittani is breathing, then falls to the ground out of pure exhaustion. The two lie on the ground for a few moments in silence.

Brittani And Bryan Arrive

Finally, Bryan rallies. He opens his eyes and looks at Brittani and asks,

"You ok?"

Brittani coughs a few times then looks at Bryan.

"Yeah. I think so..."

Bryan gets up and looks around. He sees mountains to the west and palm trees to the east. He gazes in awe at the surroundings. As Brittani wearily starts to rise he asks, "Is this it? Is this Rainbow Alley?"

Brittani takes in the waterfalls and swaying palms.

"If not, it ought to be, this is beautiful."

"Yeah," Bryan agrees. He walks around as Brittani stares out to the other side of the river.

"Hey, Bryan? What is that over there?" She points towards the boulders next to the river's edge. He squints in that direction.

"I don't know!"

He walks towards the boulders.

"Be careful!" Brittani warns.

Up above the cavern and looking down upon Brittani and Bryan, Danaë watches as Bryan gets closer and closer to the boulder. He notices that this foreign object looks a lot like a body. As he gets nearer, his heart rate begins to accelerate.

Brittani shouts from a distance, "What is it?"

Bryan hollers back, "I think it's a body."

Stunned, Brittani shouts, "A body? Don't go near it!"

Bryan ignores her and gets closer to the body.

"Bryan, don't go near it! You don't know what it might be."

Chapter 17

Bryan gets close enough to make it out. He falls to his knees screaming, "Oh my God, it's Jimmy!"

He looks directly at Jimmy's body draped over the boulder and sees the mortal wound in his chest. Next to the body lays Will's map of Rainbow Alley and the road to Ynitsed. Bryan hesitates as he places his hand on Jimmy's shoulder. The body remains lifeless and Bryan is overcome with emotion.

Distraught, he begins to wonders if it is Will's map.

He looks back to Brittani who is running towards him.

"Britt, this wasn't supposed to happen. What are we going to do now?"

She looks down at the body. Stunned, she slaps her hand over her mouth and says, "Oh my God, it is him. What happened to his body?" She, too, falls to her knees.

In a haphazard attempt to console her, Bryan places his hand on her shoulder. In doing so, he looks up to the rim of the cavern. Quickly, he looks all around the rim. With his eyes rolled upward and his head facing the ground, he murmurs, "I don't think we're alone here, Britt."

Brittani peeks up and sees Danaë and her group of warriors. They look like a band of Indians stalking their prey. Simultaneously, the strange group begins to descend into the valley. Bryan and Brittani frantically look for cover in a valley where there is none.

⋆Chapter 18⋆
Crossing The Moats Of Seren

Ever since the Sorcerer's Shadow penetrated the tranquility of Rainbow Alley, the desert sands of the village of Seren have become as hostile as they were once beautiful. With natural defenses and difficult terrain, Seren is caught up in a paradox of good and evil. Its only defense is nature.

Prior to the Shadow's infiltration, the inner sanctum of the Village of Seren was the centerpiece and final destination of any traveler to Rainbow Alley. The ultimate objective for most travelers was to enjoy the inner sanctum of Seren.

Not only was the trip through the desert sands a treat for the traveler, but the greeting each received on the way up to the sacred core would be one never to be forgotten. From streets carpeted with palm leaves to incredible buffets of fruits, candied delights and thirst-quenching liquids, the weary traveler entered the inner core feeling like a newly crowned king.

Chapter 18

Once in the inner core, the traveler was treated to a visit with Bethel, *The One Who Knows All* This visit made the traveler's journey complete.

As the trio enters the outer limits of the village, Will is perplexed by the site. He remembers his grandfather's stories of this village, but by the looks of it, this could not be the same place. Scorpions, rattlesnakes, and even fire-breathing iguanas comfortably inhabit this land. Oddly, the awful creatures create a moat-like circle surrounding the village. They begin about two hundred yards outside the village, and stop abruptly before the first dwelling. The creatures make a daunting defense from oncoming trouble. The wisest way to travel here would be by graviports, but with the electron fields above, hovering or flying over is nearly impossible. The desolate landscape does not bear any resemblance to Grandpa's description of Seren the least. It seems the Village of Seren has evolved a natural protection against in-coming violence.

Will surveys the area. He sees that Juno has the same concerns written all over his face. He then turns towards Jimmy. To his amazement, he sees Jimmy standing atop a large boulder.

Will screams, "What are you doing?"

Jimmy points over the desertscape and announces, "There is no way I am going through that."

"What happened to, I never felt so strong'?" Will counters.

"That was before I knew there were snakes and scorpions, and what the heck are those?" Jimmy point to tiny lizards that appear to be spitting fire.

Crossing The Moats Of Seren

Juno quickly responds, "The typareks...the name means 'fire within'."

Jimmy nods and says, "I'll bet it does. Nope, not for me, this is as far as I go, Will."

Will watches the typareks, snakes and scorpions spar with one another over the barren land. Shaking his head he says, "There's gotta be way. Juno, you know this land. How do we get through this?"

Juno sheepishly looks at Will as if he has disappointed a father figure. He shrugs his shoulders and crouches down in a catcher's position on the top of a small boulder.

Frustrated, Will turns away. "Aghh."

He looks back to Jimmy and with says with determination, "We're not giving up, Jimmy. We're going through this."

Dripping with sarcasm, Jimmy replies, "Really? How?"

Will walks slowly toward the moat of reptiles and they immediately begin to hiss and coil at his intrusion. The iguanas open wide to shoot fire and the scorpions scamper in delight as if they are finally going to be fed. The creatures do not step out of their invisible fence surrounding the moat. Inside the circumference, however, they are free to roam.

A few feet from the moat, Will begins to sweat and become jittery. He sees that the enemies will not step out of the circle, but he also sees that there is no way he can step inside of it. Dejected, he begins to retreat. The reptiles ease up from their attack position.

Jimmy asks sweetly, "We're going through, huh?"

Will smirks and says, "We're going through." He walks like a man possessed past Juno and then past Jimmy.

Chapter 18

Confused and stunned Jimmy says, "We are?" He turns around to see Will walk towards the graviport. He shouts, "Will didn't you hear Jubi over here say those things won't work because of he electrons?"

Juno mouths to himself, "It is Juno, please."

Tinkering with the graviport, Will ignores this.

Baffled, Jimmy continues, "Will, it ain't going to work in there."

With unbridled determination Will responds, "It doesn't have to." Will hops onto the graviport and says, "The momentum will carry us over."

Eyes wide and breathing labored, Jimmy says, "You're crazy. That ain't gonna work. We'll go down halfway through. They'll be all over us."

Will starts the graviport. "It'll carry us through."

Jimmy looks at the moat again and then back to Will and suggests, "Let's just go that way." He points in the opposite direction.

Will revs up the graviport. "You can go back that way. I'm not. I'm going through."

"Will, it ain't gonna work."

Will revs it one more time and the graviport jumps forward a bit and almost knocks him off. He challenges his friend, "You gonna drive, or am I going solo?"

Jimmy sighs and begins to growl like a Scolit breathing hard. He jumps off the boulder and walks towards Will.

"Move over. At least if I drive we'll go straight to our death instead of swerving all over the place."

He pushes Will back further on the graviport. Will shouts to Juno to get on.

Crossing The Moats Of Seren

Jimmy growls again in Scolit-like manner and says, "What are we doing with this guy?"

"He can help us. We need someone who knows the land."

Sarcastically Jimmy grumbles, "Yeah, he's been pretty helpful so far. Just look at the beach he's brought us to."

Juno begins to walk slowly towards the graviport.

Jimmy screams, "Let's go Jujitsu, the snakes are waiting."

Juno picks up his pace and says once again in a soft tone, "It's Juno, please."

Jimmy looks at Juno sarcastically and says, "Get on Jibby."

Jimmy revs the graviport up as Juno hops on the back. Will shouts, "We need a running start. Go back about a hundred yards and punch it. You hit it hard enough, the momentum's gonna carry us through."

Jimmy growls again, "Yeah, right."

He turns the graviport around and drives away from the living moat. About a hundred yards across the sandy terrain, he turns the graviport around and switches to hover. Now far enough away from the electron field, the graviport has regained its full strength. Jimmy feels the power beneath him and begins to lose himself in revving the machine.

Will shouts, "HIT IT!"

Jimmy shouts back, "Nice knowing you man! This is nuts!" He hits the throttle and the graviport takes off directly towards the deadly moat and the Village of Seren beyond. Juno grabs onto to Will with all of his might as the graviport reaches top speed. Fifty yards away, Jimmy howls as he punches down on the throttle to gain more speed. They fly through the next forty yards, wind screaming in their ears.

Chapter 18

With ten yards to go, the electrons flare and the graviport putters. They've reached the moat and realize the speed Jimmy generated is actually carrying them across. They soar over a hundred yards as reptiles and crustaceans hiss and coil beneath them.

Will shouts with delight, "We're gonna make it!"

Looking ahead, Jimmy sees the end of the moat and the village directly beyond. With only fifty yards to go, the graviport begins to slow down. Another fifteen yards, and the machine is nearly ready to fall.

Jimmy screams, "Nooooo!"

The graviport brushes the terrain and slides across the desert, pushing the excited reptilian creatures aside. It stops just five yards from the edge of the moat.

The boys scramble atop the graviport to avoid the danger below.

Jimmy screams, "Now what?"

Will replies, "go! Go! GO!"

Will jumps off the graviport and sprints into the desert through the startled creatures. Jimmy and Juno quickly follow. All three sprint the five yards to safety and collapse.

Will rolls to his back and screams to the sky, "Whooo! That was awesome!"

Jimmy rolls over and says, "That was crazy, that was completely crazy."

Smiling, Will turns to him and screams. "Aaaaaghh!" He points to Jimmy who has a typarek on his shoulder. The typarek spits fire towards Will. Jimmy screams as he grabs the typarek and throws it into the moat with the rest of the critters.

Crossing The Moats Of Seren

The two boys begin to laugh uncontrollably. Will finally manages to say, "That was great, that was great!"

Still laughing, Jimmy turns toward Juno and croaks, "Oh my God, Jubos is down."

In great pain, Juno manages to say, "It's Juno."

The boys run over to Juno who is suffering from a snakebite. Concerned, Will says, "Juno, you've been bit!"

Juno looks at Will and says, "I almost made it. He got me right at the edge."

Jimmy suggests, "Let's bring him into the village, they might be able to help."

Will estimates the village to be over two miles away.

"Do you think he'll make it?"

"We don't have a choice."

Juno softly says, "The Scolit is immune."

Will and Jimmy simultaneously pipe up. "What did you say?"

Juno points to Jimmy and repeats, "The Scolit, he is immune to the bite of the snake that rattles."

"How do you know this?" Will asks.

"It is written that the Scolit has many powers, and many allies. The snake that rattles is his ally."

Jimmy looks at Juno and says, "Listen, Jibby, I'm no Scolit, this is just temporary. And even if I did have these powers or allies, so what?"

Juno says, "The Scolit can extract the venom and save Juno."

Confused, Jimmy asks, "What do you mean by 'extract the venom'?"

Chapter 18

Will chuckles and says, "He means you can suck the venom out of his leg and not be hurt."

Over taken with emotion, Jimmy says, "Well, isn't that just great? You're not actually thinking that I...."

Will looks at him, "I don't think we have a choice."

"Sure we do. We pick the guy up and carry him into town. That's our choice."

"Jimmy, he won't make it into town."

"Oh, yes he will. Let's try."

Jimmy runs over to Juno and picks him up. Juno shrieks in pain. Will jumps in. "Jimmy, we've got to do this now."

"What do you mean *we*? I don't see 'Scolit' written on *your* head."

"Jim, please help," Juno says softly

Jimmy looks at the helpless kid in front of him. Finally, he barks, You sure this stuff isn't going to bother me?"

Juno says, "Yes. You have blood of a Scolit now, you are immune."

Jimmy looks away and then back to Juno lying on the ground. He snarls, "This day is getting better every minute."

Jimmy drops down to Juno and bends over to place his mouth over the wound on his calf, when Juno screams, "No! No, not with the mouth!"

Jimmy shrinks away.

Juno reaches for Jimmy's arm and gingerly pulls his hand towards the wound. Confused, Jimmy allows Juno to pull his arm towards his leg. His fist is clenched tightly. Once his hand is directly over the wound, Juno says, "Open your hand."

Crossing The Moats Of Seren

Jimmy looks quizzically at Will, who motions to him to do it. Jimmy slowly opens his hand. As he unclenches his fist, his hand begins to illuminate.

"What's going on here?"

Under Jimmy's open hand, Juno's leg begins to convulse. The leg begins to contract and pump the snake venom outward and streams upward into Jimmy's palm. As the venom hits his hand, it evaporates into his skin.

When the convulsions end, Jimmy rocks back and forth and then falls to the ground on his rear end. He sits up, out of breath.

Will gasps in awe, "That was awesome!"

There is no sign of venom or injury on Jimmy's hand. Concerned he asks, "What am I turning in to?"

Will reaches out his hand to help his buddy up. "Don't you worry, we're gonna get you back, I just know we are."

Once on their feet, they head towards the Village of Seren only cacti and sand dunes greet them as they trudge across the land. The sound of thunder makes all three of them turn back towards the moat.

Will wonders aloud, "Now what?"

Jimmy points up and says, "It's all around us."

The boys watch as the atmosphere changes drastically. Clouds quickly form and turn from pillow white to charcoal gray. All around, the atmosphere is changing violently. All around, except within the Village of Seren.

Winds kick up as day turns to night and rain begins to pelt the desert floor.

Chapter 18

Miraculously, the atmosphere over the village of Seren remains unchanged. It is as if the village has a protective bubble. Inside, the sun shines and the weather is beautiful.

As Will stares at this phenomena, he says, "Maybe we should get into the Village?"

Watching the winds kick up tiny twisters Jimmy agrees, "Ah, yeah. It's time to get to the village." Jimmy walks over to Juno, extends his hand and say, "Come on, Jubo, we have to get moving."

Juno cracks a tiny smile, "You saved me. How can I repay thee?"

A loud thunderous crack in the sky is heard and Jimmy quickly reaches down and pulls him up.

"Don't worry about it. Let's go before that weather gets here."

Will takes the lead. Jimmy and Juno follow him towards the Village of Seren.

⋆Chapter 19⋆
Malkuth's Plan Unvieled

There was a time when the castle on top of the Mountain of Time represented peace. During this phase villages stood as one and kings had no enemies. Malco ruled the villages, permitting free reign of power that fostered unity throughout the land.

Unity governed the land and harmony ran from east, west, north and south. This was all before the Times of Trouble. This was all before Malkuth gained access to six of the seven Tablets of Fate.

Breaking tradition in passing leadership to the first male, Malco long considered Marabus the chosen one. Her deep loyalty to her father and the land he governed was unwavering. For many years Malkuth never displayed his dissatisfaction with his father's obvious favoritism towards his younger sibling. He may have accepted it if the favoritism had been cast upon to his younger brother Abra, but the mere fact that he was being looked over in favor of his younger sister only provided more fuel to his evil fire within.

Chapter 19

On the eve of the Times of Trouble, Malkuth allowed his internal demons to take control. No longer would his younger sister have what is rightly his. Moments after his father drank the arsenic, Malkuth could feel his newfound power. Gaining access to each of the Tablets of fate would only increase his supremacy. With all of the tablets within view all Malkuth would need to do is join each of the seven tablets and his immortality would be assured.

His father's lifeless body only provided a brief obstacle for the evil intentions of the wayward son.

The tablets had been secured for centuries and were housed in the Holy of Holies, the innermost room of the tabernacle. Access was restricted to one person only, Malco, the high priest of the land. Even so, access was only permitted through sacrifice and with the blood of a goat on behalf the people of his chosen land.

The ark which housed the tablets was a small box made of acacia wood, overlaid with gold. It measured 1.4 meters long, 7 centimeters wide and 7 centimeters high. Two long bars, also made of acacia wood overlaid with gold, carried it. Safely inside the tabernacle, Malkuth pulls from a blood-soaked cloth a pouch which was attached to his waist. He carefully places the bloody cloth at the base of the ark and slowly opens the container. His eyes begin to shine. His desire and dreams are being realized by this glimpse of the contents of the ark.

As he reaches to pull the stone tablets from their housing, a look of concern crosses his face. His pace quickens as he pulls tablet after tablet out of the ark. He counts, ""One, two, three, four, five…six…six…SIX!"

Malkuth's Plan Unvieled

Blood boiling, he realizes he has been deceived. One of the seven tablets is missing. He knows that his prophecy cannot be fulfilled without the seventh tablet. And the only other one who would know this is the one being he has no power against--Bethel.

In a fit of rage, Malkuth grabs the gold bars of the ark and screams, "BETHEL! BETHEL! BETHEL!"

OUTSIDE THE CASTLE

Draped in a dark cloak with a hood covering his head, Bethel peers around a dark corner. No one is in sight. With the seventh tablet secure in his possession, Bethel mounts his horse and rides off.

⋆Chapter 20⋆
The Village Of Seren

On the outskirts of the Village of Seren a sign reads, "Η υποδοχή ένα, καλωσορίζει όλους". Carved out of acacia wood, the sign rests on top of a large natural arch of red stone, melded into the landscape.

The entrance is truly breathtaking. Dark red rock is punctuated by oddly eroded sandstone forms. It is as if this desert had its very own artist painting its form and structure.

Just inside the arch, a faint rainbow shimmers where the sun shines within the city surrounded by storms. All three of the boys stop in amazement as they peer into the village. No words can express the beauty they are witnessing. The oddity about the situation is that this village appears as unscathed as its surroundings appear to have been overtaken by darkness. Will, Jimmy and Juno stop to examine the markings on the sign.

"What do you think it says?" Will says.

The Village Of Seren

Juno looks up and begins to read, "It's Serenian. It says, υποδοχή ένα, καλωσορίζει όλου. Welcome One, Welcome All!"

Jimmy looks to Will and asks, "Should we believe it?"

Considering the storms and the circle of deadly creatures, Will replies, "I don't think we have choice." He continues to follow the footpath inside the jagged walls of Seren. The others follow closely.

Will looks ahead, "We'll you look at this."

To gain access inside the city you had better be fit for serious hiking and climbing. The red rocks may be beautiful to look at, but to cross is another story.

Jimmy begins to climb over the rocks, "Come on Will, it's just like at Zion park at home."

Jimmy makes climbing the rocks look like fun. Finally, Juno addresses Will, "What are we waiting for?"

The boys hit the rocks as if they are at their local park. They hurdle the odd shapes and structures and dive through natural stone arches creating the pathway into the village. They are having a ball running, hiking, and scaling the rock formations.

"Hey, Will watch this!" screams Jimmy, on top of a red stone arch. He slides down the arch, tumbles over once and lands his feet.

Will grins in amazement, "Aw, that was awesome, I gotta try it!" He runs to the very same arch, climbs up and duplicates Jimmy slide and tumble.

Jimmy howls with excitement. "Yeah!"

The boys revel in this newfound natural playground. Jumping, sliding and hurdling, they can't get enough of it. They lose track of their intended purpose. With only a hundred feet to go to the village, the

Chapter 20

boys keep their playful pace up. Jimmy looks up, sees one more giant arch and makes a bead on for it. He scampers up and over jagged rocks and begins to speak when. Instead, he freezes.

Watching Jimmy, Will interjects, "Jimmy, you ok? What is it? "He begins to run towards Jimmy, "What is it?"

He makes it up to the arch and peers through it. He now sees what Jimmy sees. An army of natives lined up in the center of the village. As he gets closer, he sees that the natives are everywhere, even within the rocks they have been playing on.

The boys watch as the sea of Serenians begins to descend upon them. The Serenians have dark complexions. None of them can be taller than five and half feet. Like bees swarming around a hive the natives move closer and closer to the boys.

Jimmy looks at Will, "What do we do?"

"Don't do anything, I don't think we're in trouble here."

Jimmy says in a concerned tone, "You don't? Do you see what I see?"

"Just sit tight. Don't make any moves."

As the Serenians surround the boys, they individually touch the boys in the center of their chests, and then quickly touch their forehead with the same fingers as a ritualistic gesture. The boys back off a bit, but the sheer size of the group overwhelms them. Serenian after Serenian, young and old begin approaches and salutes the boys in their strange way.

Jimmy, growing increasingly uncomfortable, chirps, "Will!"

Will whispers, "Don't make any moves."

The Village Of Seren

Suddenly, the crowd begins to shuffle. Sensing the changes, Will, Jimmy and Juno look up as the natives begins to part. From a distance the boys see a tiny man walking up the hill towards them. As he passes, the Serenians kneel. Shoulder-length silky white hair brushes his shoulders and provides a contrast to his dark skin. He carries a sense of wisdom about him. It literally emanates from the well-placed layers of wrinkles upon his face. He appears to be well into his eighties.

The boys watch silently as he makes his way up to them. The tiny man stops in front of Will and speaks in a soft, foreign tone, "Είναι σαν δεν έχετε φύγει ποτέ."

Confused, Jimmy looks over to Will. Will says, "Excuse me?"

Juno says, "He's speaking in Serenian."

"What did he say?"

"He said, it is as if you have never left."

Will looks at the tiny man and says, "What did you say?"

The aged man looks, ignores the question, and says in broken English, "Welcome to Seren. I am Bethel. You are safe within my care."

Stunned, Will says, "You're Bethel?"

The storms outside walls of the village intensify. Bethel looks outward and then points towards his village. It appears that not only are the storms increasing, but flocks of giant bird-like lizards are circling the perimeter of the village. The shrieks of these giant flying reptiles increase with every passing second.

"We must seek shelter. It has begun."

Will politely asks, "What has begun?"

Chapter 20

Looking directly at Will, Bethel says, "The Times of Trouble. Quickly, we must not be seen."

He motions to the Serenians and they quickly grab the three boys and escort them into the village.

The Serenians rush the boys into and under a red rock arch that doubles as the structural foundation for the center dwelling within the town. All the adobe dwellings and various huts that riddle the village take their form from this giant red rock arch. Once underneath the safety of the arch, the Serenians throw the boys down and scamper off and into the tiny adobes..

Jimmy, who lands against a bedrock wall, becomes irritated. He jumps up from the floor and snarls, "What is going on here?"

Will picks himself up from the ground and dusts off his pants.

"I'm not sure. But if this guy is the Bethel my grandfather has always talked about, we might be ok."

"Might?"

Will gives him a look of pretended certainty and walks over to the edge of the dwelling and peers out from the giant arch. He sees the storms outside of the city collide. "I think we need to stay put here for a while."

Looking at the flying lizards and the intense storms, Jimmy agrees, "Ah, yeah. Yeah, you might be right."

Jimmy glimpses Juno hiding behind a large boulder next to the arch, trembling. "What's with you, Jibby?"

Shear fear on his face, Juno babbles, "It's true. It has begun."

Will walks closer to Juno and demands, "What are you talking about? What's begun?"

The Village Of Seren

Trembling like a leaf, Juno stutters, "The Ttttt...."

"Come on, get yourself together. Not what has begun?"

Juno takes a deep breath and slowly intones. "The Ttttimes....the Times of Trouble."

"What are you guys talking about? What is the Times of Trouble?"

A crack of thunder blasts from the perimeter of the village. The storm is still shielded from the village, but the cracks of thunder are gaining force. Juno jumps at the noise and shields himself by curling up behind the boulder.

Jimmy turns in anger and watches the storm again. After a moment, he turns around in a controlled rage. He approaches Juno, reaches down behind the boulder and lifts him completely up and over the boulder.

"Stop whimpering and tell us what this thing is?"

Jimmy's newfound strength stuns Will.

With his back firmly pressed up against the wall, Juno begins to talk, "Th...th...the times of trouble are here."

Jimmy growls, "What are they?"

Will grabs Jimmy's arm., "Put him down, Jimmy."

Jimmy growls quietly back at Will. Not flinching, Will looks at his morphed friend and demands "Put him down, Jim."

As Jimmy looks over to Will's eyes, something mysteriously calms him down. Typically, a Scolit cannot control his emotions, but something within Will has diluted the anger and rage Jimmy's Scolit form experiences.

Chapter 20

Reluctantly, Jimmy slowly puts Juno upon the boulder. He walks away in disgust, as Will says to Juno. "Juno what is this thing? What are the Times of Trouble?"

Relaxing a bit, Juno speaks, "Dddd darkness. Darkness overcomes the light. The land…the land can bear fruits no longer, th…th…the river…she can no longer quench the thirst of its people…the tablets… they…they have been compromised."

In an instant, Will is taken back to the moment he and his grandfather were hit with the beam of light from the snow globe in his room. He sees his grandfather saying to him, "The tablets have been compromised."

Gaining his composure, he resumes questioning Juno, "What did you say?"

Looking pointedly into his eyes and speaking clearly, Juno says. "The tablets have been compromised."

A thunderous crack rattles the perimeter of the village. Juno quickly curls himself into a ball again and takes cover behind the boulder.

Jimmy questions Juno., "What tablets have been compromised? What are you talking about Jobo?"

From behind Jimmy, a soft voice interrupts. The boys turn around and see the most beautiful female they have ever laid their eyes on. Deity, a gorgeous blond-haired Serenian woman in a white toga-like dress, meets their gaze. Her beauty is breathtaking. Only five feet tall Deity features are soft and gentle. With smooth white silky skin her image almost angelic in front of the boys.

"Do not worry yourself. My name is Deity. You are in Seren. You are safe."

The Village Of Seren

Deity appears to be in her mid-twenties. Three Serenian men accompany her. Will stammers, "Uh, excuse me?"

"You are safe now. You must not worry. Bethel has sent us to care for you while he prepares himself. Please come with me."

Jimmy jumps to the forefront, "Come with you where?"

"You have journeyed long and your feet are tired. Let us care for you and fill your belly."

Jimmy looks at her with a wolfish grin, "You have food?"

Diety smiles, "Of course. Please, come."

Diety walks out of the hut and her entourage follows. Jimmy looks over to Will, "I am SO hungry."

Will smirks and says, "You're always hungry, let's go."

The boys follow Diety and the men.

Diety turns and directs, "Stay under the arch."

The boys look up and see a gigantic red rock arch that runs across the village. The arch could be used for cover from the sun or as a bridge when necessary. Everywhere they turn they see a more beauty. Tucked away in tiny adobes are gentle water falls and tropical plants plentiful with fruits, vegetables and candy-coated foliage.

Will remarks to Jimmy, "Now, *this* is what I imagined Rainbow Alley to be?"

"This is awesome. I'm glad we crashed here," Jimmy responds.

"Look!" Juno shouts. He points to a beautiful rainbow shooting through the land just above a waterfall.

Diety stops to explain, "This is the river of Seren. It is our gift from above."

"It's awesome."

Chapter 20

"Awesome?" Diety doesn't quite understand Will.

"You know it's like…out of the box…way out there…cool."

Diety isn't quite sure she understands. "Ahh , yes, yes it is very refreshing." She turns from the river and leads the boys into a large structure near the center of the village. As the boys enter, they gape at what appears to be both modern and archaic spa. Everything is made of natural elements from red bedrock, from hot tubs to large granite tables.

Deity, turns to them, "Please, help yourself to anything you would like to eat. After you have filled your bellies, please enjoy our refreshing tubs and our relaxation tables."

The boys can not believe it. "What can we eat here?"

Diety opens her arms to the room.

"Everything and anything you see is edible and meant for consumption."

Jimmy is stunned., "Are you serious?"

Diety laughs and says, "Yes, please enjoy."

Jimmy walks over to an odd looking tree and flicks his finger on a branch. Diety nods to him with assurance.

He pulls on the tree branch again, and it breaks off. He slowly takes the branch and places it in his mouth. His face lights up, "Oh my god, this is awesome. Will, you gotta try this! It tastes like a Starburst."

Will walks over and grabs a piece of the tree. He takes a bite and his eyes open up wide. "This is unbelievable."

Jimmy runs to another bush and samples its leaf. "This one taste like a Snickers."

The Village Of Seren

Will stoops and plucks a tomato-looking vegetable. "I got a raspberry sherbet here."

"This is great. Willie Wonka eat your heart out!" Jimmy takes off into the garden and begins to indulge. Will follows suit as Juno slowly sits down by one plant and very simply begins to eat.

The boys are having a ball running around and sampling the vegetation. Everything they bite into reminds them of a candy or ice cream flavor back home. They are in their own form of paradise. After about twenty minute's of this, the boys slowly come out of the garden.

Diety is waiting for them with robes. She hands the boys their robes.

"Come with me and we will help to refresh your pores."

The boys grab the robes and follow her.

"You may change over there."

"Thank you."

Each of them walk to a changing area and change into the garments provided by Diety.

When they come out, they are directed to a resting area. Two more beautiful Serenian women come out.

The women pull back a curtain and expose a gigantic pool with swirls of steam coming from it. One of the women says, "Please, enjoy."

Will looks over to Jimmy. "You ready for a dip?"

"Why not?"

Will gets up and walks the pool. He dips his toe in it and turns back to Jimmy. "It's like really warm bath water, Jimbo."

"Oh, yeah."

Chapter 20

Jimmy literally jumps over Will and cannonballs into the warm water.

"Oh! This is great! It's so warm."

Will jumps in and Juno follows.

For the next twenty minutes and the boys frolic about. After their swim, the boys are lead to a natural bedrock sauna and then to a natural steam room. Finally the boys return to the resting area and find their clothes freshly laundered. Exhausted, warm, clean and untroubled, all three fall asleep in the hut provided for them.

⋆Chapter 21⋆
Will Glimpses His Destiny

As Will sleeps, he dreams images of destruction, war and scenes of Malkuth torturing his own people. He tosses and mumbles as explosions roar and bodies are hurled through the air.

Suddenly, a brilliant white light pierces the awful scenes. Will focuses on a vision of a beautiful woman in a while silky cloak. She tries to say something to him, but cannot seem to get the words out. Finally, she is able to whisper, "The tablets…Forerunner come to…to…to…"

The mysterious woman is interrupted by images of Malkuth torturing his people and another of his grandfather falling to the ground the night of the reading. The beautiful woman still struggles to get her words out, but the images of the torture and suffering overpower her words. An explosion larger than any of the others erupts, and Will is shaken from his sleep, shouting, "Nooooo!"

Jimmy and Juno quickly jump up. "What is it?"

Chapter 21

Will looks over and says, "Sorry guys. It was another of one of my dreams. They're getting more intense."

Rubbing his eyes, Jimmy mumbles, "What was this one about?"

"Same stuff, but this time she mentioned the tablets."

Juno jumps up in fear. "Oh, the tablets! I forgot about the tablets!"

Jimmy snarls, "Don't start Jibby! What is so special about these tablets anyhow? What are they? And why are you so antsy?"

Juno looks at Jimmy fearfully, "Th…th…the tablets …."

From behind Jimmy a soft voice joins in, "They are the Tablets of Fate."

The boys turn to see Bethel standing in the archway.

Will looks at him with curiosity as Jimmy says, "The what?"

Will interrupts, "Are you really Bethel? The same Bethel my grandfather always talked about?"

Bethel looks at Will and intones, "You are, as he was."

"Excuse me?" Will says in confusion.

"I am who you say." Bethel walks over to a boulder to sit.

Will is unsure where to begin. His grandfather has talked about this man for years in a surreal sense and now, not only is everything he had told him about Rainbow Alley true, but the people are turning out to be real, as well. He fumbles for words to continue, "So…so is it all true. Everything he has told us about Rainbow Alley. Is it all true?"

Bethel only says, "Truth is one's perspective on his own situation."

Frustrated, Will says, "You're talking in riddles. If you're really the Bethel my grandfather has talked so much about, then you can heal him. I need you to come back with me to heal my grandfather."

Will Glimpses His Destiny

Bethel says, "A task that I would certainly cherish, however one that can not be done."

"Why? I thought you had great powers--powers that can heal."

Bethel looks Will directly in his eyes and says, "The power to heal is within. Joseph must find this, and he will be released."

Jimmy looks at the obviously frustrated Will and asks, "Will is that it? That's what we came here for?"

Will pleads with Bethel, "This can't be what we've traveled this far for. Please tell me that's not it."

Bethel does not respond. He simply sits on the boulder and stares.

"Unbelievable!" Will sputters. "This is unbelievable! Come on guys, there has to be someone here who can help."

The boys start to walk towards the exit of the adobe.

"It is within the tablets where he will find his strength," Bethel says softly.

Will slowly turns around. He sees Bethel sitting on the boulder with a slight smirk on his face.

"You *can* heal him can't you?"

"It is not I, it is within the word."

Confused again, Will demands, "What word?"

"The word within the tablets. It holds everything. It will release and it will confine. You must choose correctly for it will show you the way."

Jimmy pipes in, "Where are these tablets?"

Bethel opens his arms and motions to the boys. "Sit and I will explain."

Chapter 21

They reluctantly walk back towards Bethel and sit in front of him on the ground.

"If it was not for the tablets there would be nothing. The tablets hold the truth, the power, and the gifts of all. For eons, the tablets have resided on the upper portion of the divine tabernacle as the alleys of Rainbows have gone undisturbed."

Will smiles and says to himself. "Rainbow Alley".

Bethel continues, "Peace and serenity were all that we knew. Then a disturbance unlike any we've dreamed about cast its evil eyes upon our land. Within moments of the disturbance, the seven Tablets of Fate were gone, and in the hands of Malkuth on the crest of the mountain of Ynitsed. With all seven tablets in the hands of such an evil force, the disturbance can only reach epic proportions."

Juno pipes up, "We are doomed. Are we not, great Bethel?"

Bethel slowly turns to Juno. "Betrayal will only mask itself as doom."

Juno gets uncomfortable as Bethel stares at him. The older man turns his head and looks to Will.

"Great power and serenity for all is achieved when all seven tablets are in harmony. However, unspeakable destruction and devastation emerges if the tablets are destroyed. That is an act Malkuth most assuredly is preparing to consummate. By creating the chaos and destruction, Malkuth is convinced he gains ultimate power. Power that he believes can transcend multi-dimensions."

"What do you mean by multiple dimensions?"

"The type of power that can cripple even outside of the rainbow's vortex.

Will Glimpses His Destiny

I'm not following you. When you say outside are you talking about..."

Bethel stops and turns towards Will and says, "The type of power that can bring down men like Joseph."

Stunned, Will says, "What? Are you saying that this Malkuth was able to put my grandfather in a coma from here? Why?"

"The seven tablets have been in his possession for a very short time. A very short time that has produced unspeakable chaos and I'm afraid regrettable losses."

Will gets up quickly. "He's not lost yet. We can save him, I know we can. What about the tablets? You said the seven were in his possession a short time. Where are they?"

"As fate has guided us, one of the seven has been retrieved. We have managed to break his chain for the moment. However, this will not stop his effort in the destruction of the land. He will pursue until all the tablets are back in his possession."

Jimmy joins in, "What's stopping him from destroying the other six?"

Bethel looks at Will instead of responding directly to Jimmy. "My son, the tablets are what holds us all together. They can only be destroyed if the elements are in sequence and they are one. They can also bring us back to serenity if the elements are in sequence. The scrolls of the four who ride will reveal all and will provide the direction. Ultimately, it all depends on who is the holder of all seven tablets when the shadow is full."

Will stares back at Bethel. "When the shadow is full? What does that mean?"

Chapter 21

"When all the elements are in sequence, the shadow can overcome."

"What are these elements and where are the scrolls?"

Bethel walks towards the archway. He stops just shy of the exit and looks upward.

"On the night when all is new and the night sky is full, the clover of the Forerunner will provide the sequence and the scrolls will be revealed."

Will recognizes himself in the comment. "The Forerunner? Bethel, what will Malkuth do?"

"We have succeeded for the time being. But for us to stop the destruction and for you, my son, to be one with your grandfather, all seven tablets must be retrieved by the Forerunner and placed back upon the tabernacle during the shadows hour of the elements."

Will slowly reaches for his shoulder and pulls his shirt back to once again reveal his newly discovered clover mark.

Bethel watches, and says reassuringly, "Yes, Will. It is you. You are the Forerunner, the chosen one to bring order in this land of disorder."

"Why me?"

"You, my son, are the carrier of the legacy. It continues on with you."

"This makes no sense. How do we know we can trust you? I mean, how do we know you're not like Danaë and the rest of them? They also said I was the chosen one. What makes you different?"

"Trust is within. You will know who to trust and who will betray you."

Will Glimpses His Destiny

Jimmy says sheepishly to Bethel, "Can these tablets help me? Can they change me back to who I was before this?

"Time will answer all. The tablets will set your direction. Find the scrolls and the elements will begin to form."

Jimmy looks over to Will. "Will, we gotta find these things."

Nodding in agreement, Will asks, "Where's this tabernacle?"

"You are upon it."

Will looks around and sees nothing. "I am?"

Suddenly, Jimmy says in astonishment, "Oh, my gosh…"

Out of nowhere, the room begins to morph. It becomes screened off by curtains of fine twisted linen on either side of the entrance. The linens, embroidered in violet, rose, and scarlet, are suspended from white marble pillars set in bases of brass. The floor transforms into smooth and silky charcoal-colored marble.

Will says, "What going on here?"

Adjacent to the back wall an elaborate white marble altar appears with cloud- white linen lying on top of it. Above the altar, seven carved wood placeholders attach to the wall. They are all empty except for one. Inside the one rests a stone tablet with multiple engravings. The carvings appear to be symbols and markings that resemble Greek.

Now it seems to the boys that the room has always been there, but had been disguised by the dirt and boulder adobe hut. Out of sorts, Jimmy reaches over to the fine twisted linen and touches it to see if it is indeed real. The linen sways back and forth as he pushes it with his hand.

Will, standing near the altar, turns towards the wall of carved wood placeholders. He looks over to Bethel and says, "The tablets?"

Chapter 21

Bethels nods yes.

Will walks closer. Now he can see the detail within the altar. The altar actually looks as if it is a part of the adobe and the red rock that has created the arch. It appears to be an extension of the natural surroundings. It does not appear to have been carved or manufactured. It is simply part of the landscape. The tablet placeholders rest within natural grooves in the red rock of the cave. They fit perfectly into the grooves.

Will runs his hand over the grooves, and then comes to the lone tablet. He turns towards Bethel. "May I?"

Bethel nods once again.

Carefully, Will reaches for the lone tablet. At the moment he touches the stone, a thunderous roar bellows from outside the perimeter of village and lightening quickly follows. Will hesitates, but quickly returns to the curiosity of the tablet.

As he pulls the tablet from the wall, the placeholder begins to illuminate. The illumination surrounds the carved placeholder and a portion of Will's arm. Gazing at the tablet, warmth rushes through Will's body. Will's eyes open wide as he stands on the altar holding the tablet. The illumination now surrounds his entire body.

A piercing pain suddenly replaces the warm feeling, and Will screams.

Jimmy yells, "Will! Are you ok?"

Will falls to his knees and whispers, "I'm seeing things"

He has a vision of the inner sanctum of Malkuth's castle. He sees the men hanging from their arms over the pits of sludge. He can smell the fear inside the torture chambers Malkuth has scattered throughout

Will Glimpses His Destiny

the castle. He sees the raids and the slaughters Malkuth has conducted, and the relentless and uncaring nature surrounding Malkuth and his henchmen.

He sees armies of Scolits and warriors training for battle, and then he sees a tiny room. Inside the room, Malkuth hovers over an ark that holds the remaining six tablets. The evil within Malkuth's stare is penetrating. He is plotting his next move over a map of the land. His next raid, Will sees, is to be on the Village of Seren.

Will sees the walls of the village crumble, and the natives of Seren running for their lives. He sees fire and explosions. He sees an army of Scolits and warriors ready to overtake the land when suddenly the beautiful lady of his dream reappears.

Marabus stands before Will at the tabernacle and says, "Forerunner, I have limited time to alert you. You have the power within to alter what is destiny. The tablets must be retrieved. Come, I will guide you in your quest."

Will tries to speak when the image becomes clouded and is replaced by those of explosions and mayhem outside of the village. He hears her one last time, "Come, I will guide in your quest."

Will breaks from his vision. He hears Jimmy, "Will, Will are you ok?"

Will rises and places the tablet back into its natural groove within the red rock and wood casing. Out of breath and sweating, he turns towards Bethel. "I think I understand now. How can we help?"

"The tablets must be retrieved. Once they are in our possession, it is you who will bring the peace."

Chapter 21

Confused, Will says, "I don't understand. What is it I need to do?"

"When the tablets are retrieved, you will understand. For now, you must stay with my people. They will protect you."

"Who's going to get the scrolls and the tablets?" Jimmy mutters from behind Bethel.

Bethel turns and says, "My warriors are assembling as we speak. We leave for Ynitsed in one hour."

Will looks outside and watches the tiny Seren warriors scamper across the village. These men are no taller than him. He turns back in disbelief. "Bethel, are those your warriors?"

Sensing Will's sarcasm, Bethel says, "Never underestimate the strong in heart, my son. They will retrieve the scrolls of the four and provide the road to the tablets."

Will turns towards Jimmy and rolls his eyes as if to say "Whatever!"

Jimmy watches as the tiny warriors' trip over one another preparing their archaic weapons. They appear to be a small tribe of naïve warriors with no sense of direction and or balance "Is that all they have to defend themselves?"

"It is all one needs, if he believes he is victorious."

Raising his eyebrow, Jimmy says under his breath, "It's all one needs to get their butts kicked." Raising his voice, he adds, "Are you sure? I mean, I've seen some of the weapons those other guys had and…."

Bethel stops him in mid-sentence. "To worry is to not to have faith. To have faith is to have far greater tools of defense than one can imagine. Have faith and you shall see."

Will Glimpses His Destiny

Still skeptical Jimmy says, "I don't know, man."

Will looks outside and watches the tiny warriors prepare. As if in another vision, he sees the size of the warriors increase and watches their weapons transform into the latest technology. He cuts Jimmy off, and says, "Jimmy, ya gotta have faith, man…ya just gotta have faith!" He turns to Bethel and grins.

Seeing this, Jimmy looks outside again and sees the tiny warriors with the archaic weapons. He turns to the two.

"You both are nuts. Will, I'm getting worried about you."

Will laughs as Bethel smiles and walks out of the adobe. As soon as Bethel leaves, it transforms back to the cave-like hut it was before. The marble floor and tabernacle vanish.

Laughing, Will walks over to Jimmy and Juno.

Jimmy demands, "Just what is so funny?"

Will continues to laugh and Juno joins in.

Jimmy walks away, shaking his head and saying. "You're losing it, man. Here I am—half Scolit or something and I'm the only one with any sense around here."

Jimmy sits dejectedly on the boulder in the center and watches the tiny warriors outside prepare for battle. "They're gonna get crushed. This is suicide."

The warriors continue their preparation.

✳Chapter 22✳
Malkuth's Rage

Deep within Bornea, Abra assesses the damage to his underground city. He walks the platform of the bridge leading to his quarters and Watches his young warriors scampering around to hold together portions of the walls that have fallen. Disgusted, he turns his back on his men and walks within his chambers.

Once inside, he walks directly to the chair Will had been in earlier. He sits and swivels the chair around. "It appears that we have a minor setback."

An overpowering voice answers, "*Minor? That's not what Danaë tells me.*" A gigantic image of Malkuth overshadows the room.

"Danaë, my brother, stretches the truth. You know this to be true."

Malkuth's image grows larger within the room. "Where is the Forerunner, Abra?"

Abra replies tentatively, "He escaped."

Malkuth's Rage

The image on the wall grows again as Malkuth's voice carries and overpowers the chamber.

"I give you one assignment. ONE!"

Nervously, Abra attempts to save face, "We were caught off guard. No one expected his powers to be as they were. We...agghh!"

Abra is stricken with a sharp pain shooting through his lower back and up his spine. The pain is so severe he buckles over, and is forced to the ground.

Malkuth speaks, "Disappointment is a luxury I have no time for."

Abra's pain intensifies. He screams out in desperation, "We...we have his...his...aghhh!"

Malkuth lowers his hand, and the pain diminishes. He orders, "Speak."

Attempting to gain his composure, Abra pulls himself off of the floor and says, while gasping for air, "We have his sibling. Look." He points to another portion of the wall where images of Bryan and Brittani are displayed. They are shackled to one another and lie face down in a dungeon within Bornea.

Malkuth appears somewhat relieved. "Splendid, this may very well prove to be advantageous." His voice intensifies, "Now where is the Forerunner?"

Abra pulls himself up and says, "Our reports tell us they headed towards the Village of Seren."

Malkuth's voice softens. "How convenient."

Abra looks up to Malkuth, "Should we be concerned, brother? It has been written that the Forerunner shall take solace in Seren. Bethel will surely see this as a sign of strength."

Chapter 22

Malkuth's voice and image intensifies again, "The only strength Bethel will witness is my wrath. Prepare my legions."

Abra looks up at the images on the wall. "Your legions stand ready, my Lord."

"We seize Seren within the hour." Malkuth's image dissipates.

⋆Chapter 23⋆
The Dungeons Of Bornea

As rats scamper across the beams and ties holding the structure together, Bryan and Brittani lie face down in the dark and damp dungeon deep within Bornea. With their arms shackled behind their backs, and chained to one another, it is very difficult for either to move. Both of their faces are pressed up against the moist mud floor.

Trying even to lift their heads is a task. Every time they move, they pull on the other's shackle, and it tightens its grip. Each movement brings excruciating pain.

Brittani, near tears, mumbles, "Bryan, this is beginning to hurt."

Trying to keep his composure, Bryan closes his eyes for a moment. Opening them with an air of confidence, he replies, "Don't you worry, Britt, it's gonna be ok. I think I know what's going on here. We just need to stay one step ahead of these guys."

"What are you talking about? Bryan, we're shackled together in a dungeon. We can't stay one step ahead of anyone! Do you see what's happening here? We're in serious trouble."

Chapter 23

Sighing, he responds "Brittani, I don't know how this is possible, and I don't know what my grandfather was into, but we're living within a book or books here. We're inside these two stories and we're really the only ones who know how it can end."

"Bryan, that was before they were combined. Rainbow Alley on its own is peaceful. I know everything your grandfather ever wrote concerning it. And I'll tell you this, this dungeon was never in Rainbow Alley."

"It was in *The Sorcerer's Shadow*, though. I know these people, I know what their thinking. We just have to play it through and ride through the story."

"Bryan! Listen to what you're saying. It doesn't make sense. Plus we don't know if it's going to play out like it was written. You said it yourself back in your bedroom. The story is writing itself. If that's the case, all we have are elements from both worlds that have collided and are creating separate realities. If that's the case, all bets are off and we don't have a clue what to expect."

Bryan thinks it over and says, "If you're right, then we gotta find Will soon."

"If I'm right, we may not have a chance to even see Will."

"Don't even talk like that! We're gonna find a way. You may be right about what may happen, but this dungeon was in the book, and that means other landmarks are too. If we can get to the end of that corridor, I know there's a clamp that can cut these shackles. We need to try."

The Dungeons Of Bornea

At that moment, Brittani feels something on her leg. She quickly kicks away as a rat scampers up and over her. She screams. "Get me out of here, Bryan."

"Ok, ok. Just listen. We have to move together. If not, it's just going to make things difficult. On the count of three, we roll towards me and over to the corridor. Ready?"

Brittani takes a deep breath. "Ok, I'm ready."

Bryan begins to rock and Brittani tries to move towards him. Every time they move the shackles tighten. After a few tries, Bryan screams in pain as the shackles grind into his thigh. They stop.

Brittani looks at the shackles and the crease in Bryan's thigh. "Bryan, I don't know if we can do this much longer. Just look at your…"

The dungeon door flies open. Bryan quickly says, "Shhh."

The two of them place their heads back to the ground as they were before.

Danaë and a few of her henchmen come into the belly of the dungeon and walk directly towards Bryan and Brittani.

With her demeanor completely changed from her initial meeting with Will, Danaë walks up to the two and says icily, "Let's get these two out of here. We need them for bait right now. We don't have much time."

Bryan looks up and says, "Where are you taking us?"

Danaë swings her foot and boots him in the gut. "You will not speak." She grabs one of the henchmen. "Take them to Abra."

The henchmen grab Bryan and Brittani and carry them out of the dungeon. As they are carried through the corridor, Bryan sees the clamp that he knew would be there. He whispers, "Britt…look."

Chapter 23

Brittani looks over and sees the clamp. Bryan gets a reassured look on his face as the henchmen dart the two up the stairs of the dungeon.

Chapter 24
Prelude To Battle

Bethel sits, his legs crossed over one another, inside a pure white teepee in the center of the village. The teepee is roughly twelve feet high and resembles teepees the Native American Indians used in the wild. He meditates with his arms extended. A soft, white layer of wool provides a cushion for him to sit upon. He sits motionless for a few moments, when from behind him he senses a disturbance.

He remains motionless as the entrance to the teepee widens. Just as the entrance is fully opened, Bethel speaks, "A disturbance grows in your heart. What can release it?"

Will cautiously enters the teepee. "You knew it was me?"

"I knew."

Bethel remains in his meditative position. Will looks around for a place to sit when Bethel says, "My home is yours. Please find an area and rest."

Will decides to sit down near the entrance of the teepee behind Bethel.

Chapter 24

"What is it that grows in disturbance for you, my son?"

Cautiously Will stammers, "Ah…well, you saw what I saw back there when I picked up the tablet didn't you?"

Bethel does not respond.

"Because that was some pretty intense stuff. I'm not sure Jimmy has a clue what we're into here, but I'm starting to get a better idea every minute. I mean I know what is expected of me now, but I'm not sure I should involve him. Just look at what's happened to him already. It doesn't seem fair that I dragged him into this and now it can get even more dangerous."

Bethel stops him. "What is disturbing you son?"

Will scoots around and sits in front of Bethel.

"Malkuth is coming here. He's coming here because of me isn't he?"

At that, Bethel opens his eyes. "He will stop at nothing to gain complete control. You are the only obstacle within his path."

Will stands up and looks at Bethel. "If that's the case, then I can not stay here and put your people in harm. I need to go to Ynitsed to get the tablets before it's too late."

Bethel smiles. "Your concern, my son, is worthy; however, Malkuth will not stop. You being here is yet another reason for him to attack. Seizing Seren has been a task for him for quite sometime. I am afraid whether you are here or not, he will come for our Village and the seventh tablet."

"Do you know how to find the other six tablets?"

"It is not wise to search for six. Release the seals of the four scrolls and all will be revealed."

Prelude To Battle

"I'm not sure I understand. Do you know where these scrolls are?"

Bethel nods yes.

"Take me. We can do this together. And maybe if he catches wind that we're not here, he may stop his siege on the village."

Bethel responds, "War is upon us my son. We must take up arms and you must be sheltered from it all."

Dejected, Will says, "I've seen his armies in my visions and you won't be able to beat him."

"At this point our task is not to beat him, it is merely to slow him down. Time is all we have right now."

Frustrated, Will says, "I feel so helpless."

"You are far from helpless my son. Your time will come. Now you must be sheltered from the evil that is upon us."

Unsure of what to do next, Will agrees with his elder and dejectedly walks out of the teepee. Once Will leaves the teepee, four of Bethels warriors emerge from within the structure. Each has a very distinct look. The first warrior, Zechariah, is wearing a white vest of armor and is carrying a bow with him. The second warrior, Machiara, is wearing a red vest and has a long sword attached to his belt. The third warrior, Famiaria, is wearing a black vest which has a pair of scales embossed within its center. He carries no weapons. The fourth and final warrior, Hadesria, is wearing a pale white vest that has no markings. He carries with him an arsenal of weapons.

Bethel addresses the warriors, "You must stay close to him. His heart is heavy and his desire is deep. When he flees, protect him in his travels. He is wise beyond his years, but his youthful tendencies are still

Chapter 24

within. Set the path for him now, for he will flee as Malkuth ascends upon the city."

Zechariah walks forward and kneels in front of Bethel with his head down. He says with his fist over his heart, "We will guard him with all our might, my lord."

He then slowly raises his head and, with concern in his voice, says, "How long will you stay?"

Bethel puts his hand upon Zechariah's shoulder and says. "We will stand our ground against evil. Our land shall not be overtaken. We will not leave."

Zechariah closes his eyes and bows his head in respect. "I understand, my lord."

Machiara, Famiaria and Hadesria follow suit. Each of them kneels in front of Bethel to pay their respects and pledge undying loyalty.

⋆Chapter 25⋆
The Battle Of Seren

      Will walks slowly back to the adobe. He sees that the storms in the perimeter have dissipated. There is an eerie calm, as if the calm before a storm. The eerie calm begins to take affect him. His paranoia sets in as he hurries towards the hut. He sees warriors readying themselves and village people scurrying for cover. He looks at the perimeter again and sees that the sky is turning a mysterious reddish color.

    He takes off in a mad sprint towards the hut. Inside, Jimmy and Juno are playing an archaic version of paper football. Jimmy is trying to teach Juno the rules as he attempts to flick a woodchip though Juno's haphazard goal post.

    "Naw…naw….listen, Jibby, all you gotta do is keep your fingers like this. No…no…like this."

    Juno looks at Jimmy's paw-like hands and tries to mimic them. "Like this?"

    "No! Like this."

Chapter 25

Will barrels into the hut. "What's going on?" Jimmy says as he flicks the woodchip directly into Juno's head.

Out of breath, Will looks at both of them. "We gotta get out here."

Stunned, Jimmy says, "What? Didn't you hear the man? This is the safest place for us. You're the one who said not to worry, that these warriors could do what they have to do."

"I know. But no matter what we do, Malkuth is coming for us. We gotta get the rest of the tablets. We can't wait for Bethel or anyone else. We gotta go get 'em. If not, we're all doomed."

"I don't know Will. This seems to be the place for us. It's pretty peaceful here. Not to mention that spa area was pretty awesome."

"Fine, you don't have to come. I'll go alone."

Frustrated, Will turns and walks toward where the tabernacle was.

"Will," Jimmy says, trying to mend the breach in their friendship.

Will keeps on walking and begins to feel around the walls.

"What are you doing?"

Will doesn't answer.

Jimmy gets up and walks towards him, repeating, "What are you doing?"

Will keeps feeling around the wall. "I need that tablet."

Juno jumps up in fear and screams, "You mustn't take the tablet!"

"I'm not going to keep it. You heard Bethel. We need to unite the tablets before the night is full. All I'm trying to do is have them in one place."

The Battle Of Seren

Juno runs over. "No..no…no! The tablets are sacred. You mustn't take them."

"Juno, I'm not going to do anything with it. Trust me, something tells me that I need to have it with me."

Jimmy looks at Will, "Will, I know you're on a mission here or something, but I don't know about taking anything. I'll come with you on your little trek, but I don't think we should take anything."

At that moment, Will hears a voice. It's the same female voice he has heard before. It says, "Forerunner, your journey is at hand, bring the tablet and take the River of Seren north to the mountain of Time."

He looks up and says, "The river?"

Jimmy looks bewildered and says, "What? Man, are you listening to me?"

Will's hand successfully rubs over a crevice in the wall. The crevice opens and the tabernacle begins to appear. "Here we go."

A tremendous explosion rocks the perimeter of the village.

"Whoa! What in the?" Jimmy screams.

Juno runs to the opening of the adobe and peers out. He sees Bethel's warriors scampering for their weapons as a burning desert outside of the perimeter of the village increases in size. He turns towards the boys.

"It has begun. Malkuth is coming."

Will watches the tabernacle appear. He looks over to the wall and sees the tablet. He begins to reach for it when Jimmy's paw-like hand grabs his arm.

Juno stands in the foreground watching them.

Will looks at his friend and says, "What are you doing?"

Chapter 25

"You realize, you take this, and that's one more reason Malkuth will be coming after us," Jimmy growls.

Will looks over at Juno and then to Jimmy with a determined look on his face.

"You guys, you gotta trust me here. I'm supposed to take this. I know I am."

Another explosion rocks the perimeter of the village.

"You better be right about leaving this place," Jimmy complains. He looks outside as Serenians run past the adobe in a panic, "Let's go."

He lets go of Will's arm and Will grabs the tablet.

"Ok, we gotta find the River of Seren."

Will places the tablet in his shirt and the boys run outside. It's beginning to get more and more chaotic within the village. Villagers are screaming and running for cover as the boys stop and look up past the perimeter of the village.

Jimmy bellows, "Oh my God!"

A darkness creeps over the perimeter of the village. The sky has become a burnt reddish-orange plume. Everywhere they look, the sky is on fire. Explosion after explosion rips outside of the village as Abra and his warriors attempt to break through the energy field that surrounds Seren. With the explosions sending shock waves through the city, the moat of reptiles begins to flood towards the village.

Will looks over to Jimmy. "Let's get out of here."

Jimmy looks out towards the desert and sees the snakes and scorpions heading their way. "Ah…yeah. Sounds like a plan."

The boys take off towards the Garden of Seren. As they run they see the Serenian warriors heading out towards the desert in an attempt

The Battle Of Seren

to stop the reptiles from invading the village. Another set of warriors' heads towards the perimeter of the village to set up their defense against the onslaught of Abra's armies.

Based on speculation, Abra's warriors had set a course for the village of Seren in an effort to track the Forerunner's location. Abra, however, has dropped his fleet of graviports too close to Seren, which has warned them far too earlier than Malkuth had prepared. Sensing the mistake, Malkuth is carried up on a graviport towards the perimeter of Seren.

Abra notices his brother and begins to feel his rage.

"We will pull back my brother. All is not lost, we still are in good position."

An enraged Malkuth screams. "Abra you fool. This is why I have to do everything myself."

Malkuth turns towards a group of Scolits near Abra and says. "Relieve him of his duty immediately."

Sensing the worse, Abra begins to back away in fear. "Malkuth no…no…we are brothers."

Malkuth stares at Abra and with a steely expression says, "Relieve him of his duty."

The Scolits quickly engulf Abra and begin to drag him away from the perimeter.

This failure—which has turned out to be his last—has brought about his immediate imprisonment at the hands of his brother, and has given Bethel sufficient warning to raise the Seren shields against Malkuth's bombardment.

The only option left is for Malkuth to lead and land a ground force to disable the Seren shield generators.

Chapter 25

Bethel quickly deploys his infantry to buy time for his own villagers' evacuation. His troops are entrenched with cross-bow lasers and expandable rifle-like blaster swords. Graviport forces provide aerial cover. Bethel places extra coverage near his power generators, anticipating them as a primary Malkuth target.

Malkuth's plan is one of envelopment. His warriors' infantry place themselves at the center of the desert with his cavalry on either flank; two thirds are on the right heading towards the road to Seren, and one-third to the left heading towards the shield generators. The infantry is to engage the Serenians' center while the cavalry moves around the flanks to surround the village.

While this is a sound plan in Malkuth's mind, there is a flaw. He assumed that Bethel would be content to sit and wait for the attack.

As Malkuth warriors begin their siege, a huge explosion rocks the perimeter of the village. This explosion has come from within the village and surprises Malkuth and his armies. The explosion knocks the majority of them off of their graviports. The remaining warriors are stunned.

The boys fall to the ground. Will looks up and says, "Oh my God, look at this!" He points to the perimeter as the fighting begins. Dozens upon dozens of Bethel's graviports come barreling out and through the shield. Bethel's men quickly pull from their animal skin pouches a weapon that resembles a crossbow.

The Serenian bowmen kneel and pull their strings back. Instead of an arrow shooting out, an electronic pulse comes hurling like a pellet from the weapons. The pulse blasts through Malkuth's warriors and

The Battle Of Seren

thrusts them off of the graviports. At least twenty are brought down immediately.

"Which way?" Jimmy screams.

"This way, it's past the garden," says Will.

The boys continue their escape as they run through the village. Not far behind, Bethel's four selected warriors follow.

STUNNED FROM THE surprise counter-attack, Malkuth's Scolits and warriors begin to retreat. In a fit of rage, Malkuth points his jagged, sword-like scepter towards his own armies and shoots a power beam towards his troops. At least thirty of his own troops disintegrate on the spot.

Malkuth bellows, "ON YOUR FEET OR PERISH!"

The troops quickly turn and see Malkuth . His presence is daunting with His troops stop in their tracks.

"PROCEED."

He points to the desert. The warriors see the reptiles going ballistic within the moat. Tentatively, the warriors slowly walk towards the snakes, scorpions and fire-breathing iguanas. Malkuth points his scepter towards a giant boulder across from his troops. He shoots a power beam towards the boulder and hits it directly in its center. The boulder erupts and spews out hundreds of pieces. At the same moment, the troops notice that the electron field has dissipated within a sector of the desert. Malkuth knew that this boulder carried a shield generator. Its destruction created an access road for his army.

He screams, "PROCEED!"

The troops quickly turn towards the village and begin an onslaught through the access point.

Chapter 25

Heading up the siege are groups of flamethrowers who quickly create a path by torching the reptiles within the moat. Following the flamethrowers, Malkuth's infantry and cavalry, over a thousand strong, make their entrance into the moat of reptiles.

Once inside the moat, Bethel's men also proceed ahead. Crossbow electra-pellets are hurling through the air as graviport warriors careen overhead. Bethel's men manage to hold them off for only a brief moment as the ground assault gradually becomes man-to-man combat.

As Bethel watches from a boulder across the moat, he sees his men engaging in man-to-man combat. Although his warriors have transformed their energies to grow in size, speed and accuracy, they are still no match for Malkuth and his legions when it comes down to man-to-man combat. Their only hope is to fend them off with their weapons and slow their attack down.

The fighting wages on and on as Bethel's men create a sort of perimeter within the moat. Still watching, Bethel sits down and crosses his legs in a meditative state. Enemy graviport warriors blast their lasers towards his vicinity.

Miraculously, none of the beams come close to him, as the Serenians aboard their own graviports head off the onslaught by shooting the enemies down.

Bethel continues his meditation, raising his arms.

AS WILL, JIMMY AND Juno run through the garden, they see the river of Seren in the foreground. Will sees flashes of the war in a dreamlike state that is going on within the desert. It is as if he is in the middle of the action as the Serenians fight feverishly to hold off Malkuth's wrath. He even sees Bethel meditating with his arms

The Battle Of Seren

outstretched and hears him chant, "Η εμπιστοσύνη στις ταμπλέτες και μας παραδίδει από αυτό το κακό."

He can't understand the language Bethel speaks, but it seems that he is speaking it directly to him. The visions of the war get stronger as Malkuth's men near the newly-formed perimeter. Will sees the four warriors Bethel sent to help him in his quest, then he sees Bethel again. In his dreamlike vision Bethel says, again,"Η εμπιστοσύνη στις ταμπλέτες και μας παραδίδει από αυτό το κακό."

Will screams, "I don't understand." Now a dark figure hovers over Bethel. He screams one more time to the vision, "I don't understand!"

The four warriors appear for a moment. He sees them standing by the river near two small canoes, he sees Bethel on the boulder, and now he sees Malkuth standing over Bethel with his spear scepter. As Malkuth raises his scepter over Bethel, Bethel seems to look straight into Will's eyes and says, "Trust in the tablets and deliver us from this evil!"

Malkuth strikes down upon Bethel and Will's dreamlike image goes dark.

Will screams "Noooooooooooo!"

He falls to the ground near the river of Seren. Jimmy and Juno quickly run over to him.

"Will, Will are you ok?"

Tears welling up in his eyes, Will sobs, "They got him...they got Bethel."

Confused, Jimmy looks at Will, "What, what are you talking about?"

Chapter 25

Panicked, Will grabs Jimmy's arm. "We gotta go, we gotta get out of here." He looks up sees the four warriors from his vision standing by the two canoes. As explosions erupt behind them, Jimmy and Juno are increasingly nervous. Will, however, begins to calm himself as he slowly stands up and stares at the warriors.

Zechariah waves his arm to tell them to proceed. Will, now trance-like, watches as Zechariah continues to wave. Machiara, Famiaria and Hadesria prepare the canoes for departure. Jimmy and Juno turn to see what Will sees.

Will says, "They're with us."

Jimmy, disbelieving, says, "How can you be so sure?"

Will begins to walk towards them, determined. "They're with us."

The boys start off slowly towards the warriors, and then quicken their pace. After a few seconds, they begin an all-out sprint towards the warriors.

As soon as they make it to them, Will looks at Zechariah. "Are you here to help us?"

Zechariah looks at him, and in a foreign dialect says, "ναι πηγαίνετε." He nods his head with a reassuring grin.

With Machiara, Famiaria and Hadesria already in the canoes, the boys quickly head into the waters and jump in. Zechariah nods again and also jumps into the canoe. The men begin to paddle downriver into the darkness. The explosions behind them illuminate the sky as they drift away from the chaos and head towards the direction of Ynitsed and the Mountain of Time.

The Battle Of Seren

As they drift, Will peaks at the tablet and its foreign markings. He looks over to Jimmy and Juno as they stare into the darkness of the night, from the surreal environment of war behind them to the peaceful flow of water in front of them.

Chapter 26
The Four Scrolls

Months before the Times of Trouble, Malco summoned Bethel to the Mountain of Time for a summit and meeting of the minds. Although they had very different opinions on the land and the ruling of the people, they did share one common belief --that was one of unity and respect for the tablets.

Malco had ruled the land as far as people could remember. His sorcery and his vision kept the land in check and allowed for many tribes to flourish. His shared respect for Bethel was embraced by Marabus, but loathed by Malkuth.

Sensing that his eldest son may be plotting against him, Malco did something that he had never thought he would have to do; he had to conspire against his own blood in an effort to keep unity in the land and of the tablets. Knowing that Abra was not strong enough to lead, he also knew that he was not strong enough to trust. He would break if Malkuth pushed him. It had to be Marabus that Malco would trust

The Four Scrolls

with his plans. It would be Marabus who would carry the torch for him if he were removed.

With the summit only moments away, Malco knocks upon Marabus' door within the castle. Marabus, whose beauty is unsurpassed, is staring out her window at the peaceful land. She revels in the birds flying over the rainbows and the gentle waterfalls flowing throughout the land. Even with the obvious beauty and peacefulness in front of her, Marabus has a look of concern upon her face. Something or someone is bothering her.

Startled by the knock upon her door, she turns abruptly and says. "Come in."

She turns to see her father, Malco, come through the door. He immediately shuts it behind him.

Marabus looks up at her father with concern, "Father."

Malco looks at her and opens his arms. "My daughter, our time is upon us. Bethel is only moments away."

She runs into his arms. "Father, is it wise to be doing this?"

"It is our only choice. You, my daughter, are the only one I can trust with this information. We must plan for the worst."

"What is it that Bethel can do for us? And how do we know he will deliver the tablets?"

Malco smiles. "My daughter, my precious blood, do not be naïve. Remember, we must anticipate every move Malkuth will attempt. It is Bethel right now who I trust the most. Let us go now, while the men are out."

Malco and Marabus open her door and through the castle corridors towards an alcove near the doors to the dungeon.

Chapter 26

Malco grabs Marabus. "Quick, this way."

They continue near an exit that is next to a beautiful garden. Once at the exit, Malco stops. "We stop here."

"Why here father?"

"Look."

Malco points to the garden. In the midst of the lilies fluttering in the breeze like butterflies, Bethel sits upon a boulder in a meditative state.

"Is that him?"

"Yes."

In awe, Marabus looks at her father. "This is just as I had imagined him. What do we do now?"

"We greet our guest."

Malco approaches Bethel with Marabus following closely. As they near him, Bethel turns his head and says softly, "There is a disturbance we must deal with, isn't there?"

Malco, a strong and husky man of substance, appears to melt while in the presence of Bethel. "We do. One that can lead to many more, I am afraid."

Bethel turns and stares directly into Malco eyes. "Then one we must prepare to deal with. Is it your will to do what is necessary?"

"It is. My concern is that it may be too late."

"A possibility we must face, but prepare for, regardless. It is time to summon the Forerunner."

Malco looks at Bethel in disbelief. "The Forerunner will be powerless against this might. It is fruitless to attempt it."

"Powerless to a non-believer. If guided, nothing can stop it."

The Four Scrolls

Marabus feels a sense of anxiety and commitment rush through her body as Bethel stares at her. Malco turns away and then back to Bethel in a bit of frustration. "What about the tablets? How can they be protected?"

"It is not the tablets we must protect, it is the content within. The tablets are vulnerable. They will be compromised. However, it is what is retained within the scrolls that will set the direction to maintaining the integrity of the tablets."

Malco looks at Bethel in confusion. "The scrolls?"

Bethel pulls from his robe four scrolls rolled up with blood red wax providing a thick seal at the opening of each. He hands the scrolls to Marabus.

"I shall trust in you, Marabus, to position the scrolls throughout the land for the Forerunner to seek." A bit frightened, Marabus backs a way and looks to her father.

"Positioned throughout the land? Why me?"

Bethel grabs Marabus' hand. "I seek the true in heart to lead this charge."

Malco looks at his daughter and with a proud but stern demeanor and nods his head in agreement. Marabus slowly reaches for the scrolls.

"Ah,...where shall I place them?"

Bethel gives her a look of reassurance. "You will know my dear, you will know." She takes the scrolls and looks over to her father. He smiles as he whistles to a horse at the edge of the garden. The horse responds by trotting over to the three. Malco grabs its reigns and looks at his daughter.

Bethel looks to the south and sees a dark sky appearing.

Chapter 26

"It is beginning."

Fearful, Marabus looks to the sky along with her father.

"Father, I am frightened."

"Fear no evil, my sweet, now you must be on your way."

He reaches out his hand to help her mount the horse. She responds and jumps on. Looking at her father she says, "Will you be here upon my return?"

Malco looks to Bethel and back to Marabus. "Go now my dear daughter, as I will be with you always."

He smacks the horse on the rear and it takes off. Marabus fearfully looks back at her father and Bethel in the garden. She watches for a moment and then, determined, turns to face the mountain of Time.

Chapter 27
Escape

Shackled by one arm to the base of a ground transport vehicle, Bryan and Brittani attempt to shield themselves from the explosions that surround them. With mortar explosions triggering massive counter attacks from Bethel's warriors, the sky is illuminated as if it were the Fourth of July.

As the counter-attacks gain frequency the guards ordered to watch over the two jump off of the vehicle and join them underneath the transport. The explosions get closer and closer. Frightened by the chaos, Brittani and Bryan try to scoot around the vehicle to shield themselves from the mortar shells.

Bryan screams, "We have to get to the other side."

The two try to roll to the other side of the transport, but can move only a couple feet before the chains from the shackles pull them back.

Bryan screams in frustration as the explosions near. He looks over to the guards who have now jumped to the other side of the transport and look as they are going to retreat.

Chapter 27

He screams, "Unhook us. You can't leave us here like this!"

The guards glance at Bryan and Brittani as another blast explodes nearby. Panicked, the guards quickly retreat and run away from the transport and the explosions.

Bryans screams, "Hey! Where are you going? You can't leave us here. Not like this!"

He looks down at the shackles on his and Brittani's arms.

"Oh this is great…just great."

Another explosion erupts nearby. Brittani screams. "Aghhh…. Bryan, get us out of here."

Frantic, Bryan looks around like a mad man. He can only move a couple feet until the shackles pull him back. Finally, he sees a lead pipe that has broken off the vehicle lying on the ground near to them. He rolls towards it, but lands about a foot away.

He looks back to Brittani. "Brit, scoot with me…come on."

He grabs Brittani as they both try to scoot towards the lead pipe. This time he is closer, but still inches away.

Struggling he grunts, "I'm almost there."

He tries to dig his hand into the ground and pull himself closer, but the shackles won't give an inch. With his face driving into the ground he tries one more time. This time he scoots his body around Brittani, and tries to reach the pipe with his foot. He's much closer now.

"Ok, come on…just a few more inches."

He kicks the pipe with the corner of his foot sending it further away from him. "Nooo," He moans in desperation.

Brittani looks over. "It's moving away."

"I know that. I can get it. I know I can."

Escape

Brittani looks over and gets a determined look on her face. As the next explosion rocks the ground around her she mutters, "Move, I'll get it."

She jumps over Bryan, maneuvers herself on the ground and stretches her legs as far as she can. She is actually much closer than Bryan.

Bryan looks over and urges "You're almost there Britt, keep on going."

She moves the pipe with her toe... "I...think I got it."

She manages to kick the pipe and turn it more towards them. One more kick and it will be in her grasp.

"You got it Britt, just kick it this way."

Brittani scoots herself closer and is about to kick the pipe when an explosion rips though, picking up the transport they are shackled to and topples it over. Brittani and Bryan get carried with it and land on top of the vehicle as it rests upside down.

Stunned, Bryan quickly looks over to Brittani, who is hanging sideways off the truck. "Brittani! Are you ok?"

"Bryan, help me."

Bryan sees that the explosion has opened the rod that had held them to the transport. Quickly, he pulls himself up and begins to wiggle his chain off of the rod.

"Hang on Britt. We're getting off this thing."

With all his might, he rocks himself and pulls the chain back and forth until it finally frees itself from the broken rod. The two fall off the transport. The shackles have separated just enough to allow Bryan to detach the chain which connects them.

As they hit the ground, Bryan quickly picks Brittani up.

Chapter 27

"Are you ok?"

"Yes, yes."

"Let's get out of here while we have the chance."

The two quickly scamper into the darkness of the night as the explosions riddle the fields around them.

MARCHING THROUGH the village, Malkuth heads directly towards the adobe that houses the tabernacle. Amidst the smoke and debris, and in his wake, lie wounded Serenian warriors. He wanders past them without a glance. At times he's forced to clear his path with his scepter.

As the wounded warriors fly from side to side, Malkuth heads directly into the adobe. Once inside the center of the adobe, he stops. He peers around the empty shell and raises his scepter. Smoke begins to filter up from the ground below as the room begins its transformation into the hidden tabernacle.

As the pillars, curtains and tabernacle morph into place, Malkuth gets a look of satisfaction upon his face. He surveys the sanctuary. Above the altar are the placeholders for all seven tablets. Malkuth heads towards the altar. He instantly spies the empty seventh placeholder.

Enraged, Malkuth pounds his hands on the tabernacle and crushes the top half of the altar. It separates and falls to the ground. Malkuth turns in a fit of rage and heads out of the sanctuary.

Chapter 28
The Mountain Of Time

The calm within the river's canyon is eerily serene. The tablet inside Will's shirt protrudes slightly outward. Jimmy and Juno who are both fast asleep in the canoe.

The canoes glide across the smooth, motionless waters. Zechariah continues to lead Machiara, Famiaria and Hadesria down the river. No words are spoken as Will surveys his surroundings.

The peacefulness is a welcome change from the chaos he had been thrown into ever since he has arrived in this strange land. They travel in the silent of the night for over an hour when Machiara says, "Το βουνό του χρόνου."

Startled Will looks up to Zechariah. "What did he say?"

Zechariah repeats, "Το βουνό του χρόνου." He points upward and adds, in heavily accented English, "The Mountain of Time."

Will quickly looks up and sees the outlines of an enormous monolith in the red rock mountainous range. The mountains remind him of the

Chapter 28

red rock monoliths of Sedona, Arizona. Against the dark, reddish sky, the site is even more awe inspiring.

Jimmy and Juno begin to stir as the canoes float closer to this amazing landscape.

Jimmy looks up, "It's beautiful."

"I'll say." Will mutters. As the canoes get closer to a white sand beach, Juno is distracted by a reflection. He looks upward toward monolith. He waits a few seconds and sees it again.

Noticing Juno staring upward, Will says, "What are you looking at?"

"I am not sure. Look."

Juno points upward toward the mountain range as the rest of them look up. It takes a few moments and then Will also sees a bright white flash.

Excitedly he says, "I saw it. Did you see that?" He looks at Jimmy.

"I didn't see anything. Did you see anything Z?" He looks over to Zechariah who remains expressionless. "Yeah, me either, big guy. Naw, you're seeing things again, Will."

At that moment Will sees it again. "There it is again. Juno did you see it?"

"Yes, yes I did."

"See what, what did you see?" says a skeptical Jimmy.

"I don't know. Some kind of flash. We gotta go up there and see what it is?"

Still watching the mountain, Jimmy asks," What did you say?"

"You heard me."

The Mountain Of Time

Still looking, Jimmy asks, "Are you seeing the same thing I am?"

"Sure am. Zechariah can you take us up there?"

Zechariah looks up the mountain. He nods yes.

"Great," Jimmy grumbles, "Just great."

With a look of skepticism on his face, Jimmy looks at Will who looks as if he has just received a gift. The canoes are only feet from the beach when Zechariah and the others jump out and begin to pull the watercraft in so the boys can hop out. Once docked, the boys jump out as Jimmy surveys the mountain.

"Will you look at this?"

The red rock monolith of the mountain is awe-inspiring. The tiny beach provides a very small platform adjacent to the red rock cliffs above. As beaches go, this would not be one to be featured on any postcards. There really is no place to walk once on the platform. The only direction is up, and in the dark night the journey will be all the more treacherous.

Jimmy looks over to Will, who is grabbing onto the red rock.

"Where exactly do you think we are going to go?"

Will looks back as he begins to climb. "We'll be fine. Come on."

Paws on his hips, Jimmy looks at Will in disbelief. "You're going nuts…you know that?"

"What are you talking about? We gotta get up there don't we?"

Jimmy looks up and finally sees the same flash Will had seen.

"Ah…yeah. I think so. But Will, I don't know about this."

Will loses his grip and lands on the sand. Determined, he gets up and finds Zechariah in his sights. "Zechariah, you said you can get us up there. Will you lead?"

Chapter 28

Zechariah looks at Will as if he doesn't understand him. Will rushes over to the same ledge he had tried to scale a minute ago and says, as he points, "Up...up. You take us up?"

Zechariah begins to smile. He slowly looks over to the other three warriors, and they all begin to laugh.

Dejected, Will says. "What? What's so funny?"

Zechariah doesn't say anything, but he keeps laughing as he looks up at the path Will is attempting. He grabs his knapsack from the canoe and then begins to walk towards Will.

Excited, Will grabs hold of the ledge again as if he was about to get a boost. Zechariah and three warriors walk past him. Each of them is smiling as they pass.

Confused, Will says, "Hey, where you going?"

Will, Jimmy and Juno watch the warriors walk about twenty yards down from where Will had attempted his climbing. They turn towards the mountain and walk directly into the monolith. They vanish from sight.

Stunned, Will sputters, "Oh my gosh. Where did they go? Jimmy did you see that? Jimmy where did they go?"

Quickly, Jimmy follows suit and runs to the area where the warriors had vanished. He turns and rushes into the mountain. Jimmy bounces off of the mountain and falls heavily back into the water.

Sitting up quickly in the shallow waters he wonders, "What in the..."

Will and Juno rush over. "You ok, Jim?"

Frustrated, Jimmy slaps the water and gets up. "Yeah, I'm ok." Out of nowhere, he rushes like a fullback towards the mountain again.

The Mountain Of Time

Once again, he bounces off like a rubber ball. Once again, he lands back in the water.

Will watches his buddy splash into the river.

"Will you stop that. You're gonna break something."

He turns around and begins to feel the wall of mountain. "They went in right here, I think."

He rubs his hand up and down the rock. "It's pretty hard."

Jimmy looks up from sitting in the waters. "You're telling me?"

Confused, Will turns to his friends. "What's going on here?"

Just as he says this, out of the corner of his eye he sees Juno walking down a few more yards. He stops and turns towards him.

"Do you know something Juno?"

Juno turns towards Will. "We must unite."

Confused, Jimmy gets up and shakes the water from his fur, "What are you talking about, Jibby? Unite what?"

"We must enter as one."

Understanding, Will takes his hand away from the rock. "We go in together."

Juno nods yes.

"That's it Jimmy. We go in together."

"Good, maybe this time you're the one who gets bounced."

He walks over to Will. "Let's try it."

Jimmy grabs both of their hands and backs up. "Here were go again."

The three of them begin to scream as they take off towards the wall. Just as they are about to impact, they close their eyes and clench their fists. Instead of bouncing off of the rock, the boys begin to ooze

Chapter 28

through it. It is as if they are running through a wall of gelatin as the rock absorbs their bodies within its structure.

The gelatin-like impact last for only a few seconds as they pass through the width of the rocks and into an open chamber. Zechariah and the others are sitting on a boulder inside waiting for them. Because of their momentum, the boys enter into the chamber and continue to run straight into a wall on the other side. They quickly pass Zechariah and the others and hit the wall squarely. Each of them bounces off and hits the ground.

As the boys gain their senses, they see the chamber as well as a long ramped pathway ascending upward. The enclosed path resembles architecture of the ancient Egyptians. They built similar paths to through a pyramid to the burial site of a king.

Steep steps lead to an incline bordered by an iron gate. Beyond the gate is a strong white light. Behind the light, shielded by a rough board, stand life-size figures of warriors, stricken stiff by an artist, silently guarding a tomb. The warriors hold blood-soaked staffs in one hand, and a long sword in the other. A palm-leaf shield lies at hand.

Between these two statues is the entrance to an inner chamber. New timbers barricade this chamber, making passage difficult. The distance between the inner chambers and the entrance the boys are in is very small and to pass through will be a tedious job at best.

Will gets up and looks around the new surroundings.

"What is this place?" He asks Zechariah.

Without uttering a word, Zechariah stands and nods in a form of agreement. He continues on towards the inner chamber.

The Mountain Of Time

Will looks over to Jimmy and shrugs. "I guess he wants us to follow him."

Still brushing himself off from the impact, Jimmy says, "The question is *should* we?"

Will watches the other warriors follow Zechariah. He looks behind him and feels the wall he had just come through. It is as hard as a rock now.

"I don't think we have choice. Besides, there something up here I'm supposed to see. I can just feel it. Let's go."

The three boys get up and begin to follow Zechariah and the other three warriors.

Chapter 29
Road To Zanzibar

Running as if he has been through this land a million times before, Bryan leads Brittani through fields of grain and stalks of vegetation. The darkness makes this task more daunting; however, his determination on his face has never been stronger.

"This way Britt, we need to make it to the road just ahead. I think I know where we can get some help."

Bryan now knows what he's up against. He has read about Malkuth and his raids for years. It has always been a fantasy world. One he never imagined he would be in. Now in a situation he had only dreamed about before, he runs through the fields thinking of the times he played 'Sorcerer's Shadow' in his backyard with his friends. Playing in this fantasy world was their favorite pastime. From fighting off warriors to becoming Eseph and Malkuth themselves, Bryan had done it all.

But now it was real, all too real. He's not pretending to be a part of great raids alongside the great sorcerer of the written word. Now, he was in a real battle against a character that, if he was to believe what he had read, was invincible. How could he compete against so powerful and resourceful a sorcerer?

Running through the dried stalks of vegetation, Brittani trips and falls to the ground. Bryan quickly stops and picks her up. The two are reaching a point of exhaustion.

Out of breath, Brittani gasps, "Bryan, how much longer?"

"Just ahead. You see that?"

Bryan points towards a beach not far ahead. Brittani notes the orange tinted sky over the emerald blue body of water. In the distance is a small island.

"What is it?" Brittani asks as she gulps for air. Bryan ignores her question.

When they make it to the beach they stop to appreciate the serenity of the calm waters and the island in the distance. With a smile on his face as if, he has found an old friend. Bryan finally says, "It's Zanzibar."

"Zanzibar?"

"Yep, we're gonna be ok now."

Brittani looks over to Bryan. "How can you be so certain?"

"Because this is were the book ends. This is where Malkuth is defeated. All we need to do is go over and find Eseph."

"Eseph?"

"Yes, Eseph was Malkuth's arch enemy in every *'Sorcerer's Shadow'* book. He's the one who can defeat him. He's the one who has the power to take him on."

"Are you sure?"

"Absolutely."

"How do we get over?"

Chapter 29

"Good question." Bryan walks up the beach a bit. He appears more confident with each step.

If my calculations are right," he begins, moving towards the water, "we'll find, yes, there they are. Right over there." He points to several overturned canoes.

Brittani is stunned.

"Oh my gosh, how did you know that?"

"I told you. I know this thing inside and out. Come on, let's get over there. We need to find Eseph. He'll get us out of here and then we can find the boys."

The two of them rush over to the canoes. Bryan quickly pulls one out into the water, and they climb in. They begin to row towards the island of Zanzibar.

Chapter 30
The First

As Will and Jimmy follow Zechariah through the narrow halls within the chambers, Juno begins to lag behind. Noticing, Jimmy keeps looking back to keep an eye on him.

The group ascends about one hundred feet through a myriad of twists and turns. The climb is challenging, but their determination moves them past even the most difficult barriers. Zechariah stops at an area that is boarded up.

Will says, "What's wrong?"

Zechariah mumbles.

"What'd he say?" Jimmy looks to Will. "What is it, Z?"

Zechariah looks at Will and translates, "The first."

Confused, Will echoes, "The first?"

He hustles up to where Zechariah stands and peers through the boards.

He sees an empty cavern with a rounded platform in the center. Other than the platform, the cavern is an abyss which seems to descend

Chapter 30

into the bowels of the mountain. Floating in a cloud of bright white light above the platform is a scroll.

Will's eyes fix on the scroll. He is drawn to it like no other feeling he has had before. He's hypnotic for a moment until Jimmy comes up to view.

"What's in there Will, what is it?"

Still in awe, Will keeps staring through the broken wood. "I'm not sure."

"Let me see."

Jimmy pushes him to the side and peers through the wood. As he does, he accidentally knocks over an odd-shaped vase placed at the entrances of the room. The vase begins to roll down the stairs they have just climbed, making a racket all the way down.

The group watches the vase vanish into the darkness, and listens to it clanking against the walls all the way down. The sound is annoyingly loud.

Shrugging it off, Jimmy turns to gaze inside the cavern. He is not impressed. "What's the big deal? It's a floating piece of paper, why are you so freaked?"

Will slowly turns to question Zechariah. "The first?"

Zechariah nods in agreement.

At that moment, a loud shriek pierces the quiet from the cavern below.

The warriors are startled. They have heard this shriek before. Machiara says, "Ochu."

Still gazing between the boards and oblivious to the fear behind him, Jimmy turns his head, "God bless you."

The First

Recognizing the fear on the warriors' faces, Will says, "What's Ochu?"

Zechariah responds, "Go! We must go, now!"

"What about the scroll? Isn't that why we're here?"

"We must go now," Zechariah demands.

Will grabs Zechariah's arm. "No. We need to get the scroll. Please. Help me."

They hear another shriek from below. Zechariah looks at the other warriors with concern. He addresses Will again, "Now! We must go. The scroll must wait."

Zechariah turns towards the other warriors. Juno follows the men. Will and Jimmy stay behind. Sensing that they have not followed, Zechariah turns and sees Will and Jimmy still at the entrance. The shrieks are increasing in frequency and decibel as the cave begins to shake from thumps below.

Zechariah screams, "Come!"

Ignoring him, Will turns to Jimmy and says, "Knock it down, bud."

Jimmy takes his paw-like fist and wails into the boards covering the empty cavern. The boards begin to break, as the thumps from below get closer.

Zechariah yells to the others, "περιμένετε."

Machiara and the others freeze. Concerned, they look back at Zechariah and then towards the shrieking sounds below. Jimmy wails into the boards again, they break apart, and Will pushes on the wood while Jimmy hits again.

"Πάρτε την περίμετρο," Zechariah commands his men.

Chapter 30

Quickly they begin to form a shield to ward off whatever is coming up the ramp. Zechariah rushes to help the boys. Jimmy has broken a few boards, but not enough to get through to the cavern. Zechariah pushes Jimmy to the side. Will looks over in confusion, but keeps pushing the board inward. Zechariah pushes Will to the side. The shrieking sounds as if it is only a few hundred feet away.

Zechariah places one hand on his chest and the other cast outward towards the boards. "ανοικτός," he says quietly. In a matter of seconds, the boards begin to fall one by one. The cavern is now open.

Will doesn't say a word despite his amazement. His adrenalin is pumping too high right now for words. He steps inside the cavern with Jimmy and Zechariah.

From behind Machiara screams "Ochu"!

A multi-headed creature with the body of a lion, a tail like a snake and heads like a dragon and eagle emerges from the depths below. It shrieks once again as the warriors stand ready to defend them.

Zechariah turns to Will. "Go."

Will looks at the scrolls hovering within the cavern. The only way to the scrolls is a seven-foot jump onto the platform. An abyss surrounds the platform. If one would miscalculate the jump, it would send them deep into the dark depths of the mountain.

Concerned but determined, Will says "Ok.".

Ochu has begun its attack and the warriors defend themselves with their swords and arrows.

Just as Will is going to lunge forward for the platform, Jimmy scoops him up and throws him down.

Will looks up in frustration. "What are you doing?"

The First

"You'll never make it. It's too far. I'm going."

"You're going. Why you?"

"Have you seen me lately? I can make this."

The shrieks and the noises of the battle behind them are getting more intense. Will hesitates for only a second, and then agrees. "Be careful, bud."

Jimmy moves as far back as he can to get a running start, and takes off towards the platform. He soars across the abyss about six and half feet and slams directly into the platform just beneath the top. He is able to hang onto the edges, but his feet and body dangle into the emptiness below.

Will screams, "Oh my gosh, Jimmy, hang on!"

Reacting quickly, Zechariah takes off and soars across the cavern. He basically duplicates Jimmy's jump. Both of them hang from the platform. Zechariah scoots his hands over one by one towards Jimmy.

BEHIND THEM, Ochu wreaks havoc upon the warriors. He tosses them into the walls while his hissing snake-like tail attempts to strike them. Juno has run for cover while the men attempt to hold the beast off.

Zechariah makes it over to Jimmy and says, "Climb."

Jimmy grabs hold of Zechariah and pulls himself up the platform.

Overjoyed, Will punches the air and yells, "Yes!"

Jimmy turns and reaches to help Zechariah. He pulls him up on the platform just as Will is struck by Ochu's tail.

Chapter 30

He screams and falls to the ground as the whipping tail flails back and forth in and out of the cavern. Machiara and the warriors continue their onslaught upon the creature from within the passage.

Jimmy looks over and sees Will on the ground. "Will!"

Shaken, Will looks up and says, "I'm ok, just get it."

Jimmy stands and turns towards the scroll hovering above the platform. As he grabs the scroll, the platform begins to shake. Unsure he tentatively pulls down. As he pulls, the platform shakes more.

Wide-eyed, he looks back at Will. Will is not sure what to tell him to do. Jimmy turns back to the scroll, grabs it tightly and swiftly pulls it from its light source. The platform shakes wildly. Then, from within the platform a narrow bridge begins to protrude to provide a walkway.

At that moment, Ochu slams into the entrance like a demon possessed. The cavern shakes from the thunderous pressure. Ochu retreats again as the warriors continue their fight.

Jimmy turns back and screams to Will, "Get out of there!"

Unsure, Will looks back inside the passage and sees that the warriors are clearly losing this fight. He also sees that Ochu is readying himself to make another plunge into the cavern.

Will turns, takes off and plunges towards the platform. Even at his top speed, Will only manages to leap about four feet towards the platform. He's going to miss it by a mile. Seeing this, Zechariah quickly reaches for his bow, pulls out an arrow and aims directly towards Will. Seeing this, Jimmy screams, "WILL! Look out!"

As Will reaches the end of his momentum, he begins to drop. Zechariah launches the arrow directly towards Will.

Jimmy screams, "Nooooo!"

The First

The point of the arrow pierces Will's shirt as the power and momentum of the shot carry him back into the wall of the cave. The arrow embeds itself and Will hangs helplessly.

Quickly, Zechariah takes out another arrow and shoots it towards Will. This one pierces the other side of his shirt. He is now hanging securely on the wall, pinned like a butterfly specimen.

Jimmy looks over to Zechariah and in an impressed tone says, "That was awesome, dude."

At that moment Ochu comes driving through the wall. The pounding shakes the cavern and Wills shirt begins to rip. Zechariah moves fast. He pulls out another arrow and shoots this one directly towards Ochu. It hits him in his shoulder, but only affects him briefly.

Will's shirt rips a little more. This time, the lone tablet which Will carries, begins to works its way out from inside his garment. Will tries to reach over to grab the tablet, but is bound too tightly by the arrows.

Behind Ochu, Machiara and the others renew their efforts... Machiara is swinging his sword around as Zechariah hits the creature once again with an arrow. This time, the arrow penetrates the neck of the eagle.

Will's shirt tears more as he tries to reach for the tablet.

The eagle's head begins to flail about. Moving in for the kill, Machiara thrusts his sword into the other neck of the dragon. The beast squeals and falls toward the abyss.

As it topples over, Machiara leaps off. The beast passes right over Will. The wind shear rips his shirt even more. The tablet is about to fall.

Chapter 30

Will makes another attempt to grab it before it, too, falls into the abyss. He thrusts his body forward releasing one of the arrows, and catches the tablet in the nick of time, now he dangles by just one arrow.

The arrow is in the portion of the shirt that is ripping the most. In a matter of seconds, the shirt begins to give way. Will is about to plunge into the darkness. The shirt is on its last thread when Will feels two hands grab his shoulders and hoist him upward.

He looks up and sees Machiara holding onto him while Famiaria and Hadesria pull him up by his legs. Once safe, Will lies on the edge of the abyss, clutching the tablet with his eyes closed.

After a moment, he opens his eyes and sees the others crouched down, catching their breath.

Will looks up at Machiara and whispers, "Thank you."

Machiara simply nods as he breathes deeply. He looks over to Zechariah and Jimmy on the platform. They, too, are in a relieved position. They all see that the bridge is clear to the other side of the platform.

Will asks, "Where's Juno?"

Not quite understanding him, the men shake their heads.

Will screams, "Juno. Are you ok?"

No response is heard.

Will looks over to Jimmy, "Did he go over?"

Shrugging his shoulders, Jimmy says, "I don't think so. You know with all the commotion, he could have."

Will screams, "Juno! Are you out there?"

Still no reply.

The First

Will gets up and hustles over to the entrance to peer inside the cave. He screams one more time, "Juno!"

No reply. Will turns to the others, "He must have gone over."

They all somberly walk to the edge and look down into the darkness of the abyss. No one speaks. Will kneels to say a prayer. After a few moments, Will looks over to Jimmy and Zechariah. "We have to continue on. Do you have the scroll Jimmy?"

Jimmy holds the scroll up.

"Ok, we're coming over."

Will looks over to Machiara and asks, "Can you…?" He motions to Machiara to assist him over. Machiara motions to Hadesria. They both grab Will by the shoulder and the thigh, and position themselves to launch him onto the platform. Will holds the tablet tightly and announces, "I'm ready."

The warriors rock back and launch Will over the abyss and into the arms of Zechariah. Then, one by one, the warriors back up and leap over the emptiness and onto the platform. Once they all are safely on, Will says to Zechariah, "Let's go."

Zechariah takes the lead across the narrow bridge to the other side of the cavern.

Chapter 31
Devastated Paradise

The canoe skims gently across the calm, emerald-blue waters on the way to Zanzibar. Bryan paddles in the back of the canoe as Brittani watches the island get closer. She turns to Bryan and whispers, "Bryan, what do you know about Zanzibar?"

Smiling, Bryan answers, "It's the land that dreams are made of. For years my grandfather told us all about Rainbow Alley and how great a place it was, well I gotta say, when I started to read the *Sorcerer's Shadow* series and began to learn about Zanzibar, nothing could compare."

"Is this why you were so distant when your grandfather would want to read to you?"

"Well, I don't know. I guess I was just getting older and Grandpa's stories were just getting old to me. I needed my own stories. And believe me, this is one heck of a story, as you can tell," he says, settling in to the telling. "Anyways, when I first began to learn about Zanzibar, Rainbow Alley couldn't hold a candle to it. This is true paradise. It's a land like no other. Not only does it have all of the great features

Devastated Paradise

Rainbow Alley does, Zanzibar was just a more real place to me. I could picture everything in my mind. I could see the palm trees, the lush vegetation. The land of sugars and spices, I could see them all. This was the real deal to me. Not to mention, it was the land were Eseph reigned."

"Eseph?"

"He is Malkuth's arch enemy in the series. He is also the hero in every book. He and his apprentice, Cayla, well, nothing can defeat them. Nothing."

As Bryan reflects, Brittani notices something hovering over the island.

"I mean, this is the type of hero we all want to be. This guy can take on an army and probably defeat them all himself. He's a master in the martial arts, amazing with swords and…"

"Bryan! What is that?"

Bryan looks up as he continues to paddle. Squinting his eyes, he attempts to look forward in the darkness of the night. "What?"

"Right there, straight ahead." Brittani points directly towards the island.

They are about two hundred yards from the island. It appears only vaguely. Bryan looks up and says, "Oh, my god."

They see the island has been decimated. Bryan sits speechless. Brittani says, "It's the two worlds, Bryan."

Bryan looks at her in disbelief. The canoe is now only fifty yards from the island. "What?"

"It's the collision of the two worlds. Remember in your room, how the book was writing itself?"

Chapter 31

"Yeah."

"That's why it's not the same. Nothing's the same, Bryan. Nothing."

"Yeah, but the clamp was in the same place. The island's here."

Brittani turns to Bryan.

"It's here, but look at it. Doesn't look like a true paradise to me. Whatever happened here is because of Rainbow Alley colliding with the *Sorcerer's Shadow*. I'm afraid no matter how much I know about Rainbow Alley and you know about *Sorcerer's Shadow*, it's all meaningless. This is all too real, it's all too real."

The canoe brushes up against the river's floor and grinds to a stop. Bryan sits in the back, staring at the decimated city. The smell of burning cottages and vegetation lingers in the breeze.

Brittani turns to Bryan again. "What now?"

Dejected and confused, he replies, "I'm not sure."

After a few minutes, Brittani gets up and begins to get out of the canoe.

"What are you doing?"

"I'm not staying here. Let's go into the city and see if there are any survivors willing to help."

"Here?"

Determined, Brittani says, "We didn't cross this river for nothing. Let's go."

"Britt, I don't know. Malkuth's men may still be here."

"Well if they are, it's not like we haven't met them before. Now come on, we have to do *something*. We can't sit and mope."

Offended, Bryan mutters, "I'm not moping."

Devastated Paradise

"Then let's go. We need to keep moving."

Brittani sloshes through the water, and takes off across the beach toward what is left of the burned out city.

Still uneasy, Bryan jumps out of the canoe and begins to run towards Brittani.

"Wait up…wait up!"

⋆Chapter 32⋆
The First Scroll Directions

Shuffling across the platform to the other side of the cave, Zechariah leads his men and the boys to a safe landing. Once across, Jimmy sits down and looks worriedly at Will. "Are you ok man?"

Will, showing signs of relief, replies, "Yeah."

Jimmy then looks over to Zechariah. "Man, you are da' man with that bow and everything. That was incredible. *You are da' man!*"

Will sits down next to Jimmy.

"Let me see the scroll."

Jimmy hands the scroll over to Will. He takes it in his hand and begins to look it over. The worn, yellow, papery document appears to be ancient. Each end of the scroll has burnt edges. The blood red seal in the center firmly holds the ends together.

Will looks over to Jimmy. "What dya' think?"

The First Scroll Directions

"Open it dude. You didn't make those guys go extreme for nothing back there."

Zechariah and the warriors watch Will's every move.

"Ok. Here goes."

He gently grabs the edges near the seals and begins to pull. As he pulls, a soft white illumination begins to emanate from within the scroll.

IN THE MIDDLE OF the carnage and mayhem, Malkuth looks up in pain, as if he is sensing the opening of the scroll. He quickly reels around and continues his quest to decimate the land.

WILL LOOKS OVER to the group as he continues to tear open the seal. Once the seal is completely separated from the edges, a sharp, bright white light shoots from within the scroll as if it had been held captive inside of the document.

Startled, Will almost drops the scroll. After gaining his composure, he begins to unroll it. The writing inside is not language Will can understand. It reads:

"Η γνώση αυτή καταλαβαίνει"
"Διασχίστε το χάσμα"

Unsure of what he is looking at, Will looks over to Zechariah and asks, "Can you help with this?"

He hands the scroll to Zechariah. The warrior refuses to touch or even look at the inside of the scroll. The other warriors follow suit. Confused, Will looks over to Jimmy. "I don't understand. If we can't read it, what are we supposed to do?"

Chapter 32

"I don't know, let me see this thing."

Jimmy reaches for the scroll and Machiara instantly rushes over and stops Will, shouting, "No, no no." He motions to Jimmy to not to look at the scroll.

"What's going on?" Jimmy retorts.

Watching Machiara as he stands guard over the scroll, Will says, "I don't think you're supposed to see inside this."

Offended, Jimmy shouts, "Why not? What makes you so special?"

"I don't know, ask him," he says, pointing to Machiara who is hovering over Will and the scroll to defend it from Jimmy. As Jimmy bobs and weaves in an attempt to get around Machiara, Will looks at the scroll again. He sees the writing is changing.

"Η γνώση αυτή καταλαβαίνει"
Knowledge of the One is Understanding

"Διασχίστε το χάσμα"
Cross the Chasm

"Wait, wait! I can see something. It says, *"Knowledge of the One is Understanding…and…Cross the Chasm?"*

Jimmy stops trying to sneak around Machiara. "What's that suppose to mean?"

"I'm not sure," Will says, looking around. "I don't see a chasm, do you?"

The First Scroll Directions

Jimmy looks around, then turns to Will and asks, "What's a chasm?"

"Man, I was hoping you knew. Do you guys know what a chasm is?"

There's no answer from the men.

"I didn't think so. Whatever it is, we need to cross it."

The warriors gather their belongings and start to walk out of the cavern.

"Guess it's time to go, huh Jimmy?"

"Do you have everything?"

Will looks down at the tablet, rolls up the scroll, and places it in the front of his pants. "I think so."

"Let's go, then."

·Chapter 33·
The Inhabitants Of Zanzibar

The island rumbles underneath their feet as Brittani and Bryan trudge into the heart of the city. Brittani screams as the buildings begin to shake and pieces of the structures fall to the ground. Bryan grabs her and rushes them to the center of an open square. They crouch down and watch the buildings shake around them. The rumbling only last seconds, but feels much longer to them as they huddle together.

When it stops, Bryan gets up slowly. "I think it's over."

Brittani stands and looks around the town. It's devastated. There are no signs of life. It appears that an army has marched through and torn it to shreds.

"It's deserted," Brittani says.

"I'm not sure deserted is the right word here. I think these people were slaughtered."

"Yeah, but where are they? There's no bodies, no nothing."

The Inhabitants Of Zanzibar

"I don't know. I don't know."

Bryan heads for what once could have been the town market. Fruits and vegetables are scattered throughout the area. A tiny, fresh waterfall still runs through the square.

Brittani picks up an apple. "Hungry?"

"You think it's safe?"

Brittani cleans it off a bit, and bites it. "Yep."

Bryan grabs one, too, and bites into it. The two of them walk around the yard, picking up various fruits and vegetables. They meet again by the waterfall, and eat like they have never eaten before.

"I don't know what these are, but they're great. Tastes like a blueberry popsicle," Bryan says as he bites into a blue vegetable.

The two enjoy their little feast and stock their pocket with reserves. Suddenly Brittani looks up and says, "Did you see that?"

Bryan, who has blue sauce on his face looks, but sees nothing. "See what? Where?"

"Over there by that building. I thought I saw something."

Bryan looks over as he continues to enjoy his feast. "Naw, must be seeing things."

"I'm telling you, I saw something."

"Where you going now?"

Brittani doesn't answer as she walks over to the building.

"Aw man. Just when I was getting to enjoy this," Bryan mutters as he gets up to follow. When they reach the building, Brittani tentatively walks up to the entrance. The structure has been hit, but still looks solid enough to go inside.

"Do you think it's safe?"

Chapter 33

"Is anything safe around here? It looks ok, I guess. What did you see, anyhow? "

"I'm not sure. I saw something, though."

They enter the structure. As they slowly walk around a small piece of debris falls to the ground behind them. Startled, they both turn and see many small pieces that have come loose. Bryan declares, "That's all you saw."

Brittani looks up at the debris still falling from the ceiling. "You could be right." Brittani continues surveying the area. Bryan leans over and picks up some of the debris that has fallen. "I wonder when this all happened."

Ignoring Bryan, Brittani walks up some steps near the entrance. Bryan turns and sees her wandering upward. "Now where are you going?"

He throws a piece of debris onto a larger pile of debris. When it hits the pile, they hear a loud squeal. Shaken, Bryan jumps back and Brittani stops in her tracks. She turns around and asks, "What was that?"

"It came from over there." Bryan points to the pile of debris. Brittani descends the stairs and walks over to the pile. As she gets closer, she slows down. She whispers, "Bryan come here, check this out."

Crouching in front of the pile. A small panda-like creature cowers inside.

"Aw, it's ok, little guy," Brittani says.

Still standing back, Bryan says, "What is it?"

"It's a little cutie. That's what it is." She turns and sees that he is still standing back. "Would you get over here?"

The Inhabitants Of Zanzibar

"Is it an animal? I'm not good with animals."

She moves closer and the creature begins to move away in fear. Sensing the fear, Brittani moves very slowly. She coos, "It's ok, I won't hurt you." The creature scoots back further, and in doing so, exposes itself completely. Bryan walks up and asks, "Is that a panda?"

"I don't think so. It's a little different. Sure is cute, though. Hi, little fellow."

A piece of fruit falls from Brittani jacket. The creature sees this and stares at it. Seeing this, Brittani picks it up. "Are you hungry?" she purrs. "I bet you are."

She reaches her hand out towards the creature. It slowly moves towards the fruit. Soothingly she says, "It's ok, little guy, here you go."

Just as it is about to grab the fruit, the creature startles and rushes back inside the debris. Brittani tries again, cooing, "It's ok. We're not going to harm you." She reaches her arm towards the creature.

"We're not going to, but they might," Bryan says, as he stands motionless.

Brittani looks up at Bryan and asks, "What?"

Bryan motions his head towards the entranceway. Surrounding the door stands a group of men and woman who all look like they have been through a myriad of wars. They look exhausted and undernourished even as they stand at the door as if to protect their land. These are beaten people. They have no weapons other than the fragments of wood they have torn from a building.

One muscular man holding a makeshift club says, "Who has sent you?"

Chapter 33

Bryan answers, "Ah, no one has sent us. We are here looking for Eseph."

One of the women looks to the man and says, "They are with Malkuth, get them." Several members of the group step forward to pursue them.

As they back away, Brittani says to Bryan, "What did you say to them?"

Bryan shouts to the angry mob, "No, no no! We are not with Malkuth. As a matter fact, we just escaped from him."

The crowd stops and looks at the woman who gave the order. She says, "Escape? No one can escape Malkuth. Get them."

They turn back to Bryan and Brittani.

Brittani shouts, "No, no it's true. Look." She shows them the shackles on her arm.

The group stops. "Wait," says the muscular man. He walks up to Brittani and grabs her hands. He inspects the shackles and then looks up at the group.

"It's true. These are from Ynitsed." Looking at Brittani and Bryan, he adds, "How can you have possibly escaped?"

"It kind of a long story and we really need to find Eseph to help us find my brother."

"Eseph is gone. He was captured by Malkuth and is feared dead."

Stunned, Bryan says, "Dead? No way, it can't be. He's the only one who can defeat Malkuth."

The man somberly walks away from them, saying, "He is dead, I'm afraid. As are the rest of our people. We are all that is left."

The Inhabitants Of Zanzibar

At that moment, the tiny panda creature runs out and begins to snuggle up to Brittani. "As well as Moli." He motions to the animal.

Brittani reaches down and picks up the little guy. "Moli? Is that his name?" she says.

"Yes. He is the last of his kind, I'm afraid. They have unfortunately become a sport for Malkuth and his Scolits."

"Scolits, is that was those things are called?"

"They are his warriors and they are…or were…our people."

"Your people?" Bryan says in a confused manner. "Wait a second; you just said that your people were dead."

"For all practical purposes they are. The bite of a Scolit, while not deadly, will transform you. Once seduced into the shape of a Scolit, you are unlikely to be saved." asks, "How is it that Eseph can help your brother. What has he done?"

"It's not what he has done. You see, it all started with my grandfather and his old story. It's not any old story but there was this four leafed clover and my brother…"

The man demands, "What clover?"

"Well it was a four leaf clover that he used to get here. Anyways, it's too complicated to…"

"It is them," The man says to the others.

Irritated, Brittani says to Bryan, "Now what did you say?"

"Nothing, I didn't say anything."

"Take them," the man tells the others.

"Now, wait a second," Bryan says defensively.

Brittani screams as the group grabs her.

Chapter 33

"Leave her alone!" Bryan shouts, even as several people grab him. The group drags the kids out of the building.

Moli, alone again, looks around for a moment, grabs one of the pieces of fruit Brittani had offered him earlier, and takes off after the group.

Chapter 34
Crossing The Chasm

AS THEY CONTINUE through the cave, Will follows Zechariah closely as Jimmy hangs back with the other three warriors. He says to the warrior, "Thanks for your help back there."

Zechariah just smiles as they continue walking. The winding path leads them upward within the monolith past a myriad of ancient wall paintings. Will tries to read some of the markings, but the text is foreign and the images are extremely abstract. They appear to depict a brutal torture of mankind. Jimmy, too, admires the artwork along the path, periodically touching the markings that appear at intervals within the cave.

The marks are staggered, and seem to provide direction up the mountain. Each stage looks as if it's a continuation of the previous marking. Jimmy breaks the silence and says, "These are pretty brutal paintings. Look how they treat their own people."

Chapter 34

From ahead, Will responds, "I know. This is something. It's almost as if I've seen this before. Like we have been a part of it. How many are there?"

Jimmy says, "I've counted nine so far."

"Look at this."

Will runs past one more of the abstract torture scenes. The eleventh image shows a four leaf clover with a tortured man lying next to it.

Jimmy whispers, "It's the same clover you have."

Will murmurs, "Yeah…it is, isn't it."

They walk up to the twelfth marking on the wall. The image is extremely abstract and very difficult to make out. The four-leaf clover is very prominent in this image, as is the man. However, the man who was lying next to the clover is now floating above it, and looks to be hovering over a large chasm crossed by a beautiful rainbow. The remainder of the image is too abstract to make out.

Will calls to Zechariah, "Have you seen this before? What does it mean?"

In accented English, Zechariah says, "It meaning for all. A… meaning, that be lost if we do not retrieve tablets and Malkuth succeeds."

"I'm not sure I understand."

Jimmy turns around suddenly and calls, "Oh my God, Will check this out!" He moves away from the twelfth mural and points to the lower corner.

"Look."

Crossing The Chasm

Will moves closer and sees a signature in the corner. The signature is hard to make out, but as he gets closer, the writing becomes hauntingly familiar. It reads: Jo seph.

Heart pounding, Will says, "Jimmy, you don't think."

"It has to be. Will, your grandfather did this."

Will rushes up to the mural and places his hands on the paintings. He then places his cheek against the wall, and allows his emotions to pour out. He suddenly gets very warm as he closes his eyes and pictures his Grandfather Joe reading to him in his room. He is taken away for a brief moment as he recalls the gentle tones of Grandpa reading Rainbow Alley.

Jimmy says, "You ok man?" When Will doesn't respond he adds,

"Will, are you all right, dude?"

Will pushes himself away from the mural and wipes a tear from his eye.

"Yeah, yeah, I'm fine," He snuffles. Then, turning to Zechariah he asks, "How much further?"

Zechariah smiles and says. "You have reached the chasm." He points towards an opening in the cave.

Will and Jimmy run to the opening. They look out into the chasm and see a tremendous pit within the monolith. Throughout the chasm are platforms. Above three platforms, bright lights hover.

Will whispers, "The remaining scrolls."

Jimmy sizes up the cavern and its emptiness. "How are we going to get them?"

Will realizes that the platforms are virtually unreachable. Each one appears to be lower than the next. They appear to be staggered

Chapter 34

throughout the interior of the mountain and look like mini monoliths set within the emptiness.

"I don't know."

Will turns around and sees Zechariah and the others come out of the cave portion and into the interior of the cavern.

"Z, how can we reach these platforms? How do we get across?"

Zechariah examines the situation and shakes his head. "Ochu was easy compared to this."

"The sides," Machiara blurts out.

Zechariah looks at the sides of the cavern, then at Machiara. He steps onto the narrow walk along the sides of the cavern.

"Be careful. There's not much room," Will blurts.

With his back plastered against the side of the cave, Zechariah scoots along about twenty feet until he begins to run out of ledge. The only way to continue is to leap across the ledge to another ledge about ten feet away. Contemplating the jump, Zechariah attempts to leverage himself to get the most momentum on his leap. As he does this, he loses his balance and slips.

His foot pushes over the edge, but he quickly regains his balance and pulls himself up. Will and the rest of the group breath a collective sigh of relief as Zechariah readies himself again. He tries to position himself, and the same thing happens. This time he almost falls into the chasm.

Will shouts, "You can't make it. Come back."

Zechariah looks at the ledge in front of him and then to the chasm below. In frustration he slams his fist into the side of the chasm before slowly scooting back towards the group.

Crossing The Chasm

Jimmy approaches Machiara. "There's gotta be someway to get them. I mean someone put them there didn't they? What about your bow and arrows, can we use those for something?"

"No rope to attach. We need to find key," Machiara responds.

Will turns and says, "Key? What kind of key?"

Zechariah steps back to safe ground.

"Key to cross."

"Do you mean like a clue?"

The men look at each other and don't seem to understand.

Will remembers what his grandfather said to him the night he went into the coma.

"When things appear unclear, clues are the keys; all anyone has to do is open their eyes and see what they're telling them."

Will says out loud to the group, "All anyone has to do is open their eyes and see what they're telling them."

Jimmy looks at him and says, "What did you say?"

"The clues, Jimmy. They're right in front of us."

Certain that he's dealing with a nut case, Jimmy says, "What? Where? Where are the clues?"

Will takes off back into the pathway in the cave. He runs back down the corridor with the paintings and attempts to read the strange markings on the wall.

He steps back and forth between murals for several moments. The rest of the group comes into the cave and they, too, begin surveying the wall.

Chapter 34

Finally, Will sits down in frustration and mutters, "I don't know what this is trying to say." Looking up he adds, "Grandpa, what were you trying to say here? I don't get it."

Hadesria, crouching near Will, addresses him, "το κλειδί"

Hadesria repeats it twice, pointing to Will, "το κλειδί. το κλειδί."

Zechariah and Machiara question Hadesria, "το κλειδί?"

Hadesria nods his head yes.

Zechariah smiles and says it again, "το κλειδί"

Frustrated, Will stands up and demands, "What are you guys saying? What's going on?"

Zechariah runs up to him, grabs his shoulders and says, "το κλειδί" He pulls back Will's shirt and says, "το κλειδί…The Key."

Will looks down and says, "The key?"

Grinning, Jimmy says, "Yeah! The key."

Enthusiastic, Will screams "Yeah! The key." Then looking to Zechariah, he asks, "Where?"

Zechariah points to the twelfth and final mural. Remembering the warmth he felt when he first touched the wall, Will smiles and runs up to the mural. Will sees the man hovering over the chasm with the four-leaf clover underneath him. He very slowly pulls his shirt back and leans his bare chest up against the clover on the wall.

The closer he gets, the warmer he begins to feel. When he is just inches away, a light begins to shine from within the clover and from within Will. He is suddenly thrust up against the wall as if he is being pulled into it.

Jimmy quickly runs over and yells to the warriors, "Get him off of it. Get him off!"

Crossing The Chasm

The warriors run to Will but the force field of light that surrounds him stops them in their tracks.

Panicked, Jimmy calls, "Will! Will!"

After a few seconds, the wall releases him and he slides to the ground. With sweat pouring from his face, and his body slowly losing its illumination, Will looks over to Jimmy.

"You ok?"

Will responds quietly, "Yeah...yeah...I think so."

Will looks back at the mural as if it had spoken to him. He continues his reverie until he hears a loud clunking sound from within the chasm.

"Now what?" Jimmy growls.

The group runs to the opening of the chasm and stops on the platform. The chasm is beginning to transform. The platforms monoliths morph into slides connecting to each of the lower platforms monoliths holding the scrolls.

Will and Jimmy are stunned. The warriors look at Will as if maybe they should kneel in front of this kid.

The changing of the platform monoliths slides takes only a few moments. The final slide forms directly in front of them and provides an obvious path to the first monolith. Recalling their days spent on water slides at the park back home, the boys grin. Jimmy finally speaks, "You wanted your scrolls."

"Can you believe this?"

"What dya say?"

Grinning madly, Will shouts, "Let's get em', let's get them all!"

Chapter 34

He jumps onto the slide and shoots twisting and turning through a maze leading to the first platform. Jimmy quickly follows. The warriors stand for a moment, look at each other, and then jump onto the slide, too.

Twisting, turning and sliding, Will and the rest of the group fly one by one onto the first platform monolith. Will stands up and rushes over to the hovering scroll. He grabs it. The light which illuminates it dissipates as soon as he takes it from its hovering position.

"Ok, let's get the rest and we'll read them after we cross…a…this chasm thing."

Machiara hands Will a leather knapsack to hold the scrolls. Will takes it from him and reaches for the tablet and remaining scrolls, which are stuffed into his pants. He places them all in the sack and turns to the next slide.

He jumps on this one in the same manner, and the rest follow. Grinning madly, each of them slides onto the second platform. Will grabs the scroll and then jumps on the third slide, which takes them most of the way down towards the base of the chasm. At the third and final platform monolith, Will gets up one more time and grabs the scroll from its elevated illumination.

As soon as he grabs the final scroll, the slides begin to retract. Will quickly jumps on the final slide. Already retracting, this slide dumps them a few feet from the base. By the time Hadesria and Machiara make it, they fall about ten feet.

Once on the ground, they all grin at each other. Will exclaims, "That was wicked."

Crossing The Chasm

"Off the charts!" Jimmy replies. Zechariah and the warriors nod in agreement.

Once they've regained their composure, Zechariah senses something is not right. Will, still sitting on the ground where the slide dumped him, pulls out the leather knapsack and sets the scrolls out in front of him.

"Ok, let's check these out."

Zechariah turns and shouts, "No!"

Will looks up and says, "Why?" He sees Zechariah and the others in a defensive ready position. "What's going on?"

"We need to go--now!"

"Now?"

"Now!"

Zechariah rushes over and helps pick up the scrolls. As he throws them in the sack, a laser bolt from up above just misses Will. He looks up at the top of the cavern and sees Malkuth standing with Juno and Danaë. Juno is pointing downward.

Jimmy looks up and mutters, "I knew we couldn't trust him."

Zechariah commands, "Let's go." Machiara, Hadesria and Famiaria each pull out their bow and arrows and shoot upward at Malkuth and his cronies. The boys take off with Zechariah as the fight ensues. Malkuth, scepter raised, loudly commands the slides within the cavern to open once again.

Seeing this, the warriors begin to follow behind the boys all the while shooting upward and precisely hitting Malkuth's Scolits one by one.

"Where to?" Will screams.

Chapter 34

Zechariah sprints towards an opening in the cavern. One by one they jump through the opening, only to find themselves in a long, dark corridor. Will stops for a second when he sees where they've landed. "Are you sure to go this way?"

Jimmy, hearing the clanking of the slides behind them, runs by Will chanting, "Go, go, go!"

Will takes off when he sees Machiara, Hadesria and Famiaria pull up the rear, still shooting. As they run down the corridor, the light diminishes and Will has to feel his way going forward. "Jimmy are you up there?"

"Yes, keep coming, I'm starting to see some light."

Will moves tentatively in the darkness. He runs about fifteen feet in total darkness, when he begins to see some images. "I'm starting to see something. Jimmy you still there?"

There is no answer.

"Jimmy! Are you there?"

Will sees the end of the corridor which leads outside. He stops once he sees the exit. "Jimmy?"

Still no answer. He starts walking nervously. "Jimmy, are you out there?"

Nothing. Will is about ten feet from the exit when he stops again. He calls out one more time., "Jimmy?" He looks back. "Machiara? Hadesria, anyone?"

Suddenly, Machiara, Hadesria and Famiaria run up from behind. Will motions for them to be quiet. He points to the exit. Together, they slowly walk to the exit and tentatively peer out. They see nothing.

Crossing The Chasm

Will looks at them and says, "Something's wrong. We need to help." He takes off out of the cave and the warriors follow suit. The instant each man steps out, the people from the island of Zanzibar grab them.

As they struggle with their captors, Will glimpses Bryan and Brittani standing in front of him with Zechariah and Jimmy. Stunned, Will screams, "BRYAN...Brittani? "Oh my God, how did you get here?"

The men release him and he runs up to his brother and Brittani and hugs them like he has never before. Then he remembers, "Malkuth is right behind us!"

Bryan replies, "I know, follow us. These people will help."

At that moment, the muscular man says, "I am Tolar. Please come quickly."

He points out a path. They can now hear Malkuth and the Scolits coming through the dark corridor. Tolar leads the group around a large bend in the mountain. Once they make the turn, all that they can see is the river and the wall of the mountain.

Panicked, Will shrieks, "Now where?"

Tolar turns around and motions to him, "Shhh."

Each of the men walks into the wall of the mountain. The mountain absorbs them in a jelly–like state. Bryan and Brittani are stunned. They haven't seen this before.

"Is this safe?"

Hearing the Scolits around the bend, Tolar says, "It's safer than the alternative. Hurry."

One after one, they embed themselves within the wall of the mountain and stand motionless within the jellied stone. They can see

Chapter 34

and hear what is transpiring outside, but, those outside cannot see them. After a few moments, the Scolits make it around the bend and begin to search the grounds for the group. A few of them scream and squeal in anger and frustration. Malkuth slowly walks around the bend. The light from the stars illuminates him as he walks. He says nothing as the Scolits hop around in anger.

Will sees him through the jellied mountain. He watches as Malkuth looks at the beach and the river. Suddenly, Malkuth turns and walks directly towards the mountain. Wide-eyed with fear, Will looks over to his brother. Bryan shakes his head to tell him to remain motionless.

Malkuth stops and stares at the side of the mountain as if he is attempting to look through it. He is actually staring directly into Will eyes. Will holds his breath.

"Down the river," yells a Scolit.

Malkuth turns and sees the Scolits are interested by something deep in the river.

"What is it?" He bellows. A few birds flutter across the surface of the water. Frustrated, Malkuth turns back to the wall of the mountain. He stares at it again for a few moments, and says, "Come."

The evil man turns and walks towards the beach.

Two graviports careen into the area and stop near him. Malkuth looks back once again, then almost reluctantly boards one of the graviports. A few of the Scolits grab Danaë and Juno. One asks, "What should we do with them my Lord?"

Malkuth responds nonchalantly, "Bring them to *'the wall of dimension'* in Ynitsed. Danaë, you will lead my legions and replace my incompetent brother. Juno you will provide support."

Crossing The Chasm

Danaë and Juno bow in loyalty. Malkuth motions to them,

"You have served your purpose well chimeras."

He turns his back towards the mountain and looks up at the stars. One of the Scolits, drool flipping from side to side on his face, runs up to Malkuth. He barks, "What about the Forerunner, my Lord?"

Malkuth turns and points his scepter towards the mountain. He shoots a beam that penetrates the rock and begins an avalanche. Boulders fall from above as the mountain begins to crumble.

Will instinctively raises his arms. A beam of light surrounds the group. The force field he has created protects his friends as the mountain continues to crumble.

Malkuth looks up at the stars again. In a confident manner he says, "What *about* the Forerunner?

"We are now only a few hours away from total transformation; they have run out of time. Not to mention, space. Bring the chimeras, and they too can witness my ascension, just as Eseph will."

Malkuth gives a go ahead to the driver of his graviport and they take off. Like wild monkeys, the Scolits jump up and down and then onto graviports parked nearby. They evacuate the site. Danaë and Juno board a graviport. Danaë belts out a few orders to the Scolits as they fly away from the island of Zanzibar.

After a few moments pass, Will, Bryan and the rest of the group slowly emerge from the wall of the mountain. Bryan looks over to his brother and asks,

"Did you do that? How did you do that?"

"I don't know. I really don't know."

Chapter 34

Once out, Tolar addresses one of his loyalist, "Tala, Eseph is still alive. We must move quickly, our time is limited. Thanks to the Forerunner, we have survived for the moment, but we must reassemble. We must fight for what is ours. Come…come all."

Tolar takes off into the darkness, the rest of the group follows. Will runs with his brother, gasping, "Bryan, how did you know we were here?"

Bryan looks over and smiles, "We're in Zanzibar bro, I know this like our backyard. This is where dreams come true."

The boys keep running as Will murmurs, "I hope so."

✱✱Chapter 35✱✱
Reading The Scrolls

Beneath the land of Zanzibar lie shelters made in a desperate effort to protect the last remaining inhabitants of the land. These shelters provide an extensive underground channel system which Tolar and his band of survivors use to hide from the reign of Malkuth.

Tolar and his people travel through the underground systems like moles. They are quite accustomed to traveling this way ever since Eseph had been taken captive. Loyalists to Eseph, Tolar and his followers will fight to the death if it means a return of Eseph.

When they reach their destination, Will, Bryan, Brittani and Jimmy are escorted into a large resting area. Each of them quickly find a piece of furniture to sit upon. Exhausted, Jimmy puts his head down and rests with his arm over his face. Bryan sits on a cot nearby studying Jimmy. Finally he says, "How long has he been like this?"

Will looks over to his buddy and murmurs, "As soon as we got here, a Scolit attacked."

Chapter 35

Bryan scoots closer to Will so Jimmy can't hear him. "Will, Tolar says that this thing is irreversible. He can stay this way."

"Not if we get the tablets before Malkuth does."

"Forget these tablets, we need to go home."

"Bryan, you don't understand, if we don't get the tablets, there may not be a home. Not to mention, Grandpa."

"Will, you have got to accept it that grandpa is old. It's his time."

Frustrated, Will moves away and replies, "NO! You have got to accept that' is not a good answer. The only reason Grandpa is so sick is because of Malkuth."

"What?"

"That's right. Malkuth did something to him to put him in the coma. He came through the vortex before we did. Grandpa knew all about this stuff. He has left us clues everywhere. This is much bigger than you think. If we don't get the tablets Bryan, none of us may have a chance anymore…or…anywhere."

At that moment Brittani gets up. "Bryan don't you see, your grandfather has been a part of this from the start. He sent us here to make things right. This is all an effort to save Rainbow Alley."

Bryan grabs his head in frustration and shouts, "Rainbow Alley! People, Rainbow Alley is just a story…can't you see that?"

Brittani calmly points to Jimmy and asks, "Is this just a story?" She points to the cave that surrounds them. "Is this? Naw, Bryan, we're in more than a story."

Bryan glares at them, saying, "Then we need to get out of this story."

Reading The Scrolls

Tolar comes into the room. He is accompanied by a few of his men. Zechariah and the warriors remain outside the door as a protective measure.

Tolar addresses Will, "Forerunner, do you still have the scrolls?"

Voice dripping with sarcasm, Bryan says, "Forerunner?"

Will grins at his brother and says, "Yeah, Forerunner. Now shut up, stupid, and help me with these scrolls."

Will pulls the scrolls one by one from the bag. As Bryan watches, he notes the air of admiration Tolar and his men have towards his brother. He has trouble watching his little brother being admired in such a way.

"What are these scrolls?" Bryan asks Will.

"These are the clues, I think Grandpa left us."

"Let me see." Bryan takes the one open scroll from him and examines the writing. "You think grandpa left us these? What language is it.?"

Will grabs the scroll back from him. "I'm not sure, but somehow I can read it and you're not suppose too"

"Is that right?" He looks it over. "Grandpa did not leave this for us."

Will lays the other remaining scrolls out in front of him. "Maybe not, but whoever did, intended for us to find them."

Tolar tentatively walks up to the one open scroll. He nonchalantly attempts to look at it. He then asks Will, "Can you open the others?"

"Sure." Will grabs the second scroll and begins to peel back the seal. Once again, as he peels the seal, a gentle illumination emanates from within, and the ground below him begins to shake. As he rolls the scroll open, they all see that it contains just a single phrase in a

Chapter 35

foreign dialect. Will looks at it for a moment and then moves onto the remaining two scrolls. He begins to peel the seals from the other two as the ground beneath them begins to shake even more. Concerned about the rumbling, Will asks, "Should I continue?"

Shouting over the rumbling below, Tolar urges, "Yes…yes…open them!"

The walls begin to shake as Will continues to open the scrolls. With all four seals broken, the shaking subsides. Will lies the scrolls face up on the table in front of him. He stands back and stares at each of them. Tolar, still standing at a safe distance from the scrolls, "Can you read to me what they say?"

Bryan watches Tolar's odd behavior and chimes in, "Why won't you look at them?"

"They are meant for the Forerunner's eyes only."

That's crazy! I just looked at one of them."

Tolar nimbly catches a vase that almost falls because of all the vibrations and looks at Bryan with all seriousness, "It would be wise for you to listen and not react. The scrolls are meant for the Forerunner's eyes only. Can you read them, Will?"

Bryan snorts, "Fine, whatever. Read the scroll, Forerunner."

Will smirks at his brother. "I'll try." He backs up from the table and looks them over. The first one says:

"πίστη"

"πιστεψτε στο σκοπό σας"

Reading The Scrolls

The second one reads:

"Φρόνηση"

"επιτρέψτε στο σκοπό σας για να χαρτογραφήσετε τον τρόπο σας"

And the third one says:

"Πειρασμός"

"παραμονή σαφής της εύκολης διαδρομής"

Will studies them hard, but can't seem to make the out. He looks up in disappointment. "I...ah...can't seem to read these like I did the other one."

Bryan looks at Tolar and sneers, "I knew he couldn't do it. Now what?"

Brittani jumps in, "Well, if you wouldn't make him so nervous, maybe he could."

Tolar calmly urges Will, "Can you try again?"

Will glances nervously at his brother. Bryan gets defensive and shouts, "What? What am I doing? I'm not saying anything. Just do what you gotta do...Forerunner!"

Again, Will gives him a sarcastic grin. He turns towards the scrolls again and concentrates on the scrolls. For several moments he sees nothing. He runs his hands through his hair in frustration, then gazes

Chapter 35

back down upon the scrolls. Suddenly he sees the copy translating itself. "Wait…here it goes…It says:

"πίστη"
"Faith"

"πιστεψτε στο σκοπό σας"
"Believe in Your Purpose"

"The second one reads:
"Φρόνηση"
"Wisdom"

"επιτρέψτε στο σκοπό σας για να χαρτογραφήσετε τον τρόπο σας"
"Allow your Purpose to Map your Way"

The third one says:
"Πειρασμός"
"Temptation"

"παραμονή σαφής της εύκολης διαδρομής
"Stay Clear of the Easy Route"

He notices that the edges of each scroll are frayed and appear have been torn from each other. He backs away and looks. Together they might form a different message.

Reading The Scrolls

Will moves towards the scrolls and begins to reassemble them as if he were placing puzzle pieces on a board. He adjoins the first scroll to the second scroll. Instantly, the two pieces melt into one and an image begins to form. Will grabs the two other scrolls and places them neatly in their spaces and they, too, begin to melt into the others.

All four scroll pieces merge with the others and form an image of a picturesque setting. The image has waterfalls flowing in the background with palm trees and lush vegetation throughout the land. A gently flowing river runs through the land. Will can actually *see* the water flowing within the image.

Above and below the idyllic image, phrases say…

"Free the Tablets within the Wall of Dimension in Ynitsed"

"You will gain access through his Lair above the highest point in Ynitsed Castle"

"Believe in Your Purpose"

"Allow your Purpose to Map your Way"

"Stay Clear of the Easy Route"

Will turns towards Tolar and the rest of the group. "I think it's safe for you guys to look at this now."

Tolar and Bryan slowly walk towards the table with the newly formed scroll and image. No one says a word. After a few moments, Brittani breaks the silence, "It's beautiful."

Tolar explains, "Yes, this was our land before evil shed its fury."

"It's so sad of what this world has become."

Tolar nods in agreement. "Indeed. But our time has come. We need to gain it back. We need to mobilize what is left of our forces and

Chapter 35

provide you the support you need get to Malkuth's Lair and into the Wall of Dimension."

Tolar motions to Tala, "It's time to call in the Minotaurs."

Stunned, Tala responds, "The Minotaurs? They will never support our cause, that is unless…Noooo."

"We have no choice. We must."

"Tolar if we allow the Minotaurs back into society, we don't know what will happen."

"Tala, we have no choice. You heard Malkuth. His ascension is at hand. We have little time to worry about what will happen. It is time to free the Minotaurs from captivity and provide an army to support the Forerunner."

Bryan butts in nervously, "Ah…I don't mean to pry, but what's a Minotaur?"

Tolar and Tala look at each other with concern, and then leave the room.

Bryan looks over to Brittani and Will. "Well, that's comforting."

⋆Chapter 36⋆
The Minotaurs Are Freed

Standing outside a makeshift underground jail, Tolar and Tala watch with concern as Minotaur after Minotaur emerge from their captivity. The Minotaur, a large humanoid, stands around seven feet tall. Their bodies are those of muscular men with broad shoulders supporting the head and neck of a bull, complete with a set of horns.

With their size, physique, agility and attitude of self-assurance, these creatures look as if they were built for combat. It's no surprise that fighting is what they love to do. Even unarmed, they are highly dangerous. They can rain down one sledgehammer blow after another and finish off with a vice-like grip to crush the life out of a victim. In addition, these beasts are not above biting their opponents, and the horns aren't just for show, either.

Minotaurs have little time for polite conversation, preferring instead to adhere to the philosophy of "actions speak louder than words." Combined with their short tempers, this has made it difficult for them

Chapter 36

to fit in any society for any length of time. That was the main reason they have been banished from Zanzibar.

Regardless of their situation, sooner or later, the need to prove their prowess in combat grows too strong. Minotaurs don't even perform well in each other's company. Before long, competition leads to the trading of blows with each other. They have no real interest in teaming up and invading foreign lands, unless they are given something as valuable as freedom. Thus, Tolar reluctantly made his decision.

As the Minotaurs emerge from captivity, Will, Bryan, Brittani and Jimmy watch in horror as the gigantic beasts assemble in front of them. Curious as to the size and girth of the incredible creatures, Jimmy strays from the group to get a closer look. Tolar has mounted his horse in attempt to direct his newfound troops. Some are already fighting one another as they taste their freedom for the first time.

Eclipses, a large and heroic-looking Minotaur emerges from the cells below. He sucks in his first breath of freedom through his nostrils, belts out a shriek and continues outward.

Tolar calls to them, "Your time has come Minotaurs. Freedom is at hand. If you successfully provide support to the Forerunner in his quest, a Minotaur will never be held captive again!"

A roar erupts from the Minotaurs as they continue to emerge from their captivity. Eclipses maneuvers himself in front of Tolar and calls out, "How can we know this is true? What are our guarantees we will not be captive once again?"

"My word is your guarantee. From this day forward man and Minotaur walk as one!"

The Minotaurs Are Freed

Not impressed, Eclipses says, "We will need more than your word, Tolar."

"I give you my word today, and you share in the land tomorrow. What more can I offer?"

Grunting and spewing saliva and snot from his nostrils, Eclipses roars back, "Zanzibar!"

Tolar looks at him, confused. "What about Zanzibar?"

Jimmy is only fifteen feet from Eclipses.

"It is ours!" Eclipses screams.

Tolar shoots back, "You can't be serious. All of Zanzibar? No, we will share in the land."

Eclipses retorts, "All of Zanzibar, or you are on your own."

Tolar looks to Tala. He reluctantly turns back. "Zanzibar will be yours. On the condition you stay within its confines."

Eclipses smiles. "No Tolar. No conditions. We roam as we feel fit. That is our condition. Take it or leave it.

Tolar looks at Tala once again. She nods. Smiling, Tolar turns back to Eclipses. "We will walk as one and you will roam as you feel fit."

The troops cheer with excitement. At that moment, Eclipses glimpses Jimmy out of the corner of his eye. He turns and screams, "A Scolit!" He raises his massive arms to crush Jimmy.

Tolar and Will scream, "No! Stop!"

Just before his hammer-like claws reach Jimmy, he stops and looks up.

Tolar quickly explains, "He is one of us. He's simply been infected."

Chapter 36

Grunting and spewing snot and saliva, Eclipses says, "He's still a scum sucking Scolit." He raises his arm again and Tolar screams, "If you strike him, the deal is off!"

Eclipses reluctantly complies. He sneers at Jimmy and spits out, "Scolit!" Turning to his troops He shouts, "Freedom is at hand! "The troops erupt into cheers, as Tolar breaths a sigh of relief. Jimmy rushes back to the safety of Will and company.

Tolar looks over to Tala. "Ready?"

With confidence she replies, "Ready!"

Shaking his head, Bryan looks over to his brother and says, "You just had to hear all of Grandpa's stories, didn't you?"

"I'm scared, Bryan."

"I know. Me too. But it looks like we have no choice here. We can do this. Just gotta believe, just like the scroll said."

Brittani joins them. "We'll be ok, Will. Let's just stay together no matter what, and it will all work out."

Will looks at the troops assembling. "I hope you're right…I hope you're right."

Tolar calls to Tala "Get the ports!"

Tala looks to a few men standing at a broken down landing station shelter. She commands, "Get the ports" Graviport after graviport begin to emerge from the shelter. The Minotaurs roar with excitement as the graviports fly into position and pick them up. Half of the troops board the graviports while the other half board ships at the beach.

"I guess we're next." Bryan says.

Will looks over to him. "Let's do it."

The Minotaurs Are Freed

Will, Bryan, Brittani and Jimmy walk toward the landing station. Zechariah and his warriors are close behind. Each of them board a graviport escorted by one of Tolar's soldiers. They all hover over the beach, awaiting Tolar's orders.

Still mounted, Tolar commands his troops, "Commence hovercraft."

The ships that are within the waters begin to hover above the river. The Minotaurs roar with excitement. Tolar calls to the troops, "Our time is at hand. Stick to our plan and our chances increase. Stray from our plan and our time is sure to end. Discipline your actions even in questionable moments and we will succeed. We have until the night sky erases and the new sun emerges. If the tablets are not in hand by the sun's new light, Malkuth's ascension is imminent. Now go into the night and bring back the peace to our land we so all desire."

The troops roar with enthusiasm as the hovercrafts and graviports careen across the sea from Zanzibar on their way towards Ynitsed Mountain.

Chapter 37
The Prophecy

As the lighting illuminates the sky and thunder rattles the landscape, rain begins to fall. Around Ynitsed castle, Malkuth's troops begin to assemble by the thousands, Scolit after Scolit emerges from the belly of the dungeon within the castle.

Malkuth watches from above in his lair. The Scolits are readying for war side by side with the chimeras, lead by Juno and Danaë. As his troops assemble, Malkuth turns from his window and walks to a makeshift cell in the corner of his room. Inside, shackled in what appears to be a force field of energy, Marabus' arms hang above her head as she lies in exhaustion on the ground.

"If only you would have joined my forces at the beginning, my dear sister, your fate would have likely been altered. Now, you will soon join father in a watery grave in the moat of peril. That is, unless you agree to succumb to my powers and serve in the capacity you were born into. I just may spare you."

The Prophecy

Exhausted, Marabus looks up at her brother. "The evil that runs inside of your veins will never be a part of mine. I'd rather rot in this cell for eternity than ever join you."

"As much as I would love to oblige you my dear, rotting in the cell was not an option. Too forgiving in my opinion. No, submerged within the moat of peril will be your fate. After, and only after, you out of everyone, witness my ascension.

Marabus, barely able to pull her head up, raises it and mutters,

"It is written, you will never ascend!"

Malkuth looks down upon his sister and says in a sinister manner, "Well, my dear sister, the time has come to alter what has been written." He turns to his Scolits guards. "Take her to the dungeon."

Marabus watches in frustration as her brother vanishes into his hidden sanctuary. The Scolit guards grab her and begin to transport her to the dungeon within the belly of the castle.

Chapter 38
The Battle Begins

On the shores of Ynitsed, Tolar and his troops begin to land their vessels in the darkness of the rain soaked night. The remainder of the way can only be traveled by foot and or graviport. With only fifty or so graviports in their fleet, the bulk of the troops will trudge through the mine-filled land of Ynitsed to reach the castle.

Tolar walks over to Will and the rest of the group. "There is a ravine east of the castle. Underneath the bridge that provides passage into the castle is where we will meet. The Scolits can sense most any disturbance. So be quiet upon entry. Beware of the moat of peril; one dip in its waters will be the end of you."

Concerned, Bryan says to Tolar. "Meet? Are we separating?"

"Tala will lead you in. I will be along shortly thereafter. None of us move until the Minotaurs are in position."

Will jumps in. "What if we're not able to meet up?"

Tolar turns to Will. "All you worry about is gaining access in through the Wall of Dimension. We will worry about everything else.

The Battle Begins

You will have your diversion, to do what you need to do." He turns to Tala. "Tala, lead them to the ravine and past the moat."

Tala looks at him with concern. "Tolar...be careful."

Tolar looks at her. He only says, "Lead them in."

She nods and hits the throttle on her graviport. Will, Bryan, Brittani, Jimmy, Zechariah and the rest of the warriors follow. As the graviports take off towards the ravine, Brittani feels something moving in the back of her port. She turns around and sees Moli has stowed away on her graviport.

"Moli, what are you doing here?" The tiny creature snuggles up to her, and they fly through the darkness and towards the castle upon Ynitsed Mountain.

In about five minutes Tala points out the path to the ravine and the moat of peril Will looks down and sees murky waters bubbling around the base of the land. He senses pure evil as they hover over the liquid death and breathes a sigh of relief once they pass it.

They fly in utter silence, low enough to the ground to avoid any disturbance. As they get closer, they see legions of Scolits outside the castle. Bryan looks at Will with concern.

The ravine is about five hundred yards from the castle. They hover down and into the base of the gorge. They manage to fly into the gorge undetected. The meet at the base of the ravine.

Each of them dismounts their vehicles. Tala rushes up to each of the graviports and triggers a lever on the handle. The graviports vanish.

Will turns around. "Where did they go?"

Tala whispers, "They're still there, just undetected. Now follow me."

Chapter 38

The group quickly follows Tala into the belly of the gorge. Brittani pauses to reaches down for Moli. "Come on little guy, it's not safe for you to be out here by yourself."

TOLAR MOVES into position as he glides his graviports south of the Ynitsed castle. He careens down a tiny river and travels about a mile down away from the castle. He sets his graviport down and waits for his troops and the Minotaur warriors. After what seems like an eternity, Tolar sees in the distance the movement of what appears to be the Minotaurs heading towards their designated position.

Unsure they were even going to follow his orders, Tolar is overjoyed to see that the creatures held captive for so many years have agreed to fight and have followed his directions. Like a proud general, Tolar stands upon a large boulder so his troops will see him as they arrive.

WITHIN THE WALLS OF DIMENSION, Malkuth stares at a large hologram of Tolar awaiting his troops. He looks at images of the Minotaurs and then Tolar with his proud expression. He says to himself, "Fools."

IN THE RAVINE Tala has lead the group to an empty cavern. As they reach their dead-end, Will turns to Tala. "Where to now?"

Tala looks up as she wipes the rain from her brow. "We wait for our signal."

Bryan chimes in., "Then what?"

Tala replies, "Up and over."

Bryan looks up the ravine. "We're climbing?"

"It's the only way. Malkuth would see the graviports in a second."

At that moment a loud explosion is heard in the distance.

Jimmy looks over. "The signal?"

The Battle Begins

Tala, looking confused says, "No…no, it's too soon."

STANDING UPON THE BOULDER awaiting his troops, Tolar is struck in the back with an arrow. He can now only watch in horror as Scolit after Scolit charge gleefully into a counterattack of his miscalculated surprise attack. He sees the Scolits launch laser bombs and explosive arrows into his ill-prepared troops. The Minotaurs scramble, some even fight one another, as they attempt retaliation.

Chaos ensues as a few Scolits rush past a defeated Tolar and into the field of Minotaurs. The battle begins as Tolar slowly sinks closer to the ground.

Chapter 39
The Miscaculated Battle

With the night sky lit up like a firework display from the lasers and the continuing storm, Tala can only imagined what has happened. She tries to reach Tolar on her wrist talk set, "Tolar. Are you there?" They hear nothing.

The sky erupts again with massive explosions as Tala screams, "Tolar…Come in…Tolar!" Nothing is heard for a few moments, then a weak crackling sounds comes from her receiver. It's Tolar.

In a faint voice, he warns her, "Ambushed…we…we were ambushed."

Tala yells into the receiver, "Tolar, what's going on? What should we do?" All the group hears is the sounds of war from the receiver. Tala screams again, "Tolar…Tolar!"

She turns to the group. "Something has gone wrong. Terribly wrong, we must flee."

Brittani says, "Flee? Flee where?"

The Miscaculated Battle

Tala begins to rush back towards the graviports. "Our only chance now is to head back to Zanzibar. It's the easiest and safest route. We must flee to fight another day." As she heads for the graviports, her warriors follow. Bryan and Brittani, confused by all this, slowly follow behind.

Will watches the groups dissolve into complete chaos, unsure of which direction to go. He plays back in his mind Tala's words, and says to himself, "The safest and easiest route." He then says it out loud, "Stay clear from the safest and easiest route."

Bryan stops, and turns to his brother. "What...what?"

"Bryan, stay clear from the safest and easiest route, it was written on the scroll."

"Ah, Will, I don't know, bud. This is pretty intense. This isn't going right, we gotta get out here." He begins to follow Tala again.

"Bryan!" Will shouts. "No. We have to continue on. We must stay clear from the safest and easiest route."

Bryan stops again and looks at Tala reactivating the graviports. They are all visible again. He looks at his brother, who has not moved. Bryan then looks over to Brittani and Jimmy.

Seeing this, Jimmy walks over to Will. He turns around and says to Bryan, "Stay clear from the safest and easiest route."

Brittani picks up Moli, walks over to Jimmy and Will, and says to Bryan,

"We must stay clear from the safest and easiest route."

Zechariah and the three other warriors all stand behind Will. Bryan turns towards Tala and her group. She says to them, "We must go now, before it's too late."

Chapter 39

He looks back at Will and the ragtag group and says to himself, "This is nuts. This is really nuts." He strides back to his brother and looks at him straight in the eyes. "I'm with you, bro. Let's go do what we gotta do."

Will has a huge smile on his face as Tala takes off and yells back to the group.

"Don't be fools; we can live to fight another day."

Will looks at Tala, and then at his group. "No, we live to fight today. You guys ready?"

They all nod in agreement.

"Let's go."

As they begin to walk, Will's knapsack falls to the ground. Jimmy quickly reaches down and picks it up. He looks at Will. "I got it, let's go."

With Zechariah in the lead, the warriors and the children begin to climb the ravine towards Ynitsed castle. The night sky grows more and more illuminated from the miscalculated war on its banks.

Tala and her group careen up and out of the ravine on their graviports.

COMPLETE CHAOS ENSUES on the banks of Ynitsed Mountain. Trying to gain some coordination, the Minotaurs attempt to gain a foothold as the massive barrage of arrows and lasers riddle the field from the Scolits up above. With the few final ships still arriving in port, the Minotaurs and Tolar's remaining troops are heavily outmanned.

Malkuth's troops increase in size as the Scolits are joined by Malkuth's chimera loyalists lead by Danaë and Juno. The competitions

The Miscaculated Battle

between men and beasts have the surroundings of Ynitsed castle in an uproar.

Scrambling to compete, the Minotaurs and additional Tolar troops quickly dismount from their carriers and rush into the field of battle. It is truly a baptism by fire. They are instantly greeted with intense warfare.

Eclipses dismounts the ship he has rode in on and witnesses the destruction in front of him. As he surveys the area, he sees Tolar lying hunched over on top of the boulder. Seeing the complete chaos in front of him, he quickly assumes a leadership role and begins to bark orders as he trots heroically towards the field of battle.

Eclipses also brings down Scolit after Scolit as he moves to a central position within the battle. Sensing, reinforcements and leadership, the Minotaurs and the troops of Tolar regroup and begin an offensive attack upon the oncoming Scolits.

A QUARTER OF THE WAY up from the center of the ravine, Zechariah leads Will and the group. Trudging through the murky, rain-soaked landfill is not helping them rush to the top of the cliff. Roughly fifty feet from the surface, Jimmy stops and motions to Will.

"What wrong?" asks Will.

Jimmy looks back down at the ravine and then up at the lit up sky. "This isn't gonna work."

"What are you talking about, what's not gonna work?"

"Face it man, as soon as we get to the top of this thing, we don't know what to expect. Tala was supposed to lead us in and she bailed for some obvious reasons."

"Yeah, so?"

Chapter 39

"So. We need to see what's up there before we get there."

"Oh, ok, "Will says, "Should I just fly up and have a peek? Just exactly how do you propose we do that?"

Jimmy begins to climb back down the ravine. "Just keep moving, I'll meet you up there."

"Where are you going?"

"They left us one graviport, we should use it."

"Jimmy no, they'll see it. It's too dangerous."

Ignoring him, Jimmy scoots down the mountain like a monkey, and screams back up, "I know what I'm doing, just keep going."

Machiara runs up to Will and grabs his shoulder. "Continue, I will get him." He follows Jimmy. Will watches them vanish into the darkness of the ravine.

Bryan whispers loudly, "Come on, Will, keep moving."

Will reluctantly turns towards the top and continues his way up the muddy passage.

ONCE AT THE FLOOR of the ravine, Jimmy darts back towards the original landing spot. He kicks around, trying to find the final invisible graviport. I know it's here. I know she left one behind."

He grabs a stick and starts brushing it in front of him in an effort to strike the port. "Where is this thing?"

He's still swinging wildly when Machiara runs up and orders, "Come with me."

"No way Macky. Someone needs to create a diversion. They're going to be lame ducks if I don't."

The Miscaculated Battle

Machiara tries to reason with him as Jimmy continues swinging his stick, searching for the graviport. "No, it isn't wise. We must ascend with the group."

CLANK!

Jimmy hits the invisible graviport. Smiling he puts the stick down and walks over to where he senses the graviport. "Mac, we need to create a diversion."

Jimmy fiddles around for a second until he hits the switch that Tala had activated. The graviport reappears in the center of the ravine. Smiling, Jimmy turns to Machiara. "Wanna go for a ride?"

Machiara looks up at the sky above him lighting up like a candle. He says, "A diversion?"

Smiling, Jimmy says, "A diversion."

Machiara unhooks his bow from his belt and prepares his arrows as he jumps on the back of the graviport. Jimmy fires it up and hits the throttle.

"Let's go."

The two take off and head out of the ravine.

Thirty seconds into the flight, they look down and see Tala and her group crashed below. There appear to be no survivors.

Jimmy looks down and says, "Not going that way." He quickly turns his graviport to fly in the direction of where Will and the group are climbing. As they fly by the group, they, see about fifteen or so Scolits at the top guarding the posts.

After swerving out of line from his friends and the Scolits waiting for them, Jimmy hovers in the dark with no sounds coming from the

Chapter 39

graviport. He asks Machiara, "Do you think you can take them from here?"

"ναι."

"I'll take that as a yes."

Jimmy pulls the graviport a bit closer. "Ok, they can't see or hear us here. On the count of three, you start firing. I'm not moving until we have to."

"ναι."

Machiara pulls out his arrows and aims directly at the Scolits guarding the perimeter.

"Ok, one, two, three…go, go, go!"

Machiara fires off three arrows with precise accuracy and impales three Scolits directly through their foreheads. The remaining Scolits quickly turn in the direction the arrow came from and respond with fire streams that light up the area, narrowly missing Jimmy and Machiara.

Dodging to the left, Jimmy says, "Ok, leaving now." He hits the throttle and takes off as Will and the group, only feet from the top, turn towards the distraction.

Machiara again pulls out his arrows and shoots towards the Scolits as Jimmy dodges the blasts of fire and an additional onslaught of arrows. Seeing this, Zechariah, Hadesria and Famiaria, pull out their weapons and quickly ascend to the top of the cliff and to return the fire.

With precision, Zechariah, Hadesria and Famiaria, quickly hit three more Scolits standing in the wing. The Scolits scream with anger as two more fall from the blows of the warriors. Will, Bryan and Brittani watch from below as the amazing warriors showcase their

The Miscaculated Battle

ability. Within no time at all, the Scolits guarding the gates have been taken out. The four warriors turn and nod to one another.

"Whooooo!" Jimmy howls with enthusiasm.

He shouts to Will, "Not bad for a monkey, huh?"

Bryan looks up and smiles, "Not bad, Jimmy, not bad."

From out of nowhere, a laser blast barrels into Jimmy's graviport.

"Whooo!" Jimmy yells as the graviport spins out of control. He tries to control the machine, but it has been hit too hard and quickly careens out of control. He's headed directly towards the area where Tala and her group were knocked down.

Will jumps up on top of the cliff. "Jimmy…nooooo!"

The graviport quickly vanishes. Will turns to see where the laser blast came from. He drops to his knees in fear at what he finds.

Will sees that something or someone has brought down Zechariah, Hadesria and Famiaria. An ominous figure stands in the entranceway of the castle.

Malkuth has been watching from his sanctuary and waiting for Will to arrive. As he stands at the entrance of the castle, he appears to be hovering over the land.

Will cannot speak, in a voice that makes the boy shiver, Malkuth says, "I have been waiting for you, Forerunner. Now, my quest is near complete." Malkuth turns to a new set of Scolits and commands, "Gather them. Gather them all."

The Scolits rush over and grab the warriors. Several head for Will. Malkuth turns and walks back into the castle.

Chapter 39

Bryan and Brittani have embedded themselves into the muddy side of the cliff. Their bodies are covered with wet mud which acts as a natural camouflage.

Bryan whispers to his brother, I'm here, bud."

Will turns his head slightly and whispers back, "Get us out of here. "The Scolits grab him and carry him inside the castle. A few remaining Scolits look over the edge to see if there are anymore enemies about.

Bryan and Brittani do not move a muscle. After a few moments, the Scolits, satisfied that they have all of them, rush back inside the castle. Bryan waits a few more seconds before he slowly peels himself away from the wall of the ravine. He watches Brittani as she, too, peels herself off the wall. He whispers, "Now what?"

"I don't know, I just don't know."

✶∗Chapter 40∗✶
The Unveiling

Malkuth gleefully watches the scenes upon the Wall of Dimension. The fields in front of Ynitsed castle are flooded with loyalists and Scolits. The battle has erupted into a full-fledged conflict. He smiles as the Scolits and Minotaur decimate each other.

For him, this is more of a sporting event than anything. It doesn't really matter if a Scolit or a loyalist wins or not. All Malkuth is concerned about is that within one hour he will have positioned himself to ascend to the ultimate reign of all kind. The power that he will soon possess will span multiple dimensions.

As he watches the war from within his hidden sanctuary, he actually takes pleasure in seeing a Scolit go down. The sport of the competition is what is drives him. He sits and watches two figures battle for a few moments, and actually cheers when a Minotaur is successful. While he watches, his loyalist and Scolit guards also watch over him. They are confused to see him laugh and take pleasure in the pain on the field.

Chapter 40

Malkuth focuses on Danaë and Juno leading their troops near the edge of the Moat of Peril. He sees Danaë and Juno both fall victim to the moat when Eclipses and his mighty Minotaur forces bring them down. Malkuth actually grins as Danaë and Juno sink into the murky waters of the moat.

Having had enough entertainment, he turns away from the hologram upon his wall. His mood changes drastically. He walks to a side room within his sanctuary. There he has housed a replica of the original tabernacle.

He begins to ready the elaborate tabernacle, which he has created for his rite of passage. The tabernacle resembles the altar and structure within Bethel's adobe, but this one has a dark and ominous feel to it.

It also features an ark, which holds the six remaining tablets.

As the warriors outside continue to fight to the death, Malkuth neatly prepares an offering of incense. Next to this altar, Malkuth has constructed yet another altar. This altar measures 7.5 meters long and 4.5 meters high. It was fashioned of acacia wood and overlaid with bronze. A Minotaur horn marks each corner.

Admiring his work, Malkuth walks to the base of the bronze altar and lights a fire, which begins to surround it. He backs away and turns to a few of his loyalist within the sanctuary. "It is complete. It is now time to prepare the sacrificial lamb."

Large, muscular servants clothed in roman gladiator attire acknowledge his orders, "Yes, my lord, at once."

They turn and head for the chamber which houses the tortured men who hang across the swampy pits. Malkuth watches the flames.

The Unveiling

THE ELABORATE CHAMBERS which set inside a passage within the Wall of Dimension provide a rich backdrop to the tortures and atrocities conducted within its walls. From medieval tortures such as "the rack" which stretches an individual until they are at their breaking point, to shackled iron crosses, to poisoning chambers, there is devious contraptions of suffering for anyone deemed not fit to grace Malkuth's regime.

The chambers reek with the unmistakable stench of death. Men hang over and into the swampy pits. Some lie helpless, shackled and starved.

Will and the warriors are deposited in a glass chamber which hovers over the swampy pits. Through the glass they can see most of the chamber within the complex. They see the men hanging, they see the rack, and they even see the gas masks used by the loyalists after they trigger the poisonous gasses.

Will approaches Zechariah. "What is that smell? I can barely breathe!"

"θάνατος...death."

Eyes wide open and fear running through his bones, Will remains silent.

Sensing his fear, Zechariah, places his hand upon his shoulder in an attempt to comfort him.

"Be strong in your faith, Forerunner. Believe in your purpose."

Will looks at him in despair. "I'm trying." He takes a deep breath as tears begin to well up in his eyes. He watches as the men below him wallow in pain and misery. The lines of men seem to go on forever.

"It doesn't seem like it ends. There are so many."

Chapter 40

Zechariah answers, "They are lost souls in search of their meaning."

Will fires back, "Lost souls? They're prisoners! Prisoners of a mad man. How can they be lost?"

Zechariah quietly responds, "Yes, they are lost."

Confused, Will turns away and again looks into the field of horror beneath him. He sees a group of Malkuth loyalists and Scolits walking across the bridges, which lead to the swamps. Zechariah and the others also turn to watch them. They walk over bridge after bridge until they reach a platform about a hundred feet from the glass chamber.

The Scolits quickly jump into the sludgy water and trudge over to a man hanging in the center. They unhook this man from his iron shackles and drag his limp body to the bridge platform. They toss him on the bridge like a piece of meat. His face is smashed against the floor.

One of the Scolits boots the man in the ribs. He buckles in pain and slowly rolls over. Seeing this, Hadesria excitedly says, "It's αυτός!"

Zechariah turns to Hadesria and then looks at the man lying on the ground. He smiles. "It is."

Frustrated, Will says. "Who is it?"

Zechariah answers, "It's Eseph."

"Eseph?"

Will looks at the man on the ground. He can't quite get a good look at his face because the Scolits are in the way. When the Scolits pull Eseph upward, his head drops down in pure exhaustion. Zechariah and his men stand up and try to move closer for a better look. Will tries to fight his way through the behemoths to watch what's going on.

The Unveiling

The Scolits drag their victim across the bridge. They walk a few feet as one of the Scolits rushes over and for no reason blasts Eseph in the stomach with the butt of his weapon. He buckles over and stops. The Scolits whip him from behind and scream, "Get up."

Horrified, Will yelps, "What are they doing to him?"

They continue to whip him as he lies on his knees with his head down.

Another Scolit grabs him by the shoulders and pulls him to his feet. Once on his feet, Eseph's head his jerked backward and then upright. His face is now in clear view.

Stricken to the core, Will stares down at his grandfather. "Grandpa?" He screams.

Eseph looks up and sees Will. He but clearly recognizes his grandson.

Looking around wildly, Will asks, "How can it be?"

✳✲Chapter 41✲✳
The Rescue Begins

Leaning his full weight against the graviport, Jimmy feverishly attempts to lift the crashed graviport from Machiara's leg.

"I...can't....lift....it!" Jimmy blurts as he pushes and pulls on the machine. He makes several attempts before he falls to the ground in exhaustion.

Machiara looks down at his leg, wedged under the graviport. He glances over to the wreckage of the other graviports where Tala and her group lie. He points to the wreckage and says in pain, "χρησιμοποιήστε τους άλλους λιμένες."

Jimmy looks up says, "I don't understand."

Machiara points again to the wreckage. "χρησιμοποιήστε τους άλλους λιμένες."

"You want me to go there?"

Machiara nods. Jimmy quickly gets up and trots over to the wreckage. He turns back to Machiara. "Now what?"

"έναρξη μια."

The Rescue Begins

"What?"

"έναρξη μια...start."

Finally getting it, Jimmy says, "Ohhhh. I get it. See if they start. Ok." Machiara nods as Jimmy tries to start the graviports. One by one they fail. He reaches the one that Tala was riding. He hits the throttle, with Tala lifeless body still on top of the vehicle. It begins to hover.

"Yes!" Jimmy screams. He turns back to Machiara enthusiastically. Machiara points to a rope near one of the graviports. Too excited to focus, Jimmy doesn't see him pointing to the rope. He continues to jump around. Then he pushes Tala off the graviport and begins to hover in the craft.

Machiara sees what he's doing and gets concerned. "No..no,...το σχοινί...the rope...the rope!"

Not paying attention, Jimmy begins to back up the graviport. "Hang on, Macky!"

He hits the throttle and darts directly towards the helpless Machiara.

"No!" the pinned man shouts in broken English. "Get the rope!"

Ignoring him, Jimmy blasts his new graviport directly into the graviport resting on top of Machiara leg. Machiara closes his eyes and puts up his arms in self-defense. The impact scoots the graviport off of his leg and into the brush about five feet away.

Jimmy smiles proudly as he hovers over Machiara like a pro. Machiara slowly opens one eye and sees Jimmy floating above him. Jimmy smiles through the fur on his face, flashing his fangs. "Never underestimate Jimmy, your friendly neighborhood Scolit/boy."

Chapter 41

He stands on the graviport and heroically bends down and extends his hand to his fallen companion. Machiara reluctantly reaches outward to the renegade Scolit/boy and grabs Jimmy's paw. Jimmy hoists him up on the graviport. In obvious pain, Machiara is not sure what to make of Jimmy's methods.

"Hang on, Macky, I've got an idea."

Machiara, looks to the sky in concern as he prays, "να είστε με μας ο Λόρδος μου."

Jimmy hits the throttle and takes off. As they careen upward, Bryan and Brittani carefully walking along the ledge of the ravine. Brittani shouts to Jimmy as he whizzes by, but they pass too quickly to hear and or see the mud camouflaged pair.

Bryan looks up, "Where's he heading?"

"He's going directly into the battle."

"He's crazy. He's always been crazy. Ok let's go. If we can't go up, I think we're going to have to go down."

"Down?"

"Yep, it's the only way. We need to go through the sewers of the dungeon."

"You're not serious."

"Britt, my brother is in trouble. I've never been more serious. These sewers lead to the dungeons and then into the castle. It's the only way."

Brittani sighs. She looks over to Moli, and crouches down. "This is where we are going to have to say good bye little one." Moli looks up at her with her soft brown eyes and tilts her head sideways.

"It's ok. Now go on." Brittani puts her down. Moli stays put.

The Rescue Begins

"Go ahead. Go." Brittani prods Moli. She doesn't move. After a few more prods, she takes off like a rabbit.

Brittani watches sadly as she scurries away. "Good bye, little one."

She turns back to Bryan and says, with conviction, "Lead the way."

Chapter 42
Will And Jimmy Regroup

Inside the glass chamber, Will watches as his grandfather is carted away. He pounds on the glass frantically, but all his grandfather can do helplessly raise is head in exhaustion.

Near tears he turns to Zechariah. "What's going on? How can this be? How is my grandfather here?"

Zechariah crouches down next to him. In heavily accented English he says, "Eseph, you papa -- one."

Confused, Will asks, "One? One what? I don't understand, Eseph was never part of Rainbow Alley. He was always part of Bryan's *Sorcerer's* books. This doesn't make any sense. We're talking my grandfather here."

"What is written has been written."

"You're not making sense. If my grandfather is the Eseph that has been involved with *The Sorcerer's Shadow* all these years, where does Rainbow Alley come into play?

Will And Jimmy Regroup

Suddenly Will pictures the mural within the mountain of time. He starts to review the images in his mind. He sees the beautiful settings, the torture scenes and the images of the man hovering over the rainbow. Then he sees the Jo seph signature. As he focuses on the image, he sees the Jo seph changing into Eseph. He realizes that the image is that of a sacrifice and that Eseph is the sacrificial lamb. According to the image, the sacrifice will allow for the rainbow to rise again.

Will breaks from his thoughts and quickly gets up. "They're going to sacrifice him aren't they? And he wants them to because he thinks it will bring back Rainbow Alley."

Zechariah reluctantly agrees with a nod of the head.

"But he's wrong, a sacrifice won't do anything. It's the tablets. Isn't it?"

Zechariah leans up against the glass wall and murmurs, "It's both."

Wills' eyes open wide as he jumps up. "No! No way!" He pounds on the glass.

"No way, I didn't come this far to see him sacrificed. It's not going to happen, No way!"

As he pounds pathetically on the glass, the shaking releases something from his pants pocket. The tiny four leaf clover he used within his bedroom floats out of his pocket and falls to the ground of the glass chamber.

Exhausted by his outburst, Will slides to the ground. The clover lies next to him. He doesn't notice it as he stares mindlessly into the torture chambers of within Walls of Dimension.

Chapter 42

AS THEY RETREAT towards the shores in an attempt to regroup, small bands of Minotaurs and Tolar's troops find a safe zone. They are no match for the sheer size of the Scolits and Malkuth's sorcerer ways. The battle has waged on, but their attempts have been fruitless. With less than a hundred or so remaining troops, Eclipses attempts to regroup his warriors.

They are all beaten and bruised as they gather by the river. Eclipses walks over and drinks from the running waters. Exhausted and defeated, the men sprawl on the ground as the Minotaurs roam about in a state of frustration and anger. A few of them reload their weapons. Some tend to the wounds of others. The rain has stopped, but the murky red sky begins to form dark clouds directly over Ynitsed Castle.

Eclipses sits upon a boulder by the bank of the river. The quiet desert air absorbs the men's moans and Minotaurs' grunts. In the distance, the Minotaur sense a silent murmur. A few of them shuffle as Eclipses gets up and grabs his club.

"Don't shoot! Don't shoot!" Jimmy shouts as he careens into the camp. Eclipses runs towards the graviport like an angry bull.

"No! Don't shoot! It's us. We're one of you."

Eclipses swings and misses as Jimmy hits the throttle and swirls around. He turns the port back around and hovers above Eclipses. "It us. Remember? We're on your team."

Eclipses simply grunts and screams to one of his warriors, "Shoot them down."

"No please stop! We're on your team!"

Just as the Minotaur readies his blaster, Eclipses says, "Wait." Jimmy and Machiara sigh with relief. "What do you want Scolit?"

Will And Jimmy Regroup

"I am not a Scolit! Well, maybe I kind of am, but I *am* on your side. Don't you remember you tried to eat me back there before Tolar stopped it?"

"What do you want, Scolit?"

Jimmy looks down at Eclipses and says, "I think I know how we can get into the castle."

What are you talking about, Scolit?"

Jimmy holds up the knapsack and pulls out the seventh tablet.

Chapter 43
The Sewers Of Ynitsed

Already covered in mud, Bryan and Brittani have found the sewers which lead inside the dungeons of Ynitsed Castle. Peering in, Brittani once again looks over to Bryan in disbelief. "You're sure this is the only way in?"

"I'm positive. Now I was right on the other stuff, there's no reason why this one would be different. This sewer leads directly into the dungeon and torture chambers of Ynitsed. It's in every *Sorcerer's* book."

"What else is in the book?"

Bryan looks over confused. "What do you mean?"

"What's *inside* the sewers?"

Bryan looks at the round entrance, which is about four and a half meters in circumference and mutters, "Ah, nothing. Nothing we should really be concerned about."

"That doesn't sound too comforting, Bryan."

"Don't worry, Britt. We'll be fine"

The Sewers Of Ynitsed

He begins to climb inside the sewer's entrance as he finishes his sentence to himself. "I think!"

Brittani reluctantly follows Bryan into the sewer system. They make their way down the dark and murky tube. The further they travel, the more the light diminishes.

"Bryan, I can't see anything."

"It may be better this way, don't you think?"

"Not funny, Collins. Slow down so I can hold onto your foot. I don't want to lose you."

"Ok, here," Bryan says as he reaches his foot back.

"What do you mean here?" she says.

"Here, grab my foot."

"Don't be funny, Bryan."

"Brittani, what are you talking about? Grab it and we can go."

"Bryan, I've been holding onto you foot since we got in here."

"Ah. Britt?"

Realizing that she is not holding onto his foot, Brittani screams and lets goes of whatever she has been holding onto. They both hear something scoot away in the sludge below them.

"What was that?" Brittani screams.

"I don't know, I don't know. Must've have been friendly though, you were holding onto it for a while."

She screams, "Give me your foot!"

Bryan reaches back. "Here!"

Brittani grabs hold and pinches down with all her might. Bryan screams,

"Aghhh, what are you doing?"

Chapter 43

"I just wanted to make sure it was the right thing. Ok, let's go."

"Yeah...right."

They continue through the sludge and muck of the sewers.

⋆Chapter 44⋆
Believe In Your Purpose

As he lies dejectedly on the floor of the glass chamber, Will watches the hellish tortures below. With fire and brimstone burning within the chamber walls, his senses are overloaded and tears flow from the corner of his eye.

He is defenseless and he knows it. With his cheek wedged to the glass floor Will stares blindly in a state of confusion.

His mind wanders as he recaps his experiences thus far. He thinks back to his grandfather reading him the story of Rainbow Alley in his bedroom. He remembers his brother's infatuation with *The Sorcerer's Shadow* series. He pictures the vortex he and Jimmy traveled through, the experiences with Danaë and Bethel and, finally, Zechariah and Tolar.

He pictures the scrolls and recants the messages on them:

"Believe in Your Purpose"

"Allow your Purpose to Map your Way"

"Stay Clear of the Easy Route"

Chapter 44

He closes his eyes and thinks to himself, "Why is all of this happening to me? I'm just a kid. What can I possibly offer here? It's too big for anyone, let alone a kid who never could even stand up for himself."

He thinks back again to the first two messages upon the scroll:

"Believe in Your Purpose"

"Allow your Purpose to Map your Way"

"How can my purpose be the way? I'm just a kid, I'm just a kid." He begins to hear a familiar female voice. It's the same voice he has heard throughout. The voice says:

"You must believe in your purpose."

He opens his eyes to a holographic image of Marabus. Not sure if he is asleep or awake, Will quickly sits up.

"Who are you?"

"I am the one who has guided you through. You must believe in your purpose, Forerunner."

"My purpose! You keep saying this. What is my purpose?"

"Allow your purpose to map your way."

Frustrated, Will stands up and screams, "I don't understand, what is my purpose?"

Marabus' image begins to dissipate, but before she is gone, she waves her hand downward and points in the direction of the clover lying on the base of the chamber.

"Don't go! I don't understand."

Believe In Your Purpose

Marabus' image is completely gone now. Will follows where she gestured and sees the clover. Will crouches down to take a closer look. He falls to his knees and whispers, "Believe in your purpose."

He looks at the clover on his chest and murmurs, "Allow your purpose to map your way."

Then, as he gazes at the clover, the image alters itself. Each of the four clover leaves straightens out and forms a perfect image of a crucifix.

The powerful image causes Will to lose his breath. Overwhelmed, Will grabs his chest and reaches down to pick up the clover. As soon as he touches the clover, it, too, begins to transform. The transformation of this clover is quite different. The four clover leaves expand outward and form a long sword with a crossed handle.

Stunned, Will grasps hold of the crossed handle and picks up the mighty sword. He stands up in front of Zechariah and the others, and each of them falls to one knee and bow in front of him.

Will notices the shaft of the sword has begun to glow. Curious, he takes the sword's blade and places it on the glass floor. Immediately, the glass begins to burn open. Will proceeds to burn a large hole in the bottom of the chamber. Once it is large enough for them to squeeze through, they escape into the inner chamber.

Hadesria is first. He jumps onto a small platform below. Famiaria quickly follows, then Zechariah. Will jumps into Zechariah's arms.

"Where to?"

Zechariah points and they all rush in that direction.

✦Chapter 45✦
The Diversion

With the tablet securely inside the knapsack, Jimmy rides through the fields as if he has no care in the world. Machiara rides shotgun. As they near the castle and the Scolit troops, Machiara reaches into the knapsack and pulls out the tablet. He hands it to Jimmy, and Jimmy begins to wave it wildly.

"I have the seventh tablet, I have the last one," He screams as they approach. As the graviport gets into firing range, the Scolits prepare to fire. Jimmy and Machiara are sitting ducks.

Just as the Scolits are about to fire, a messenger comes running over. "Wait! Hold your fire!"

"Macky, I think its working."

"Oh, it's working all right," Malkuth says inside his chambers. He backs away from the holographic image, presses a button on a control panel and says, "Let them fly all the way in. Bring them to me, and keep the tablet out of harm's way. And watch for the ambush, once they land. It is sure to come."

The Diversion

Inside his lair, Malkuth turns from the images of the field to his tabernacle. A ring of fire has been lit and surrounds the platform where Eseph now lies. Within the circle of fire is the ark, which holds the six remaining tablets. The ark is closed and rests at the Eseph's feet. The fire is at a safe distance from them both. It simply provides a backdrop as Malkuth moves towards the altar.

He sees Eseph sweating from the flames that surround him. Eseph looks gaunt and dehydrated. His arms and feet are shackled to the altar.

"It's the heat within the fire that drives the hearts of many, Eseph. Many that you have looked to save. But no longer. You see on this day, the day of my ascension, the fire shall live within all that had believed in you. The same fools that had looked to you will now become mine. I give you one last opportunity to join me. One more chance, to live, and serve under my guise."

Eseph turns his head in Malkuth's direction and says, "Το δίκαιο άτομο θα ζήσει από την πίστη."

Malkuth screams in anger, "You had your opportunity. You had your opportunity!" He looks over to what looks like an ancient sundial. He sees that the shadows within the dial are separated slightly. He turns away and heads back inside his lair.

From a safe distance leading into the belly of Malkuth's tabernacle chamber, Will and Zechariah peer downward as Malkuth walks away from the altar. Will whispers, "He speaks in foreign tongue, too. I've know him my whole life and I don't think I knew him at all. What was he saying? Who is he?"

Chapter 45

Zechariah points to the guards outside the chamber. "What's our plan?" Will says to Zechariah.

"Wait. Too many."

"I don't think we have much time, though."

"We wait."

Will looks back at his grandfather and shakes his head in disbelief.

JIMMY LANDS SUCCESSFULLY in front of the castle as Scolits and Malkuth's troops await his arrival. As soon as they land, the troops, about twenty strong, head over to them.

"Not so fast. You come any closer, the tablet goes over." Jimmy acts as if, he is about to toss the tablet into the ravine.

Malkuth's lead solider comes to the forefront. He is cautious as he approaches. "Put the tablet on the ground. You have no chance here."

"You come any closer, it goes over." Jimmy holds the tablet over the ravine.

A Scolit in the background says, "Shall I take him out, sir?"

The soldier holds up his arm. "One moment. Wait until the tablet is safely away from the ravine." He looks around and sees no sign of ambush.

"It appears he has come alone. We will…"

At that moment an arrow slices through the soldier's chest. He falls to the ground. The Scolits chatter in confusion as a barrage of arrows shoot from thin air. Scolit after Scolit falls to the mysterious arrows. The remaining Scolits and troops are not sure where to fire back. Jimmy and Machiara have taken cover under their graviport.

The Diversion

Chaos reigns as the troops run and shoot wildly. One Scolit notices that his arrow bounced off of something. He takes aim in the same direction and gets off a lucky arrow of his own, shooting it ten feet from where Jimmy and Machiara lie. Jimmy hears a loud groan and turns to his right to see one of Tolar's soldiers emerge from his camouflage hideaway. The soldier had been hidden under an invisible graviport which had flown into position next to him.

Jimmy remembered how Tala hid the graviports in the ravine by activating its invisible screen. His suggestion, and in his mind perfect plan, to Eclipses was to have the troops ride underneath the guise of the graviport while its invisible shield is activated. The plan called for the soldiers to ride under the carriage of the invisible port. Jimmy and Machiara would then lead the way, and the remaining would set the ambush.

Now, with one of the soldiers hit, the jig is up.

The Scolit who hit the soldier with his renegade arrow yells, "The ports are invisible, aim directly ahead." The remaining Scolits shoot their blasters and successfully hit some of the hidden ports and soldiers hiding within them.

A couple of the graviports are hit by so many blasts that they begin to lose their transparency. When this happens, Jimmy yells, "They're on to us."

Eclipses emerges from his camouflage hideaway and yells, "Attack!"

The remaining Minotaurs and Tolar's troops come out from their bunkers and attack the Scolits. All out man-to-man combat ensues as the Minotaurs club anything and everything in their path.

Chapter 45

The Scolits resort to fighting with their swords and blasters, as the fight is too close for their arrows to be of use. Seeing this, Machiara looks over to Jimmy.

"This is our chance, let's go."

Watching the mayhem in front of him, Jimmy says, "Now?"

Machiara grabs his arm. "Now!"

The two dash for the entrance of the castle, followed by some alert Scolits.

Just as they reach the entrance, the Scolits intercept them. Machiara jumps in front of Jimmy and wields his sword like a master.

It takes him only a few seconds to bring them down. Jimmy admires the masterful display, "That was intense." Three more Scolits appear as Machiara prepares to take them on as Jimmy tries his best to not get in the way. Once again, it only takes a few seconds for Machiara to defeat the Scolits. As soon as the third one falls, Machiara turns to Jimmy.

Jimmy sees another Scolit coming at him, "Look out!"

Without enough time to react, Machiara can only lift his blade over his head. He actually closes his eyes in anticipation of a blow. But another blade falls to the ground with the Scolit falling quickly behind.

Machiara and Jimmy look up and see Eclipses standing over the Scolit with his club-like blade drawn over him. With his deep, overpowering voice he says to Jimmy, "Go. We will hold them."

"Awesome E, thanks man…I mean bull…I mean…" Eclipses grunts. "Forget it! Ok. Let's go," Jimmy takes off. Machiara nods at Eclipses with gratification and then quickly follows Jimmy into the

The Diversion

castle. Eclipses turns and takes on the remaining Scolits outside of the castle.

✶✲Chapter 46✲✶
The Dungeon Of Ynitsed

Through the sludge and muck of the sewer system, Bryan and Brittani finally see a light at the end of the tunnel.

"Britt, I'm starting to see something."

"Me too. Hurry. I'm starting to freak out in here!"

The two of them begin to pick up the pace. As they get closer to the end of the sewer, Brian slows down. Brittani runs into him.

"What are you doing?"

"Shhh. I think I hear something up there."

They creep closer and closer to the end. Finally, only a couple feet from the end, Bryan tries to peak his head outward.

"What do you see?"

"Not much. It looks like an old dungeon. Not much in here though."

Growing impatient, Brittani nudges him, "Ok, so is it safe?"

Bryan looks around again. "I, ah, I think so."

"Good!"

The Dungeon Of Ynitsed

Brittani pushes Bryan with all her might. He lands in a pile of mud on the dungeon floor.

Quickly he gets up and hisses, "What was that for?"

"I'm sorry Bryan, but this place is freaking me out. I need to get out! Whoooo!"

She grabs hold of the sides and thrusts her way out of the sewer and into the waiting arms of Brian. They both fall to the ground once again as she lands on top of Bryan. Bryan looks up awkwardly. They both stare for a few moments directly in each other eyes and then quickly jump up and off one another.

Bryan stammers, "Ah. Are you ok?"

Brittani responds. "Ah, yes. Yes, I just needed to get out of that thing."

They brush themselves off as best as they can and look around the empty room.

"What is this place?"

"I think it's their dungeon."

"Have you read about this before?"

Looking disappointed, Bryan says, "I thought so. But it doesn't look like what I had imagined. The dungeons in the books were more elaborate. They had more gadgets and they were loaded with…"

"People?"

"Yeah. People. How did you know?"

White as a ghost, Brittani stands staring at Bryan. "Bryan…I didn't say anything." Bryan and Brittani slowly turn towards the corner of the dungeon. Shackled and behind a cage created from beams of light, sits Marabus.

Chapter 46

"Who are you?" Bryan says nervously. Marabus sits up and only stares at them.

Bryan and Brittani slowly walk towards the caged woman.

Bryan asks, "Are you ok?" He reaches towards the beams of light that have created a cage around Marabus. Brittani quickly grabs his arm.

"What are you doing? Are you crazy? You don't know what this thing is."

"What? It doesn't look that bad."

"Oh no? Watch?"

Brittani bends down, picks up a stone and tosses it towards the cage. The stone disintegrates as soon as it touches the beams. Bryan backs away from the cage.

Marabus reaches her hands outward and then turns them palm up. She tilts her head and stares at Bryan in a defeated and exhausted state.

Suddenly they hear a voice say, *"Go to the Forerunner, he is in need."*

Bryan and Brittani turn around to see where the voice has come from.

"Who said that?"

Bryan points and says, "Look over there."

They can't find a soul other than Marabus in the dungeon.

Confused, Bryan comes back to the cell. He whispers, "Who else is in here?"

Marabus, too weak to move, simply bobs her head backward in exhaustion.

The Dungeon Of Ynitsed

"What's going on here Britt?"

Staring at Marabus, Brittani says, "It was her."

"What are you talking about?"

"I don't know how she did it, but that voice came from her. Isn't that right? Was that you?"

Marabus opens her eyes and as her head bobs once again.

"It was her. Bryan we have to get her out of there. She can help us."

Bryan looks around. "How are we going to do that? You saw what those beams did to that rock."

Suddenly they hear the voice again, *"Do not agonize over my being; the Forerunner shall possess its strength soon. Find him now, he is need."*

Bryan and Brittani stop their bickering and turn towards Marabus.

"It is you. How can we find him? How can we find Will?"

"Bryan, something is happening to her. Look."

Marabus appears to be fading fast. Her strength is being stripped from her as the voice begins again, "You will find him within the Wall of Dimension. Take the clover, it will show you the way." She drops to the ground and passes out.

"Oh my god! Is she dead?

Bryan moves closer to the cell. "I'm not sure."

He crouches down in front of the cell and stares at Marabus lying on the ground. Next to her on the ground is the same four-leaf clover Will had in his glass cell. Bryan sees it.

"Britt come here."

"What?"

Chapter 46

"Look. Look next to her."

"It's a clover."

"Yeah…How we going to get it, though?"

Brittani runs over to an old torture rack which appears to have been used for stretching an individual and the impaling them with a spear.

"Bryan, will this work?" She pulls a long spear-like tool off the rack.

"Perfect."

Bryan runs over and grabs the tool from her. He darts back towards the laser beam cell and prepares to retrieve the clover.

Chapter 47
Transfer Of Power

Staring at his grandfather on the altar, Will feels a weird sensation all over his body. He feels stronger and more confident every second. Energized, he is ready to move.

Trying not to make a sound, he looks over at Zechariah who is patiently waiting for the guards to move from their posts. Will's eyes begin to roll in his head as the sensation grows. At one point, Will has to kneel down on one knee to regain his composure.

Soon the sensation becomes over-powering. It brings him to the ground. He sprawls on the floor near Zechariah's feet.

Zechariah whispers with concern, "Will. Will, are you ok? Will!"

Will lies paralyzed for one long minute. Zechariah shakes him to revive him. Will slowly regains his composure. Behind them, a group of guards run into the sanctuary. They know Will and his band have escaped and rush to inform him Malkuth. The sorcerer, who had been viewing holographic images, becomes irate.

Chapter 47

As Will gets up, he sees Malkuth strike one of his guards in anger and then rushes over to a control panel. Immediately, a screeching siren blasts through the complex and red flashing lights appear everywhere. Malkuth rushes out of his lair followed by a group of Scolits.

"Where's he going?" Will asks Zechariah as they try to take cover within the sanctuary.

Chapter 48
The Seventh Tablet

Safely on the second level of the castle, Jimmy and Machiara have made it past the first wave of Scolits and troops. As they hustle up the steps, Jimmy turns and watches Eclipses and his troops take on the remaining Scolits and loyalists below. Then he hears the sirens and tries to gauge where it is coming from.

"Keep going." He urges Machiara. "I'm right behind you, Macky. Let's go." The two take off up the stairs and make it safely up two more levels. Finally on the fourth and final level they scamper up the steps only to be met by another group of Scolits.

"Oh boy," Jimmy growls. "This doesn't look good."

Machiara pulls his bow and arrow out. He says to Jimmy, "Stay behind me."

He unleashes three quick arrows and brings down three Scolits. He manages to push the corpses back enough for them to make it away from the stairs. Unfortunately, they see another fifteen Scolits and Malkuth loyalists waiting.

Chapter 48

"Here." Machiara tosses Jimmy one of his swords. Jimmy looks at the sword and immediately gets excited, glad that he can finally get into the fighting.

"Nice."

Machiara rushes the Scolits and puts on another display with his sword. Jimmy, increasing impressed by Machiara's skills, tries to jump into the chaos. But every time he is about to strike a Scolit, Machiara strikes it down first.

After three or four failed attempts, Jimmy gets frustrated. "Macky, don't be so selfish here."

Machiara looks over for a brief second and then ignores Jimmy as he continues to bring down Scolit after Scolit. Jimmy, on the another hand, keeps on trying to engage, but is constantly and instinctively protected by Machiara. Suddenly, Machiara freezes in mid swing. Seeing this, Jimmy looks up. "Macky, what's wrong?"

Machiara is frozen. He can't move a muscle. Out of the corner of his eye, Jimmy sees Malkuth standing in the wing with his scepter extended. He also sees a Scolit coming directly towards Machiara with its blade extended.

Jimmy jumps in front of Machiara just as the Scolit is in range and thrusts his sword into the Scolits ribs. The beast topples.

As soon as they Scolit falls, Jimmy turns to Machiara. The warrior can only give him an expression of gratitude. Everything else is frozen. Jimmy quickly turns towards Malkuth and pulls the tablet from his knapsack.

"Stop them right now or I'm going to shatter it in a million pieces."

The Seventh Tablet

Seeing the tablet, Malkuth raises his other arm and the Scolits stop in their tracks.

Gaining confidence, Jimmy continues, "Ok. Ok, good. Now, unfreeze my buddy here."

Malkuth smirks.

"I don't see anything funny here. Unfreeze him and give me my friend back or the tablet's history."

Malkuth takes a step toward Jimmy.

"Hey what are doing? I'm serious. If you don't release my friends, I'm gonna break this thing."

Malkuth continues his silent walk

"You don't think I'd do it. Take another step, and it's gone."

Malkuth looks at Jimmy with all his evil might and sneers, "Go ahead, destroy it."

"You don't think I will."

"Destroy it."

"Let Will go, and unfreeze my friend and it's yours."

"It's mine already."

He continues to walk toward Jimmy.

"I warned you."

Jimmy pulls his arm back and is about to throw the tablet to the ground when Malkuth extends his scepter and freezes him in place.

Jimmy murmurs through clenched lips, "It's gone." With all his might Jimmy tries to free his fingers from the tablet. One by one he is able to pull them away. The tablet slowly begins to fall from his fingers. Just as the tablet releases from his hand, Malkuth's hand comes in and catches it before it even has a chance to fall.

Chapter 48

With Jimmy and Machiara frozen in front of him, Malkuth holds the seventh and final tablet in his hands. He intones, "It is complete. My destiny is now at hand."

He turns to the remaining Scolits. "Bring them both. We will need them as leverage now. Seal off all the levels."

The Scolits grab Jimmy and Machiara as one of their loyalists runs over to a small entrance. He hits a series of levers on the wall. The floors beneath them begin to seal themselves off from the levels below.

Jimmy watches in horror as Malkuth rushes to his lair and steel walls seal them from any assistance below. Eclipses and his fighting troops now have no way of gaining access to the upper level of Ynitsed castle.

Chapter 49
Access Denied

With the long, thin tool penetrating its way through the laser jail cell, Bryan, sweat pouring from his forehead, attempts to pull the clover towards him.

"Be careful Bryan. Don't hit the beams."

"I know, Britt. Please stop reminding me."

"I'm just trying to help."

"I know, just let me concentrate."

Lying on his stomach, Bryan extends the long pole into the cell. It gets closer and closer to Marabus.

"You're close, Bryan. Just a little bit further."

He keeps extending the pole. "Just a little bit further," he says to himself. Suddenly he extends it too far and accidentally hits one of the laser beams. Immediately the beams send off a shock that throws him across the room and instantaneously disintegrates the pole.

"Bryan!" Brittani screams as she rushes over to his aid. "Bryan, are you ok?"

Chapter 49

Trying to gather his senses, Bryan slowly looks up. "Yeah. Yeah, I'm fine. Whoo, that was intense."

"Now what?"

Bryan takes a deep breath. "We need to get this thing. Let's get another pole."

Brittani smiles and gets up. "You would do anything for your brother, wouldn't you?"

"He's my brother." Bryan grimaces as he tries to gain his senses again.

Brittani rushes over to the same wall to retrieve another pole. She comes rushing back with a replacement. She hands it to Bryan. He shakes his head one last time to regain his senses, and then heads back over to the cell to make another attempt.

FROM AN elevated platform above the sanctuary, Will, Zechariah, Hadesria and Famiaria watch the guards scramble about. The sirens have been turned off as the guards run through the complex looking for the escaped prisoners. Will is stunned to see Malkuth walk into view with the seventh and final tablet in his hand. He then sees Jimmy and Machiara being carted in behind him.

"Oh, Jimmy," Will whispers. "What did you do now?" He sees that Jimmy is not moving. "What's wrong with him?"

Zechariah replies, "They will be fine. It's Malkuth's sorcery."

"We need to get down there, Z. And we need to do it now. We are running out of time. He has all seven tablets now. Bethel said this can be devastating."

Zechariah looks over to the two other warriors. "Προετοιμαστείτε για τη μάχη." The two prepare themselves for battle. Zechariah looks

Access Denied

over to Will and barks, "You stay, we will create a diversion. You get Eseph and the tablets."

Will watches Malkuth head into his sanctuary. He takes a deep breath and grabs hold of his sword. "Ok, I'm ready."

The three warriors descend from the rock platform where they have been hiding.

ECLIPSES AND HIS warriors have defeated the Scolits inside the castle. However, their ascension to the upper levels has been stopped by the steel walls. One of the Minotaurs screams to Eclipses, "There is no access, Eclipses. It is totally sealed off."

"Break through it." Eclipses replies.

The Minotaurs take their clubs and anything else they can find in an effort to break through the steel wall. No matter how hard they pound, the structure doesn't budge.

BRYAN IS ONLY inches away from the clover once again.

"You've got it, Bryan! Be careful."

"Just one more inch and I…"

The pole brushes up against a laser beam and creates an electrical response. Bryan pulls it away from the beam just in time to stop the reaction. He stops and looks at the beams.

"That was close! Be careful, Bry."

Bryan doesn't even respond to Brittani's continual commentary. He takes the pole and extends it further into the cell. This time he makes it to the clover. Gently, he begins to nudge the clover back towards him.

It is an extremely tedious process and Bryan is making every effort to move slowly and precisely in an attempt to pull it towards him

Chapter 49

without damaging its leaves. He only has about three feet more until he can reach it with his hand.

ECLIPSES TROOPS BEGIN to grow weary as they pound on the steel foundation. Nothing is working and they're beginning to lose steam. Sensing their exhaustion, Eclipses walks up to the steel and shouts, "Move aside."

He begins to pound on the steel with all his might. Seeing the drive and tenacity he is displaying, the rest of the Minotaurs gain a second wind and begin to pound on the structure in an effort to break through.

✦Chapter 50✦
The Four Leafed Wonder

Will watches as the three warriors descend into the sanctuary. He begins to talk to himself in an attempt to motivate himself. "Ok Will, this is it. Don't screw this up."

He watches Zechariah jump from a platform in front of a Scolit and quickly and quietly overcome the creature. Swiftly, he grabs his weapon and rushes towards the others. Hadesria and Famiaria follow behind and duplicate his efforts. The three warriors begin an impressive stance against the Scolits and soldiers within the sanctuary.

Will plots his course towards the altar and his grandfather. As the men below successfully bring down the Scolits, he senses that now is the time to make his move. Just as he gets up he sees Zechariah, Hadesria and Famiaria all fall to the ground, as if, they have been hit by a bolt of lighting. Each of them falls at the same time and lies motionless on the ground. Will freezes in his tracks, then creeps back to his hiding spot. He peeks his head out to see what's going on.

Chapter 50

Malkuth walks out in a confident manner and shouts, "It's over, Forerunner. The time has passed and you have run out of resources. You can not stop what is destiny."

He motions to his troops. "Put them in the pit. All of them."

The Scolits rush over and grab the three warriors. They drag each of the men, including Jimmy and Machiara, to hang in the sludge pit with the other tortured souls. Will can only watch in horror as the men are carted away and hung, as if, they are drying upon a line.

He turns his back to them and closes his eyes in fear. "Oh, my God. Oh, my God. Now what?"

Malkuth heads back into his lair to prepare his final element. He heads over to the tabernacle and quickly begins to position the tablets over the altar. Just prior to opening the ark, he looks over to the sundial, which has moved closer to a full shadow. When the full shadow is complete the ascension process can begin.

Seeing that he is only minutes away from his ascension, Malkuth gets a proud and secure look on his face. In his mind, nothing can stop him now.

He opens the ark as Will watches in horror. Malkuth unlatches the handles and a beam of light emanates from within the inner sanctum of the golden crate. Malkuth smiles broadly as he pulls open the top portion of the ark.

As soon as he opens it, the light shoots out in all directions, illuminating the dark sanctuary within the Wall of Dimension. A cool breeze begins to flow from the inside the ark.

Will stands there, chastising himself for being a failure. Malkuth now has all seven tablets and the darken shadows is only moments away.

The Four Leafed Wonder

As Malkuth pulls the tablets from the ark and places them in their assigned position upon the altar, Will sheds a tear.

ONLY TWO FEET away from actually grabbing the clover, Bryan begins to sweat profusely. His nerves are getting the best of him. He stops once again as the pole nearly hits a beam. Brittani looks at him. "Are you ok, Bryan?"

"Yeah...I'm...I'm fine."

"Do you want me to try?"

"You know what? Yes. I'm getting too close to these beams. If you can pull this closer, maybe I can grab it." Bryan drops the pole and backs away from the cell. He takes a deep breath and wipes the sweat off his brow as Brittani gets on her knees and grabs hold of the pole. She looks back. "Ok, you ready?"

"Yep."

Brittani begins to maneuver the pole. Quickly she, too, gets very close to the beam.

"Whoa, be careful, Britt."

Defiant, Brittani continues. "I got it." She maneuvers the clover closer and closer to the edge of the cell.

"Just a little bit more, Britt, you're getting it."

Starting to get sore from the awkward position, Brittani begins to sweat from exertion. The clover is less than a foot away.

"Can you get it, Bryan?"

"Couple more inches, Britt. Come on, you're doing great."

Drumming up all the strength she can, Brittani makes a final nudge and pulls on the pole. She brushes the clover close enough for Bryan to grab hold of it.

Chapter 50

"I can get it Britt...don't move." As Bryan reaches for the clover, Brittani begins to lose grip of the pole.

"Hurry Bryan, I can't hold this much longer."

"A couple more seconds, Britt."

As Bryan grabs hold of the clover, Brittani loses her grip. The pole slips out of her hand and rolls towards one of the beams of light. As soon as the pole touches the beam, it generates an electric current. Bryan quickly pulls his hand and the clover out of the cell in the nick of time. The pole disintegrates right before their eyes.

Bryan and Brittani roll away from the cell to avoid the electrical fall out. Bryan quickly gets up and sees that the clover had fallen on the ground between them.

"What do we do now?" Brittani asks.

Propping himself on his knees in front of the clover. Bryan admits, "I don't know." He reaches down and grabs the four-leaf wonder. The room begins to illuminate.

"What's happening, Bryan?"

As a wind kicks up within the dungeon, Bryan holds the clover away from his body. Brittani points at something on the wall directly across from them. Bryan sees the wall transforming into a holographic image of Will looking down upon the tabernacle. He is completely dejected.

"It's Will."

The images get stronger as the wind within the dungeons increases in power.

AT THE SAME moment as Eclipses and his troops are ready to give up trying to access the upper level of the castle, they too see an

The Four Leafed Wonder

opening and an image on the steel that has prevented access. Eclipses stops his troop and watches the images become a real access point into the sanctuary.

BRYAN AND BRITTANI realize the image is so solid that it looks as if they can enter the sanctuary through the hologram. The wind kicks up enough that Bryan is having difficulty holding onto the clover.

Bryan looks over to Brittani. "What do you think?"

"We have to try it. Don't drop the clover."

"Ok. Go. I'll hold it as long as I can."

Brittani runs toward the image. Without hesitation she jumps directly into the image and is immediately transported into the sanctuary. Seeing this, Bryan quickly follows.

Bryan rolls as soon as he lands upon the rocks above Malkuth's lair.

Back in the dungeon, Marabus lies peacefully on the ground with a satisfied look upon her face.

When Bryan and Brittani stop rolling, Will turns around in fear. He wields his sword around and nearly slices through his brother.

"Whoa! Will, stop! It's us."

"Bryan! Brittani! How did you?"

Bryan looks at his hand. The clover is gone. "It's a long story. Are you ok?"

"Yeah. I'm fine, but Grandpa's in trouble."

"Grandpa? What are you talking about, Will?"

"Bryan, Grandpa is Eseph."

Chapter 50

Confused, Bryan says, "Eseph? The great warrior and Malkuth's nemesis in *The Sorcerer's Shadows* books? Are you crazy? Eseph is a character in a book."

"Bryan, I'm telling you, they are one and the same. Look!"

Will points down to the tabernacle. On a ridge overlooking Malkuth's lair Bryan and Brittani creep their way up to the rocks where Will has been peering in. Suddenly they all hear a ruckus on the other side of the Wall of Dimension.

"What's that noise?" Will says as Bryan tries to peer down to the altar.

As the ruckus gets louder he sees that Malkuth is distracted by the sounds that are coming from within the castle and quickly rushes over to grab his scepter. A few Scolits come rushing in and scream, "They have broken through! We have been penetrated."

Angered, Malkuth rushes out of the sanctuary to deal with the ruckus. Bryan keeps trying to see the man on the altar.

As Malkuth leaves to confront the intruders, he commands a group of Scolits, "Stay within the tabernacle."

Bryan watches as the man on the rack turns his head in their direction. Stunned and speechless, Bryan sees the face of Eseph. It is his grandfather. Rocked by the fact, Bryan falls to the ground. "Oh, my God, it's true. Eseph is Grandpa."

Brittani gets up and looks at both of the boys. "Yes, it's true. Your grandfather is Eseph, our great leader, our great savior. And I, I am Cayla."

"What?" Bryan shrieks. "Are you saying that you are Cayla, Eseph's apprentice?"

The Four Leafed Wonder

Brittani stands up proudly, "I am. I have been sent to look after you on this great journey."

"No way, you're our neighbor."

"A guise that I have cherished for many years."

Bryan looks over to Will. "This can't be. This is wacked!"

"Just look around Bryan."

Bryan looks at Eseph one more time, then back to Brittani. "You're really Cayla?"

"Bryan, I'm sorry I have deceived you for so long."

"Will, can you believe this?"

"Bryan, I've been freaked out about this from the start. At this point, I believe anything." Will says. Then, turning to Cayla he asks, "So Brittani…or…Cayla, whatever your name is, you know what's going on here, don't you?"

"I do."

"Why are the tablets so important? What's in them?"

"It is the tablets that bring us the good word, the only True Word."

Will echoes, "The good word?"

"The stories of our time center around one path. One path to reach eternal happiness. The tablets are the blueprints to our eternal happiness. They must never be destroyed. If destroyed, all hope is lost, and our faith and eventual ascension erased."

Bryan chimes in, "Are you talking about the Bible?"

"The word comes in many names, Bryan, it is the contents that need to be preserved and understood. To destroy them would devastate us all. You're grandfather has been the keeper of the tablets for many years.

Chapter 50

Malkuth somehow figured a way to clash the worlds of good and evil together in an effort to compromise the tablets. The two books in your room that evening represented an opportunity for him to activate his evil. As evil prevailed, his strength increased. Now, with more people turning away from the tablets or the true Word within this world and ours, he gains more and more power. As you can see this world, the world of Rainbow Alley has been infected by the evil that spawns from Malkuth and his desires. It is only a matter of time that it affects the world you have come from. If he destroys the tablets, all hope and faith will be erased. We will all be doomed.

"Will, you have been chosen. It is your fate to deliver the tablets from the evil that possesses them."

"*The tablets of fate*! Bryan, this is bigger than I thought."

"What are we supposed do?" Bryan says to Cayla.

Cayla addresses Will, "Will, you have known what to do from the start. Your grandfather has educated you and Marabus has filled you. The power has been placed within you. You must call upon it."

She looks at the sword Will holds.

Will looks down to his sword. He then looks over to the tabernacle and sees that Malkuth is on his way back. Malkuth has successfully created a barricade with his scepter, which has stopped Eclipses and his troops from gaining further access into his sanctuary behind the Wall of Dimension.

Will looks at his brother and his friend. "I know what I have to do. Hang on guys. This could get interesting."

Will stands up and grabs hold of the sword with both hands. He climbs on top of the boulder and clutches the handle end of the sword,

The Four Leafed Wonder

as if it is a javelin. Balancing the blade end of the sword with his other hand, he reaches back. He is now ready to launch the sword towards his grandfather.

Alarmed, Bryan yells, "Will, what are you doing?"

Ignoring his brother, Will reaches back and with all his might he launches the sword like a javelin directly towards his grandfather who lies on the altar.

Bryan screams. "Nooooo!"

The sword flies through the air, towards the tabernacle. The blade is heading directly towards Eseph, but it flies past his body and penetrates the shackles that confine his arms. The shackles break open and the sword sticks into the headboard of the altar.

Shaken, Eseph reacts quickly, and grabs the sword. He immediately slices through the shackles on his feet. He looks up and sees Will standing in the rafters. With a gentle smile, he turns away from his grandson and looks in the opposite direction.

Bryan looks over at his brother in utter disbelief. "Unbelievable! Not bad…Forerunner."

A bit overwhelmed, Will grins back at his brother proudly.

Malkuth has already grabbed his scepter and is heading towards the tabernacle. Seeing that Eseph has been freed, he screams to the Scolit guards, "Close the perimeter."

From behind Malkuth, a quiet voice says, "That won't be necessary, Malkuth."

Malkuth stops in his tracks and smiles. He turns around. "You should have run, Eseph."

"Not likely Malkuth. Your time has come."

Chapter 50

Malkuth raises his scepter and points it towards Eseph. "Yes, it has, and you will be my witness, Eseph."

He points the scepter and blasts a ray of energy towards Eseph. Eseph raises the sword in defense and the energy ray bounces off the sword. Confused, Malkuth shoots another blast towards him with the same result.

"Looks like you're going to have win this one with your hands, Malkuth."

Frustrated that the scepter isn't working, Malkuth screams to his guards,

"Seize him." The Scolits rush towards Eseph. He responds with an amazing display of martial arts. In a matter of seconds he dispatches four Scolits as if they were moving in slow motion.

Will and Bryan high five one another to celebrate their grandfather's skills. "Will you look at him," Bryan says in awe.

"He's amazing." Will responds.

As s Eseph finishes off the final Scolit guard, he jumps off the tabernacle platform and rushes to the sludge pits and where Zechariah and the warriors hang. He takes his sword and slices through their shackles, freeing them from their bondage.

He looks at each of them and says, "πηγαίνετε και παλεψτε." The warriors react as if they are accustomed to following him. Quickly, they jump from the sludge pits and rush towards the sanctuary with Eseph. Machiara and Hadesria join Eseph. Jimmy and Famiaria stay behind to free the other hostages in the pit.

The Four Leafed Wonder

Malkuth glances at the sundial, which shows that it's just moments away from his ascension. He then summons more Scolits as the war within the sanctuary continues.

Led by Eseph, Zechariah, his warriors and a group of freed hostages wage war on Malkuth and the Scolits. The fighting continues as more and more hostages gain their freedom, and more and more Scolits come out of the woodwork. The fighting grows intense as Eseph wields his sword like a master in an effort to make his way towards Malkuth.

Still watching this from up above the mayhem, Will says, "Bryan, we need to get the tablets."

"Let's go."

Will, Bryan and Cayla attempt to make their way to the tabernacle as the fighting wages around them. Seeing Malkuth also heading towards the tabernacle, Eseph strikes down three more Scolits in his path. As the third one falls, he calls out, "Malkuth!"

Malkuth turns towards Eseph. "I had figured it may come down to this. And to think I was going to give you an opportunity at eternal life." Malkuth points his scepter once again towards Eseph, but instead shooting an electrical blast, it morphs into a sword of equal size to his.

Eseph readies himself. Malkuth takes one last look at the sundial and sees that it is almost at a complete shadow. He waves his sword over the tabernacle and, in a matter of seconds; winds begin to swirl around the altar. A large whirlpool of quicksand appears in front of the entrance.

Malkuth turns from his altar and raises his sword. "Prepare for the end, Eseph!"

Chapter 50

He races towards Eseph, sword raised high, and thrusts it downward towards Eseph. Eseph reacts brilliantly, and he spins away while deflecting the powerful thrusts from Malkuth's sword. The two dual like masters of martial arts. Though Malkuth is much larger than Eseph, his quickness makes up for Malkuth's powerful thrusts.

Bryan, Will and Cayla dash in, trying not to be noticed, and head directly for the tabernacle. Just as they reach the inner core of the sanctuary, three Scolits appear and corner them. Cayla yells as Bryan jumps in front of her to protect her. Unfortunately, none of them have weapons. The drooling Scolits approach them with confidence.

Just as the first Scolit raises his sword, Will points his hand towards the Scolit and the creature's weapon flies out of his hand. Bryan looks at his brother and grins. "Get the other two, quick."

Will repeats his hand gesture. Both Scolits lose their swords immediately. The creatures look to one another, then scream and squeal and rush towards the three of them.

"Get ready, you guys. This can get ugly," Bryan says.

Just a foot away from them, the Scolits raise their fists in rage and get ready to pounce. A horrifying shriek fills the air as Zechariah, Machiara and Jimmy jump into the sanctuary, swords in hand. Each of them wields their sword them like masters and bring down the Scolits in a matter of seconds. Proud of his actions, Jimmy turns around towards Will and says, "How dya like them apples Will?"

"Not bad Jimbo."

Bryan looks over to Jimmy and Will and says in a sarcastic manner, "Who are you guys?"

The Four Leafed Wonder

Will looks at the tabernacle and screams, "The tablets! We need to get the tablets!"

Bryan shouts to Zechariah and Machiara, "You help my grandfather. We'll get the tablets." Zechariah and Machiara rush over to Malkuth and Eseph as Will, Bryan, Cayla and Jimmy run over towards the tabernacle.

As they reach the front portion of the tabernacle, they are brushed back by intense winds Malkuth has created above the altar. They stop in their tracks when they see the whirlpool of quicksand in front of the entrance.

Bryan calls out, "What now? How are we going to pass through this?"

Will looks at his brother in confusion and realizes the winds have kicked up even stronger and the whirlpool of sand is growing.

MALKUTH AND ESEPH continue their duel.

"This will end tonight for you, Malkuth!"

"You will not stop me again, Eseph. I won't have it." Malkuth swings down hard and knocks Eseph off balance, sending him reeling into the sludge pit. Eseph loses his grip on his sword as he falls.

Malkuth confidently walks over towards the sword and says, "Not this time, Eseph." He kicks the sword into the sludge pit and watches it sink. He then turns towards Eseph and points his sword directly at him as the sword morphs back into the scepter. As the scepter begins to illuminate Eseph begins to rise above the sludge pit. "You didn't really think you would win this time, Eseph."

Malkuth moves his scepter in a circular motion and Eseph begins to twirl in midair.

Chapter 50

"It is time for my sacrifice, Chosen One!" Malkuth shouts as he swings his scepter in the direction of the tabernacle. Eseph is whisked up and away towards the altar. His body is hurled up into the swirling winds that hover over it. Eseph helplessly hovers over the altar.

Will and Bryan scream, "Grandpa! No."

Malkuth marvels at his handy work. With a sly smirk on his face, he checks the sundial and sees that he is only moments away from a total shadow. He says, "I have done what you requested, empower me, O dark one!"

Malkuth's eyes open wide and his face cringes in excruciating pain. He arches his back upward; his eyes begin to water as his teeth clench.

Like a rock falling from a cliff, Malkuth falls face first into the sludge pit below. The two swords in his back form a cross as Zechariah and Machiara stand victorious in the wake of Malkuth's demise. The two warriors watch this great sorcerer sink deep into the sludge he had forced so many to be tortured in. Zechariah grabs Machiara's shoulder in a gesture of acknowledgement. Simultaneously, they hear screams from Cayla.

The two warriors rush over to the alter. The quicksand barrier in front of the alter is rising in height as it whirlpool-like appearance increases in size and speed.

Will gasps, "Z, do you think can throw me again?" The warrior nods. Cayla shouts, "Hurry! Something is happening to Eseph."

Streams of light swirl around Eseph and shoot upward through a new hole in the ceiling. The roar of the winds increases as Will rushes over to Zechariah. "Throw me, Z. Throw me over the quicksand."

The Four Leafed Wonder

Zechariah looks at the expanding quicksand barrier one last time and then grabs Will. He says, "It's too far."

Will demands, "We have to try, we're running out of time."

Thunder cracks and the room begins to shake. Zechariah grabs Will and twirls around once before flinging him towards the altar and over the quicksand barrier. Will flies over most of the sand, but lands short. His upper body hangs on the rim of the altar, but his lower torso is caught up in the swirling quicksand below. Instinctively, he grabs a piece of the alter and hangs on.

"Hang on, Will." Cayla screams.

The swirling quicksand pulls Will more and more as it continues to grow in size. "Help!" He screams. His grip is growing weaker by the second.

Zechariah looks over to Machiara and says, "δίκαιο άτομο θα ζήσει από την πίστη." He takes his bow and arrow and hurls it up and over the sand. It lands about five feet from the altar. He takes about three steps backward and then rushes towards the sand and leaps with all his might towards Will. The force of his lunge is so powerful, he is able to crash his body into Wills,' sending him forward and safely out of the sand.

Once safe, Will looks back for his friend. He sees that Zechariah is submerging in the swirling quicksand. Will calls out, "Z!"

Zechariah, sensing that his fate is at hand, shouts to Will, "Be one with the tablets, Forerunner." Will rushes to the edge of the sands as Zechariah submerges and disappears.

Will screams, "Noooo."

Chapter 50

As if reacting to Zechariah's loss, the winds within and above the alter begin to get fierce. Lighting shoots in every direction while the wind tosses Eseph back and forth. In a matter of seconds, Eseph is tossed to the base of the altar. He appears unconscious.

"Will, get to the altar," Cayla screams.

Will is not sure if he should tend to his grandfather go directly to the altar or search for Zechariah. He looks back at Bryan who shouts, "Go, Will, get the tablets!"

Will sprints towards the tabernacle. He see the tablets on top of the alter. He is now just a few steps from his goal. When out of nowhere, Malkuth appears in front of him.

Completely stunned, Will stops in his tracks and croaks, "I thought you were..."

Malkuth stares down at Will. In an ominous tone he replies, "It's convenient to have siblings that resemble you. I believe you know my dear brother, Abra, Forerunner."

Malkuth extends his scepter towards the sludge pit. He raises the body within, and turns it around. Will watches as the corpse's facial features change from Malkuth's to his brother, Abra. After a few seconds, Malkuth tosses the body back into the pit.

"He was quite useful. It's over, Forerunner. My ascension has begun." Malkuth raises his arms as the lightning and thunder become constant.

Will screams and rushes Malkuth. Malkuth raises his arm and stops Will dead in his tracks. Will can not move his legs. He cries out, "No... Stop this. You can not destroy the tablets."

"It is done, Forerunner. You have failed!"

The Four Leafed Wonder

Malkuth raises his arms and as the winds swirl around his head.

"Noooo," Will screams again.

An arrow hurls through the air and penetrates Malkuth's chest. His eyes open wide as he screams in pain. He looks to see where this arrow has come from.

Standing in the wing is Wills' grandfather, Eseph. He has picked up Zechariah's bow and arrow and stands ready with another arrow pointed directly at Malkuth.

"Eseph!" Malkuth says in obvious pain.

Eseph looks directly at Malkuth and says, "This is the ending we've all been waiting for." He shoots the arrow through Malkuth's neck. The force drags Malkuth back and up against the alter. The arrow embeds itself into the wall with Malkuth hanging from it.

Stunned, Will turns towards his grandfather, "Grandpa!"

Eseph commands, "Will, get the tablets. Hurry!"

Will rushes to the altar, grabs each tablet and places them back in the ark. He grabs six of them and turns around. "Grandpa there's only six."

Eseph turns and looks at Malkuth. The winds are howling. He rushes to the impaled body. Eseph searches Malkuth and finds the seventh tablet hidden in his cloak. With the winds unbearable now, Eseph grabs the tablet and rushes back to Will on the altar.

The tabernacle begins to crumble as Eseph makes his way to Will. "Grandpa hurry!"

Sensing that he may not make it in time, Eseph calls to Will, "Will, catch it." He launches the tablet toward the altar. Will opens his arms in anticipation. The tablet almost floats across the altar. Will lunges

Chapter 50

and catches it just before it hits the ground. Proudly he yells, "I got it! I got it!"

"Put it in the ark!"

Will lunges once again, this time for the ark, and tosses the seventh tablet inside. He slams the ark shut and hangs onto it with all of his might. The ground begins to shake uncontrollably. "Grandpa!"

"Hang on, Will!"

The shaking grows fiercer and an explosion of epic proportions erupts outside the complex. The very ground begins to crumble. Will, Eseph and the rest of the group all grab hold of pieces of the alter in an effort to stabilize themselves. Jimmy rushes over to grab a corner piece when globs of sludge from the pits hit him with enough force to bring him to the ground.

As the eruptions begin to travel through the complex, Eclipses and his troops also grab hold of pieces of the building. Outside, the same affect grabs hold of the land. The land begins to ripple and shake uncontrollably from Ynitsed castle all the way to Bornea.

Back inside what's left of the castle, Will and Eseph feel the shaking subside. As the environment begin to calm down, a slight drizzle of rain begins to fall across the land and the sun begins to rise.

Will slowly lets go of the ark as Eseph rises to his feet. Bryan, Cayla and the warriors also stand up and to stare at the site now in front of them.

Will and his grandfather start to laugh. Will shouts "We did it! We did it.!"

The Four Leafed Wonder

Will rushes jumps into his grandfather's his arms. They all laugh and watch the dark lands of *The Sorcerer's Shadow* morph into the wondrous paradise of Rainbow Alley.

Everywhere they look, the genesis of a natural paradise begins to emerge. Will can't help but think that he has seen this image before. He contemplates a few seconds and then remembers the image created from the four scrolls.

He smiles at the memory. Then, seeing a pile of dirt trembling, he stops. As he peers closer, Zechariah emerges from the pile of dirt and sand.

"Z...you made it!"

Zechariah gets up, smiles and begins to brush himself off. Will rushes over to Zechariah and jumps on him. Zechariah laughs as Will ruffles his hair on his head. He puts Will down. Will turns to his brother and Cayla. Standing in amazement, Bryan smiles and opens his arms. "That was awesome, bro, truly awesome." Will rushes to his brother. They high five one another and then hug as if they have never hugged before.

"Jimmy! Where's Jimmy?"

"Look." Cayla interrupts. Emerging from the sludge, Jimmy snarls and coughs his way to his feet. Will eyes get wide as he shouts, "Jimmy! You're back!"

"What?" Jimmy grabs his face, and then his arms and legs. He is stunned. He has changed back into his human skin. "It's me...It's me. I'm back I'm really back!"

Chapter 50

They all high five one another as Eclipses and his troops enter the area and join in the celebration. As they all congratulate one another, Eseph notices something in the sky. Gradually, they all turn to a bright light floating in the sky above them.

The light begins to descend towards them. Curious, and a bit concerned, they all begin to back away. As it floats down, the light grows in size. As soon as it touches the ground, it transforms into an image of Bethel.

"You have done well, my son," Bethel says to Will.

"Is it over?"

"Peace has been brought to this land by your perseverance and your faith."

"My faith?"

"It is faith that carries us all. You, my boy, have set the tone for generations to come. Go and tell your story to all that will listen. Carry the tablet within you and witness to all that will hear. For it is the tablets and the contents within that will deliver us all."

They all smile as a beautiful rainbow appears behind Bethel. Cayla sees Moli rushing towards her from behind Bethel. "Moli! You made it, too!" Moli jumps into her arms.

Will gets a concerned looked on his face. He asks Bethel. "How will we get home?"

Bethel looks at Will reassuringly. "She has guided you through, she will guide you home." Bethel waves his hand and points to his side. He then slowly disappears as his life force vanishes.

"He's gone." Jimmy says.

The Four Leafed Wonder

Will looks over to where Bethel had pointed. Near a palm tree, by a gently flowing river, Marabus stands. She is dressed in a white silky cloak. She appears heavenly. They are all speechless.

"Is that?" Bryan questions.

Cayla says. "Yes, it's her."

Will smiles, realizing she has been his guardian angel through out his entire journey. They walk over to her. Her beauty illuminates the entire setting.

Will asks, "Can you take us home?"

Marabus simply smiles.

Will turns to the rest of the group. "Well, what dya say, gang?"

Bryan and Jimmy quickly say, "Let's do it."

Cayla doesn't say anything. Neither does Will's grandfather.

Will asks, "You ready, Grandpa? You ready to go home?" Eseph gets an awkward look on his face.

Bryan says, "Grandpa, what's going on?"

"Boys, come here for a moment."

"Grandpa, don't play around, let's go home."

"Sit here for a moment."

The boys sit on a boulder near the river as Eseph walks in front of them. "Boys, this may be hard to understand, but I cannot go back."

"What do you mean, you can't go back? You can't leave us now."

"I would never leave you. You will always be able to see me, talk to me and even read about me. Rainbow Alley is place that is always open. All you have to do is open the door and read."

"Grandpa, we came here to save you and heal you."

Chapter 50

"You have not only saved me, but you have saved so many in more ways than you know. By maintaining the tablets and spreading its Word throughout the land, you have delivered new life. My time in your world has passed. This is my home now. My eternal home."

Will looks over to Bryan, and then back to his grandfather. "Grandpa what is Rainbow Alley?"

"It is everything you can imagine…and more!"

"Grandpa, I don't want leave you."

"Don't think about it as leaving. Think about it as a short vacation. We will be together again after your vacation."

Will gets a tiny smirk on his face. "A vacation, huh?"

"A vacation."

"What do you think, bro?" Will turns to his brother who has a slight tear in his eye. "Bryan, are you ok?"

With a smile on his face, Bryan looks to his grandfather. "Yeah…yeah I'm ok! No more *Sorcerer's Shadow,* huh, Grandpa?"

"There's nothing wrong with a good adventure, Bryan. Just make wise choices on where your allegiance lies."

Will hugs his grandfather as Bryan looks to Cayla. "You, too?" Cayla smiles and nods in agreement. Bryan teases, "Protecting us, huh?"

"Always there, Bryan. I'll always be there."

Bryan smiles, and he looks over to his brother and Jimmy. "You guys ready?"

Will looks at his grandfather one last time. He hugs him one last time. Bryan does the same. Feeling a bit out of place, Jimmy walks over and throws his arms around them, too.

The Four Leafed Wonder

As they separate, Will turns to Marabus. "Ok, I think we're ready."

Marabus nods and waves her hand. Behind her, and through the palm trees, a vortex of colors begins to appear. The boys look at the whirling mass of color and smile.

Will turns to Zechariah and the warriors and rushes over to them for a farewell hug. When he gets to Zechariah He whispers, "I'll never forget you."

"Nor will I forget you, Forerunner."

Bryan and Jimmy also say their goodbyes and the boys can't help but run one last time to hug their grandfather. As they unclench their embrace, Will looks over to Bryan and Jimmy, grins, and says, "Let's do it."

They boys take off for the swirling vortex and jump into the vibrant colors as they are thrusted upward and into the rainbow current.

ONE MONTH LATER

Reading in his bedroom, Bryan has his study light on his new fantasy adventure novel, *The Pirates Revenge*. He can't take his eyes from the pages. As Bryan holds the novel in one hand he fiddles with a shining black stone in his other hand. Someone pounds on his door. "Bryan, Bryan open up."

"What is it? It's open."

Will opens the door. "Come on, are you playing? We need one more guy."

Bryan looks up at Will, then to his book. He contemplates for a second. "Yeah…sure. I'll play."

"Then come on, we'll give Jimmy the ball every down. Nothing can stop him when he gets his Scolit face on."

"Yeah, I bet."

"Let's go."

Will rushes outside. Bryan follows after tossing the shining black stone and his novel, *The Pirate's Revenge*, on his study table next to the window. The novel and the stone lands on top of another book entitled, *The Island Where Magic Began* .

The End…Or Is It?

⋆About the Author⋆

John Cicero's passion for writing is driven from the joy he receives from reading his stories to his children. Watching the expressions on their face as he takes them on a journey through the magical pages of his imagination is what drives him to find the time to write. With over 18 years of experience in healthcare, technology, and professional sports marketing, John Cicero lives with his family in Cleveland, Ohio.